The resemblance between and Christian was too obvious.

He watched her as she approached the counter. Tall and yet slight to the point of appearing fragile, Dana Stewart wore her honey-blond hair in some kind of twist on the back of her head. Her bone structure echoed her son's—no, it was the other way around. Her cheekbones were almost too sharply defined, leaving hollows beneath. There was a tension to the way she carried herself, shoulders squared, head high, as if she wouldn't let herself relax in any way. The hand not clutching a purse was curled into a fist.

She was a beautiful woman now, but he wondered how much more beautiful she'd been before her son's disappearance damaged her in ways both visible and invisible.

Needing to be battle-ready, Nolan slid off the stool and stood before she reached him.

"Ms. Stewart."

"You're guessing," she said, in a distinctively throaty voice.

"No." He made a sound even he couldn't decipher. "You look like him."

Pleasure showed on her face. "I do, don't I? Thank you for emailing the pictures. I know you were annoyed at me—"

"I'm not that petty," he broke in.

Her teeth sank into her full lower lip. "I...would have understood."

Nolan had to momentarily close his eyes to recover his resolve. *I'll fight dirty to keep you, if it ever comes to that.* Of course it would come to that.

No, he might not be petty, but inevitably he would hurt this woman.

Dear Reader,

If you're a longtime reader of mine, you'll know that *A Mother's Claim* isn't the first book I've written about an abducted child. An earlier Harlequin Superromance novel, *The Family Next Door*, began after the heroine's daughter had been restored to her, too. I think that story must have been at the back of my mind when I started plotting this one. In it, the daughter was young and hadn't been gone nearly as long as is the case in *A Mother's Claim*. Long after writing that book, I began to wonder what would happen if so long had passed that the very young child was nearly a teenager and had no memory whatsoever of his real mother and father. Who *is* this woman, asking him to betray the only mother he remembers?

Dana has dreamed for eleven long years that a miracle could happen. Sure enough, it does, with a phone call letting her know her son is alive and well. *After* the miracle, though...well, that's when the real story begins. As always, I love wrestling with the aftermath of trauma. What more confusing time could there be to fall in love? Plus, as a fiercely protective parent, I identified powerfully with Dana.

I hope you're as moved by her journey as I was.

Janice

USA TODAY Bestselling Author

JANICE KAY JOHNSON

A Mother's Claim

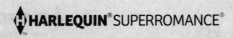

HARLEQUIN® SUPERROMANCE®

Recycling programs
for this product may
not exist in your area.

ISBN-13: 978-0-373-61013-6

A Mother's Claim

Printed in U.S.A.

An author of more than ninety books for children and adults, **Janice Kay Johnson** writes about love and family—about the way generations connect and the power our earliest experiences have on us throughout life. An eight-time finalist for a Romance Writers of America RITA® Award, she won a RITA® Award in 2008 for her Harlequin Superromance novel *Snowbound*. A former librarian, Janice raised two daughters in a small town north of Seattle, Washington.

Books by Janice Kay Johnson

HARLEQUIN SUPERROMANCE

Brothers, Strangers

The Baby He Wanted
The Closer He Gets

Because of a Girl
The Baby Agenda
Bone Deep
Finding Her Dad
All That Remains
Making Her Way Home
No Matter What
A Hometown Boy
Anything for Her
Where It May Lead
From This Day On
One Frosty Night
More Than Neighbors
To Love a Cop

Two Daughters

Yesterday's Gone
In Hope's Shadow

The Mysteries of Angel Butte

Bringing Maddie Home
Everywhere She Goes
All a Man Is
Cop by Her Side
This Good Man

A Brother's Word

Between Love and Duty
From Father to Son
The Call of Bravery

SIGNATURE SELECT SAGA

Dead Wrong

Visit the Author Profile page at Harlequin.com for more titles.

To my dearly loved daughters, Sarah and Katie.

CHAPTER ONE

IDIOT BOYS.

Having gotten Christian to the emergency room, Nolan Gregor was trying hard to be mad instead of sick to his stomach and scared out of his skull.

As a former army ranger, Nolan would have felt concern if he'd seen this much blood in the field. Panic—no. But this was Nolan's eleven-year-old nephew with the ugly ax wound to the shoulder, which made everything different.

Yeah, he'd done his share of idiot things when he was a kid and later put his life at risk for his country. But even with a bullet wound he had never bled like this. Christian's shirt was saturated by the time the EMT cut it off. Blood continued to flow despite the efforts to stanch it.

It took everything Nolan had to pretend non-chalance, to keep his posture confident and reassuring. A big man, he had retreated to a corner to be out of the way of the medical personnel clustered around Christian. He braced a shoulder against a wall of the emergency room cubicle. Nothing and nobody could have made him leave.

Face taut with pain, Christian kept his gaze fixed on Nolan, who was the closest thing to a father he'd ever had.

The doctor straightened, his eyes sharp above the mask. "Mr. Gregor, do you know Christian's blood type?"

The question ramped up Nolan's tension.

He frowned. "No. His mother is AB, but I have no idea about his father." Or who Christian's father was, for that matter. Nobody but Marlee knew, and she wasn't saying.

To one of the nurses, the doctor said, "Let's go with universal, but type him, too."

Christian tried to rear up, restrained by the team working on him. "Am I bleeding to death?"

"No, I'm just being cautious." The doctor laid a gloved hand on the boy's uninjured shoulder and squeezed. "You've learned a good lesson. Chop yourself open, and you might end up needing a transfusion."

A nurse was already pulling blood to check its type. Someone else was on the phone just outside the room requesting a unit of O neg.

Christian knew the rules: he used an ax *only* under the direct supervision of his uncle or, on occasion, a friend's parent. Today, after overhearing Nolan grumble about the cold and whether he'd split enough wood to last until spring, Christian and his buddy Jason had decided to surprise Nolan. They got cocky and did some roughhousing. Somehow, Jason swung an ax that dug into Christian's shoulder. Blood spurted. Jason ran screaming to the house.

Nolan wouldn't soon forget his first sight of Christian, crumpled to his knees, his thin shoulder sliced to the bone, blood gushing. He hadn't felt sickening terror like that since an IED had killed two men in his squad and left three others missing body parts. As he had then, he'd forced himself to calm down and done his damnedest to stop the bleeding while he waited for help.

Now, watching the doctor and nurses work on Christian, he saw that they were finally having success. The strain gradually leached from his muscles.

Sure enough, by the time the unit of O-neg blood arrived, the doc waved it off. He did decide to keep Christian for the night to recover from the blood he'd lost.

Eventually, Nolan and his nephew were left alone while overnight arrangements were being made.

"It wasn't Jason's fault," Christian said in a desperate voice. "Don't blame him."

"Safe to say, we'll let you share the blame," Nolan said drily. He felt sure Jason had already caught hell from his dad.

Christian seemed reassured. His eyelids sank, but he mumbled, "We were dumb, weren't we?"

"Yep." Now standing right beside the bed, smoothing the boy's dark blond hair back from his forehead, Nolan said, "We'll talk about it once you're in fighting form again."

Christian made a fist with one hand and managed to raise it a few inches.

Nolan chuckled. "Oh, I'm scared."

The small smile on the boy's face caused relief and something sharper to squeeze his heart. Nolan didn't have much family: his sister, Marlee, and her son. And Marlee... He loved her, but she was a constant worry and aggravation he had inherited when their parents were killed by a drunk driver. Medication gave her stretches of stability, but more and more often she refused to take it, which meant her mental illness dominated all their lives. Nolan could deal with the ups and downs, but watching her put her son through so much enraged him.

After their parents' deaths, he'd given up his military career to take care of his sister and her kid. When he came home to Lookout to stay, he told Marlee that, from here on out, Christian would be living with him. She was welcome, as well, or they'd arrange occasional overnights. He hadn't wanted to hurt her, but the boy he loved had to come first. He'd made sure she knew that if she didn't agree to his conditions, including her signature on papers giving him the right to make decisions for Christian, he'd challenge her in court for guardianship. Neither had any doubt he'd win.

So they'd made an uneasy peace, with her coming and going but Christian gaining in confidence now that he had a stable home and someone he could count on.

Thank God for that agreement. Today was typical. Nobody had been able to reach Marlee. Nolan hadn't seen her in a couple of days. She might be holed up in the apartment she maintained with disability payments, or she might have hitchhiked to Portland or somewhere else. In the grip of her schizophrenia, she tended to wander. If she could get her hands on drugs, she took them. He knew she spent weeks and months at a time living on the streets in one city or another, vulnerable to predators. It was almost inevitable that someday she would disappear for good. His parents had tried to gain guardianship so that she could be committed to an institution when she was at her worst, but they had failed. Nolan wasn't sure he loved that idea, anyway.

When an orderly appeared to take Christian upstairs, the boy was sound asleep.

Not liking his pallor, Nolan decided to stay behind and corner the doctor again. Maybe the boy should have received that unit of blood.

He hadn't caught the doctor's name but spotted him in the nurses' station scrutinizing something on a computer monitor.

He looked up as Nolan approached. "Mr. Gregor. I'm glad you're still here."

Ice trickled down Nolan's spine. "Something's wrong."

The doctor's expression cleared. "Not with Christian's condition. He should be fine. He's going to hurt for a while, though."

Relaxing a little, Nolan shook his head. "Hell of a lesson." He glanced at the badge pinned to the other man's scrub top. Dr. Karl Soderberg. "You must have a concern."

"Not at all. Just wanted to let you know that Christian's blood type is O positive."

"Must have gotten that from his father," Nolan said slowly, although something tugged at his memory.

"He might have. It does mean his mother isn't AB, though."

"What?" Nolan said, almost soundlessly.

"A parent with blood type AB can have children that are A, B or AB, but not O, even if the other parent has type O. It's just not possible. You might want to ask your sister again for her blood type."

Nolan was too stunned to speak. He'd taken leave and flown home after the car accident that killed their parents and left Marlee injured. He'd always known they had the same blood type as their mother, a fact confirmed when Marlee received a transfusion.

All he said was, "Thanks. Will you print that off so I can keep it with Christian's vaccination records?"

"You bet." A moment later, Soderberg handed over the piece of printer paper. Summoned by a nurse in the door of another cubicle, he walked away.

Nolan was left to stare at a couple of lines of basic information that carried the force of a grenade capable of wiping out his small family. He wanted to believe the lab had made a mistake, mixed up two samples of blood. He would, of course, take Christian to his own doctor for verification. But Marlee wasn't your average, everyday mom. A part of him knew.

Christian could not be her biological son.

ONE MONTH LATER, almost to the day, Nolan buried his sister.

When their parents died two years ago, he had acted on intuition—or had it only been fear?—and purchased not two cemetery plots but three. Now he laid Marlee to rest beside her mother.

He'd seen too much death and devastation himself to gain any comfort from that—he'd ceased to believe in an afterlife or the rosy fiction that Mom had met Marlee with outstretched arms. But Christian seemed to find it some consolation, which was all that mattered.

Christian had insisted on staying to watch as earth was shoveled atop the casket. Only two cemetery workers in rain gear remained with them. Friends and the minister who'd said a few words over the grave had all given the man and boy kind, pitying glances and walked away, sheltered by black umbrellas. Nolan held the same kind of umbrella and kept Christian close to him with an arm around his shoulders. Cold rain dripped from the bare branches of the maples that lined the paved cemetery lane. The heap of soil beside the grave had been protected by a tarp.

As the first shovelful pattered down, Christian's body jerked.

"That's enough," Nolan said harshly and turned him away.

To his relief, Christian didn't protest.

They walked across the squishy ground to Nolan's SUV, decorated on each side with the logo of his business and the name: Wind & Waves.

Shivers racked his nephew's thin body. "I can't believe..." he mumbled.

That his mother was dead? Nolan had no trouble believing that. What he struggled with was the knowledge of how she died. Marlee com-

mitted suicide after Nolan insisted she tell him
the truth about Christian. He, who had vowed
to care for her, had killed her.

When he first confronted her, she screamed,
"That's a lie! That's a lie! That's a lie!" and covered her ears with her hands. He had insisted
she stay with them so she couldn't run from
questions she didn't want to answer. He'd also
figured that with Christian out of school recuperating, she could be there to help while Nolan
was at work. Nolan had grown grimmer, Marlee
more hysterical. He had become reluctantly convinced that she truly believed she had carried
Christian for nine months and borne him with
the help of a midwife rather than in a hospital.

Did that mean Christian had no birth certifi-
cate? Hadn't Marlee or their parents needed one
to enroll him in school?

Nolan would forever be thankful that he—not
Christian—had found her dead from an over-
dose. The law had required an autopsy, and
Nolan had asked if the pathologist could tell if
she had ever borne a child.

The pathologist's report had left no doubt, de-
tailing changes childbirth made to a woman's
body. Marlee Gregor had never birthed a baby.

And she'd taken to her grave any answers
about who Christian's biological parents were
and how she had come to claim him.

She had also left Nolan with a shattering emotional and moral dilemma.

He loved Christian like a son. Any effort to trace those parents, to find out whether his sister, in the grip of her madness, had stolen a baby boy, could result in Nolan losing Christian.

Reason said he should keep what he knew to himself. Christian had experienced too much turmoil already in his life. As it was, he could cling to the belief that, despite everything, his mom had loved him, that the grandparents he still missed had been his, that he was safe with his uncle Nolan.

And Nolan couldn't imagine his life without the boy who was his only family.

And yet...what if somewhere were parents who still mourned their lost child? He didn't want to think his sister had been capable of snatching a baby from a loving family, but he couldn't be sure.

Christian's DNA might have been entered in databases of missing children and been waiting all these years for a match.

Perhaps the boy's biological mother had been a teenager living on the street, unable to care for him. Marlee might even have found him abandoned.

God, how Nolan wanted to believe in that as an explanation.

In the weeks that followed, he had trouble

thinking about anything else. His heart and his conscience engaged in silent warfare.

It's the right thing to do.

I could lose him.

If his parents pop up and want him back... what will that do to Christian?

He told himself constantly that he could take his time, think about the consequences of every conceivable choice. That baby boy had become Christian Josiah Gregor a very long time ago, which meant there was no hurry for Nolan to make a decision. A few weeks, months, at this point, what difference did it make?

FLOATING ON A cloud of well-being, Dana Stewart didn't want to open her eyes. The aftereffects of a dream lingered. She could feel the precious weight of her son in her arms, smell baby powder and his natural sweetness. The sensation of happiness was so rare she would have given anything to hold on to it.

But, inevitably, she woke up and the glow succumbed to crushing pain and guilt.

Still she lay there, refusing to open her eyes. If she did, she'd have to see her empty, lonely bedroom, the one she'd once shared with her husband. She and Craig had divorced a year after Gabriel's disappearance.

Too awake now to hold on to the dream, she opened her eyes at last to see her bedroom door open to the hall, as always. She never closed her door or the one into Gabe's room, not anymore. Dana knew how irrational she was being, but she couldn't fight a desperate need to…hear.

She followed her usual routine: check her phone to be absolutely sure she hadn't somehow missed a call or text, get out of bed, choose something to wear, shower, force down some toast or a bagel with peanut butter.

It had taken her years to do more than snatch a few hours of interrupted sleep. Even now, she didn't sleep deeply.

She didn't enjoy eating anymore, either. It had always puzzled her that she hadn't gone the other way; she'd loved food, once upon a time, loved to cook and had been just a little plump. Now…she ate to sustain life. She doubted Craig would recognize her. Occasionally, she encountered an old friend and saw shock.

Really, she was healthier than she'd ever been. She ran up to five miles a day, usually when she got home from work. Her diet consisted of whole grains, vegetables, fruit and nuts. She had a runner's thin body but didn't care how she looked.

On the surface, she lived—had friends, spent time with her family, held a fulfilling job. But she would sacrifice every other relationship to find Gabriel. That hole inside her, the search, secretly consumed her.

She haunted websites devoted to missing children, posting reminders of her lost son wherever she could. Once a year, she called the detective who had investigated fruitlessly, even though he was now a district commander in the Aurora, Colorado, police department. He was always polite and sympathetic; yes, he would do some follow-up. He always called a few days later to say that nothing new had come up. Although she knew he was thinking it, he didn't say, *Lady, your son is dead. You need to deal with reality.*

If she had believed, truly believed, that Gabe was dead, she wasn't sure she'd have reason to live. But if Gabriel ever was found, he would need her. She couldn't surrender entirely to despair.

She would go to work, immerse herself in other people's problems, try to find them help, soften their burdens. She'd come home, run until her body ached, eat what she must, read or watch some meaningless television show and finally go to bed, where she would only allow herself to sleep lightly, listening for the faintest of sounds.

She would keep doing it.

But every hour, every day, every week and month and year, scoured her out until less and less of the old Dana survived.

UNCLE NOLAN HAD been really quiet since Christian got home from school. Well, not *home*

home—most days, if he wasn't hanging with friends, he rode his bike to his uncle's business, which had a private beach on the Columbia River. Uncle Nolan had bought the business when he came back from Afghanistan for good, and immediately made a deal with a really cool small inn to take over an old boathouse and expand it on land leased from them. Then he'd sold the original building on the main street.

It wasn't like he'd been busy today; hardly anybody wanted to rent windsurfing gear or a sailboat or kayak in late January, when the weather was this cold and wet. Usually Uncle Nolan didn't seem to mind slow stretches; he said the busy seasons more than made up for them.

But today he'd been sitting behind a computer and barely looked up when Christian walked in. All he said was, "Homework."

Uncle Nolan used as few words as possible, listening more than he talked. This was kind of different, though. Usually he at least said hi and asked about Christian's day. He'd been more withdrawn since Mom died. He brooded a lot, which was okay. Christian did, too, going up to his room to lie on his bed, stare up at the ceiling and wonder how Mom could have done that. Hadn't she worried about him at all? He knew she was sick, but hadn't she loved him? What if she had changed her mind at the last second but it was too late?

Was dying like they said, following a white light? In killing herself, had she committed such a sin she was condemned to a horrible eternity? Or was she just...gone? Erased? Uncle Nolan had talked with him about what different people believed and had shaken his head when Christian asked what *he* thought.

"I wish I could tell you." He'd stared into the distance, but not as if he was seeing anything. "You know what I did in the military."

Christian nodded.

"I saw a lot of men killed."

Christian knew his uncle had probably killed a bunch of those men. Sometimes he thought that's why Uncle Nolan was so quiet. Maybe those dead men haunted him.

But what he'd said then was, "I've never seen a ghost. Never had a hint of one of my buddies coming back to let me know he's okay on the other side. Not sure I believe it when someone claims Grandma appeared the day after the funeral to say goodbye. But I can't discount the possibility that there is an afterlife. Any minister will tell you there is, and most people believe it."

"I wish—" Christian wasn't even sure what he'd meant to say. He wished Mom hadn't done it? Or that she was watching over him, like people had claimed she was? Or that she hadn't been crazy to start with?

But Uncle Nolan had pulled him into a tight hug and said, in his deep voice, "I do, too, son."

And Christian knew he really did understand. That he had all the same wishes, never sure which one to go for, because he had loved Christian's mom even though he got really mad at her, too.

They had sat there long enough Christian should have been embarrassed, but he wasn't, because Uncle Nolan wasn't. Nobody could say Uncle Nolan wasn't a really tough guy. If he thought it was okay to hug, then it was.

Today Christian didn't argue. He had a bunch of homework. He was in a pullout program to take an advanced math class, and they were doing some algebra and geometry, which he really liked. Today's problems were hard, and he was still working on them when Uncle Nolan said, "Closing time."

He threw Christian's bike in the back of his Suburban, then said, "I ordered a pizza."

"Cool!"

They picked up an extralarge with practically everything on it. Uncle Nolan cooked broccoli, too. They always had a vegetable with dinner, no matter what else they were eating. Then they sat down and gorged.

Uncle Nolan did finally ask about his day and

grimaced when Christian asked if he'd done any business at all.

"Sold a couple of Naish sails because I have them discounted. Harness lines, a vest, some little stuff." Then he grinned. "Couple of cocky young guys rented a Hobie Cat." That was a kind of small sailboat. Uncle Nolan thought they were ideal for rentals. "Came back an hour later with blue lips and chattering teeth, real sorry they hadn't accepted my recommendation and rented wet suits, too."

Christian laughed.

Like always, they cleared the table and loaded the dishwasher together; Uncle Nolan didn't like anything left lying around, especially not dirty dishes.

Christian headed for the stairs. "I've still got homework to finish."

Uncle Nolan said, "I need to talk to you first." The way he said that scared Christian. It was kind of like when he'd had to tell Christian Mom was dead.

He went back to the table and sat down.

Uncle Nolan pulled out a chair, too. He sighed, rubbed his neck and sighed some more. Finally, he met Christian's eyes. "I don't know any way to soften this, so here goes. When Jason whacked you with that ax, I found out your blood type."

Christian nodded.

"You have O positive. That's pretty common." He obviously didn't want to say the rest. "It shook me up, because it meant my sister couldn't be your biological mother."

On an explosion of fear, Christian shoved his chair back. "That's not true!"

Lines that weren't usually there creased Uncle Nolan's forehead. "I'm afraid it is. You know I had Dr. Santos draw your blood the week after you were hurt."

Still not having risen to his feet, Christian went very still. He'd kind of wondered why, when he was seeing their family doctor to make sure the wound hadn't gotten infected or anything like that, he'd had to give blood. Especially after he'd lost so much.

"The lab he sent the sample to verified the result. I requested your mom's medical records to be sure I wasn't misremembering."

He lectured then, about blood types and why someone with AB blood couldn't have a child with O blood, even if the other parent had it. He said he'd tried to get Marlee to tell him how she'd come to adopt Christian but she wouldn't. Christian had heard enough to know they were arguing, but not what it was about. Now he did.

Scared like he'd never been, even when he was bleeding so much he thought he would die, Christian whispered, "But if she adopted me, it's legal, right?"

"I can't find any paperwork." Worry and sadness made Uncle Nolan look different than usual. "I can see her not bothering to go to court for a decree. She had trouble following a bunch of steps or conforming to what people expected of her."

"But…if she didn't…where did she get me?"

"You know she lived on the streets sometimes. Your biological mother could have been a teenager or an addict she met there, unable to take care of you. Marlee would have known that Grandma and Grandpa and I would help if she brought you home."

He swallowed and made himself say, "Does that mean I can't stay with you?"

"No." Uncle Nolan's jaw muscles bulged. "I'll fight dirty to keep you, if it ever comes to that. And if there's one thing I learned at Fort Bragg and overseas, it's how to fight dirty."

Christian let himself breathe out and nod.

"Here's the thing, though." Uncle Nolan squeezed the back of his neck, like it hurt. "There's one other possibility we have to think about."

Christian got scared again. Really scared.

"You know when your mom was off her meds, she didn't always know what she was doing. She'd think things were true that weren't."

He nodded numbly.

Uncle Nolan had these bright blue eyes. Right now they were really dark, and Christian saw that he did hurt.

"I need to make sure she didn't steal you."

"She wouldn't!"

Uncle Nolan didn't say anything. He didn't have to. Mom had gotten arrested a few times for shoplifting. Confused, she forgot she had to pay for things she wanted.

So…she did steal sometimes.

"I've wrestled with myself about this. A big part of me doesn't want to do anything about what we know. You're mine, and I want to keep it that way."

Christian waited, fire scorching his stomach.

"But then I imagine how I'd feel if you disappeared and I never knew what had happened to you. What if you had parents who loved you deeply and you were taken from them? How can we go on the way we are and leave them suffering?"

Christian didn't care about anybody else, so long as he could stay with Uncle Nolan.

"I'm not asking your permission." His uncle's blue eyes were regretful now. "I can't live with myself if I don't do this."

He shrank back. "What's…*this*?"

"We need to take a DNA sample—which we can get from some spit, so it's no big deal—and have someone at the sheriff's department list it in a couple of databases."

"So…somebody can find me." He was shaking.

"So if your DNA is already in one of those databases, a match will come up."

"You'll let them take me, won't you?" Suddenly he was on his feet shouting. "You *can't* say no if they come! They'll just take me." He backed away. "You lied. You're just like Mom. You're both liars!"

And he ran, not caring that it was dark and cold and raining outside. He didn't slow down even to slam the back door behind him. He just kept running.

CHAPTER TWO

"PHOENIX HAS BEEN ACCEPTED." Dana smiled at the very young woman across from her. "His enrollment starts at the beginning of the quarter. The child-care facility is right off campus, which makes drop-off and pickup easy for students. It won't cost you a cent, as long as you stay in school full-time and receive passing grades."

This was the best part of her job working at a nonprofit focused on helping single women with children find opportunities. Lucy Evans had been considerably easier to help than many of Dana's clients. Not quite twenty, she had a two-year-old boy. Her mother lived at a subsistence level and was unable to help except for babysitting evenings when Lucy worked at a bar. Lucy and her little boy drifted from shelters to cheap by-the-week motels back to shelters. Her income gave her no hope of anything better. So far, she had avoided the trap of going from man to man, smart enough to recognize that the men she met in those bars and run-down motels couldn't offer economic and emotional stability. What she had over many of Dana's clients, besides common sense, was a high school diploma and grades that would have won her admission to a four-year college had she not become pregnant her senior year.

After struggling since her son's birth, she had finally come to A Woman's Lifeline and begged for help. Since Dana had first talked to her, Lucy had been accepted into the local community college nursing program, starting summer quarter. Scholarships would cover the cost of tuition and books. She could continue her evening job, taking advantage of her mother's willingness to babysit. Because of the child-care program Dana had secured for them, Lucy could devote breaks between classes to studying. Dana had also found her subsidized housing at a cost she thought Lucy could handle.

This was one young woman, Dana believed, who would make it and emerge strong and capable.

Dana was intensely grateful that A Woman's Lifeline provided free on-site child care while its clients met with their caseworkers. She had seen Phoenix when she first talked with Lucy, and the sight of him had been like a stiletto to her heart. His brown eyes, blond hair and grin couldn't possibly look as much like Gabriel's as her first reaction suggested. Even so, it was far safer to avoid seeing him at all.

Lucy jumped to her feet as Dana stood and threw her arms around her. "Thank you!" Tears shimmered in her eyes. "You've done so much for us. It's like a miracle."

"You're very welcome," she said. "Watching you succeed is going to give me more satisfaction than you can imagine. And, just so you know, I have no doubt whatsoever that you *will* succeed."

Lucy was still wiping her eyes when she exited. Dana was surprised to find she had to blow her nose, too.

Fifteen minutes before her next appointment gave her time to have a cup of coffee. She was leaving her office when her mobile phone rang, the sound muffled because her purse was in a desk drawer. Knowing she was most often with clients during the day, friends and family rarely called during working hours. Heart pounding, she went back to her desk, fumbled the drawer open and delved into her handbag until she came up with the phone. She hated the hope that rose every single time the damn thing rang. Eleven years of painful, useless hope. It would be a neighbor letting her know she had a package UPS dropped off, or her dentist's office urging her to schedule a cleaning.

She didn't recognize the number, but it was local. She answered with a simple "Hello."

"Ms. Stewart?"

The familiar voice made her dizzy enough to grope for the arm of her desk chair and then sink into it.

"This is Commander Knapp from the Aurora PD."

As if she wouldn't know who he was. Dana could not summon a single word.

"I'm happier than I can say to tell you we've had a hit on NamUs." He knew he didn't have to explain anything about the National Missing and Unidentified Persons System, not to her. "Your son is alive and well in a small town in Oregon."

Something that should have been happiness but felt more like anguish swelled in her, pressing against her rib cage, rising in her throat, burning in her sinuses. She tried to speak, but she seemed to burst open at that moment, sobbing as she had never sobbed before. She couldn't stop herself. She sat there, gripping the phone, and cried without even trying to check the deluge.

"Ms. Stewart?" Commander Knapp's tinny voice rose from the phone. "I'll give you a few minutes to process the news and then I'll call back."

She couldn't even say thank you. The phone slipped from her fingers and dropped to the desk blotter. Tears kept gushing. Snot ran down her upper lip. A box of tissues kept for clients sat on the corner of her desk, but she couldn't so much as reach for it.

Why did this feel so much like grief? Or was she letting go of an overload of grief that had built, day by day and year by year, until it was too much to contain?

Someone knocked. When she didn't answer, the door cracked open. Jillian Markham, who had the next office, took one look and then rushed in.

"Oh, my God! Dana, what's wrong?"

Dana's face contorted and she cried harder.

Jillian saw the phone. "Bad news?"

Dana managed to shake her head.

"Oh, honey." Jillian bent to hug her, deftly swiping her nose and cheeks with a tissue at the same time. "Just let it out."

Dana couldn't have said why that struck her as funny, but suddenly she was laughing and crying at the same time. Her body shook even as she soaked her coworker's blouse, but Jillian only held her tighter.

Slowly, slowly, the storm abated. Maybe she'd run out of tears. Exhaustion swept through her, and she sagged. She felt as if she could slither to the floor, becoming a puddle.

"Honey?" Jillian pulled back a little, her face

worried. "Let me get a wet washcloth and we'll clean you up a little."

She couldn't have been gone a minute. The slightly rough cloth, wet with cold water, felt astonishingly good. Dana couldn't remember the last time anyone had babied her like this—and that included her mother. She wouldn't have permitted it. Yet here she sat, docilely accepting it.

Finally, Jillian patted her face dry, then perched on the edge of Dana's desk. In her thirties, too, she was a curvaceous brunette whose husband was a physics professor at the University of Colorado. Dana always tried not to look at the framed photos of Jillian's husband and two children on her desk.

"Can you tell me about it?" she asked.

Could she? Dana scrunched up her face and worked her mouth. The muscles were still obedient, if oddly numb.

"My son was abducted when he was a baby. Eight months old." She could talk after all. Until now she'd only ever spoken of Gabriel to other parents who had lost a child. None of her coworkers knew, not even the ones like Jillian she considered to be friends. If they had, they might have worried about her. Pity, sympathy, might have broken her. "He was stolen from his crib. Police never found a trace. Nobody noticed anyone around the house." Her mouth was dry. She finished, "That was eleven years ago."

"I wish I'd known," Jillian whispered. Suddenly tears glittered on her lashes. "I'm so sorry."

"The phone call. It was the police detective who investigated." Pressure built in her chest again. "They've found him, Jillian. Gabriel is alive. I don't even know why I cried." The words were so stunning, so beautiful, she had to say them again. "He's alive!"

And, just like that, the pressure became a radiance that was surely visible through walls.

"He's alive." She smiled, she laughed and she cried again, Jillian doing the same. "I've waited eleven years to say this. My Gabriel is coming home."

A MAN WHO'D once melted into the shadows and waited without moving for hours on end when he'd been hunting bad guys, Nolan couldn't make himself sit down. He prowled the downstairs, wound so tight he expected to snap. Why hadn't the woman called?

"Crap." He rolled his shoulders. Maybe she'd never call. Maybe she'd had five more children by now and written off her firstborn. He could hope.

Christian was huddled upstairs in his bedroom. He'd promised to come down when he heard the phone ring, but he hadn't promised to speak to Dana Stewart. His mother.

Nolan reached the living room wall and spun to continue his restless pacing.

The news had come a lot faster than he'd expected and could not have been worse. Either Marlee herself had stolen Christian—whose name had been Gabriel Angus Stewart—or she'd gotten him from someone who'd done the stealing. Either way, Christian had parents. Parents who had searched desperately for him, who had loved him, mourned him. Parents who had never given up.

Or, at least, a mother who hadn't given up. Evidently, Gabriel's parents had split up after his disappearance. Nolan knew that a tragedy often led to that outcome. People didn't grieve the same way or at the same pace. They turned inward. They had to focus their rage on someone, and who was more available than a spouse?

It was the mother who was supposed to call any minute. Nolan had no idea what to say to her. He remembered his promise to Christian.

I'll fight dirty to keep you, if it ever comes to that. And if there's one thing I learned at Fort Bragg and overseas, it's how to fight dirty.

But panic stalked him. How was he supposed to fight a woman who'd done nothing wrong? Who only wanted her little boy back?

His phone rang.

He closed his eyes for a moment, gathering himself, before answering. No sound came from upstairs. No eager or even reluctant feet thudded down the staircase.

"Nolan here."

There was a small silence. Then a soft woman's voice said, "Mr. Gregor?"

"That's right." It wasn't in him to help her.

"I'm Dana Stewart. Gabriel's mother."

"He's been Christian for a long time, Mrs. Stewart."

"Ms.," she said, almost sharply. "I've been divorced for a long time, too."

"Why did you keep your husband's name, then?" He threw it out, a challenge.

"Because it's Gabriel's."

The simple truth in a tremulous voice made his head bow, his face twist.

"I understand."

"Will you tell me more?" She sounded humble. "I mean, about how you ended up with my son?"

He couldn't deny her this much.

"I'm former military. I was overseas when my sister emailed to let me know she was pregnant and expecting anytime. She was living in Denver." He rubbed a hand over his face. "My parents and I weren't thrilled. Marlee was mentally ill. At the time, she seemed stable. She responded well to medication but wouldn't always stay on it." He paused. "She returned to the West Coast about the same time I came home on leave, her little boy eight months old."

"She planned to steal a baby." This voice wasn't tremulous. It was lent resonance by rage.

"It...would appear so. When I confronted her after finding out Christian's blood type, though, she denied anything like that. I think she really believed that Christian was hers. That she'd gone through a pregnancy and had him the usual way. She told me how many hours she'd been in labor."

"She lied."

"Her truths weren't the same as most people's."

"You're excusing her."

Suddenly angry, he said, "I'm explaining her. Do you want to hear it or not?"

In the silence that followed, he felt her grabbing for calm. He wondered what she looked like. Had Christian's blond hair come from her or his father? Christian was a strikingly handsome boy, embarrassed because girls liked him. Did his looks come from her? His height?

"You're right," she said, with what he suspected was hard-won poise. "I know this can't be easy for you. She's your sister."

"She was my sister. Marlee died a month ago."

"Oh," she whispered.

"Christian has lived with me for a couple of

years anyway, and I spent as much time as possible with him before that." He might as well lay it all out there, he decided. "As far as I'm concerned, he's my son."

"And yet he's not."

"He's a good kid. He loves me."

"That doesn't make him yours."

The fear of losing Christian would crush him if he let it. "He's not your baby anymore, Ms. Stewart. You have to understand. He's five foot six. Doing advanced math. Summers, he teaches windsailing and kayaking classes. He's damn near a teenager."

"Why did you put his DNA online if you feel this way?"

The question rocked him. *Because it was the right thing to do.*

"Because I understood that you might be out there, clinging to hope, fearing he was dead. I couldn't let you keep hurting."

"Thank you." The softness was back, the undertone that spoke of devastation, of an unexpected miracle. "You can't imagine what it felt like to get that call."

As an opponent, she'd be hard to knock down. She had too much on her side.

"Have you let Christian's father know?"

"Yes." Constraint could be heard. "He's as thrilled as I am. Needless to say, he's eager to see Gabriel, too."

"I assume you want to talk to Christian," Nolan said abruptly.

"Yes. Oh, yes. Please."

Damn it, damn it, damn it.

"Hold on." He went to the foot of the stairs, covered the phone and called for Christian.

After a minute, a door opened and the boy appeared. He took the stairs slowly, shoulders hunched, expression mulish but his eyes showing how scared he was.

"Your mother," Nolan said, and held out the phone.

DANA WAITED, ALL of her focused, hungry, listening for a voice she'd feared never to hear.

"Uh…hi." The *uh* was deep, the *hi* a squeak. *Damn near a teenager.*

Her breath came faster. He wasn't her baby, hadn't been for a long time. He was almost twelve years old. How could that be?

"Hello—" she made herself say it "—Christian. I'm your mother."

"I don't know," he mumbled.

"Accepting what you do know can be hard."

His "I *have* a mom!" sounded angry, almost violent. Then he went quiet for a moment before saying more softly, "Had a mom."

"I have missed you every day since you were taken."

"Mom wouldn't have done that."

"Somebody did." Dana knew she'd said it too sharply, but how could she not let him know how angry *she* was. "You were asleep in your crib in your bedroom. It was spring. The weather was nice. Your window had a screen, so I…left it open." Craig had never let her forget that by doing so, she had left their child vulnerable. He didn't quite say, *It was your fault*, but he didn't have to. "You'd had a restless night, so I took a nap, too. When I woke up and went into your bedroom, your crib was empty and the screen on the window had been removed."

Not only removed: stomped on, twisted. In unwary moments, she still saw the window screen lying mangled on the lawn. It had epitomized the worst of her fears. What kind of person had taken the time to destroy the window screen only because it had briefly gotten in the way?

Gabriel didn't say anything. Even in her turmoil, she knew how torn his loyalties had to be. How could he accept that the woman he'd believed was his mother had committed a crime so awful?

"May I speak to Mr. Gregor again?" she said politely.

Her son didn't even say goodbye. He probably felt a rush of relief as he handed off the phone.

The slow, rumbly voice was back. "If you'll give me your email address, I'll send you some pictures."

She trembled. To see his face!

"If you would—" more that was hard to say "—I'd be grateful." She gave him her email address.

"Consider it done."

His kindness was reluctant but real, she thought.

She steeled herself. "Mr. Gregor, I have already bought an airline ticket. I will be arriving tomorrow. Can you recommend a place to stay?"

"Don't you think you should give this longer before you get pushy?"

"I can't read him when we're on the phone."

"Our computer has a camera. You could Skype."

Anger punched through all the other emotions. "If you were me, would that satisfy you?"

Silence. He didn't want to say no. Admitting as much would give the advantage to her.

"The Lookout Inn," he said abruptly. "It's a nice place. With this being out of season, you shouldn't have any trouble getting a room."

"Thank you," she said. She didn't care if she had a nice place. Eleven years of longing had coalesced into one driving need: to see Gabriel. "Then you can expect me tomorrow."

"Doesn't sound like we have any choice," he said.

She looked at her phone suspiciously and saw that her guess had been right; he'd ended the call.

Would he still email the photos? Her heart drummed. *Please, oh, please.*

With a shaky hand, she dialed Craig's number. She'd promised to let him know once she'd talked to Gabriel and what her plans were.

Dana desperately did *not* want him to insist on coming to Lookout, too. She had no desire to see him, but it was more than that. He had gone on with his life so quickly. He had two other children. Losing his son? Hardly a blip in his life.

She rarely wasted thought on her ex-husband, but bitterness seared her now. Craig had given up on Gabriel. So who was he to pretend to care now?

UNFORTUNATELY, THE MORNING dawned sunny. Nobody would be going out on the river without a wet suit, but that didn't stop most ardent wind- or kitesurfers. A powerful wind that funneled between banks of the Columbia River Gorge was the draw. It wouldn't be like summer, but a sparkling spring day would have Nolan busy from the minute he opened. If not for the business, he'd have been tempted to go out on the water himself.

He wished he'd thought to ask when Ms. Stewart expected to arrive.

Christian had exploded the minute he learned his biological mother was coming.

"You said you wouldn't let her take me!" he had yelled.

"I said I'd fight her," Nolan responded, weary and, yeah, freakin' terrified he would lose. "And she isn't here to take you away. What she wants is to see you. Talk to you."

"I don't have to talk to her if I don't want."

Shit. Nolan had pressed the heel of his hand to his breastbone to suppress the pain beneath. "Christian, this is a woman who has hurt for a very long time because she loved you so much. Think about how you want to treat her."

Too many confused emotions crossed the boy's face before he bolted upstairs. Nolan had let him go.

Wind & Waves didn't offer lessons until mid-April. There wasn't enough call for them. He rented a lot of windsailing packages and Hobie Cats as the morning went on, though, and sold a bunch of accessories, too.

Midafternoon, he had a lull. Over the winter and early spring, he covered the store with minimal additional staff. At the moment, Amir was out helping a couple launch a small catamaran-style Hobie Cat, leaving Nolan alone inside. The growl of his stomach reminded him he hadn't had a chance to take lunch. Since he'd been so tied in knots this morning, he hadn't managed to swallow much of his breakfast, either.

Nolan was reaching for his phone to order delivery from a local deli when the bell on the door rang and a woman walked in. He froze, hand outstretched, and watched her look around as she approached the counter. She might be a customer…but he was betting not.

No—he knew she wasn't. The resemblance between this woman and Christian was too obvious.

Tall and yet slight to the point of appearing fragile, Dana Stewart wore honey-blond hair in some kind of twist on the back of her head. Her bone structure echoed her son's—no, he supposed it was the other way around. Her cheekbones were almost too sharply defined, leaving hollows beneath. There was a tension to the way she carried herself, shoulders squared, head high, as if she wouldn't let herself relax in any way. The hand not clutching a purse was curled into a fist.

She was beautiful, but he wondered how much more beautiful she'd been before her son's disappearance damaged her in ways both visible and invisible.

Needing to be battle ready, Nolan slid off the stool and stood before she reached him.

He met wary gray eyes, which she hadn't bequeathed to Christian. His were a warm brown.

"Ms. Stewart."

"You're guessing," she said, in a distinctively throaty voice.

"No." He made a sound even he couldn't decipher. "You look like him."

Pleasure showed on her face. "I do, don't I? Thank you for emailing the pictures. I know you were annoyed at me—"

"I'm not that petty," he broke in.

Her teeth sank into a full lower lip. "I…would have understood."

Nolan had to momentarily close his eyes to recover his resolve. *I'll fight dirty to keep you, if it ever comes to that.* Of course it would come to that. No, he might not be petty, but inevitably, he would hurt this woman.

"Christian is still in school."

"I assumed he would be. Someone at the inn—" she gestured behind her "—told me where to find you."

Nolan waited.

"You don't want me here."

"He's not ready."

The pain in those eyes could rip him in two. "Mr. Gregor, do you know how long I've waited to see my son?"

His jaw tightened. "Are your needs more important than his?"

As if he'd struck her, she fell back a step, making him feel like an asshole. But then she squared her shoulders again and lifted her chin. "Do you have any concept of the connection a woman feels with her unborn child? And then when she sees him, holds him, nurses him? What happens to both of them when that connection is snapped?"

His gaze lowered to her breasts, full despite her overall thinness. He saw her, a breast bared to a blond baby who had latched on. Her head was bent, her hair falling forward, her tenderness palpable.

When his eyes met hers again, he wondered what his face betrayed.

"If I hadn't understood, I wouldn't have put his DNA online," he said roughly. "What you have to understand is the power of the bond he and I have. I've been his father in every meaningful way."

"Every meaningful way?" Dana Stewart's voice could have cut glass. "You are not his father either biologically or legally."

He hadn't meant to issue threats, not yet, but heard himself say, "The legal part is...still a possibility."

Temper glinted in her eyes. "We'll fight you tooth and nail."

"We? I thought there was no longer any 'we'?"

"Divorced doesn't mean we aren't united as Gabriel's parents. And I should warn you that Craig is a wealthy man." She flicked a glance around the store, a suggestion of disdain putting his back up. "He can afford the best legal team."

That possibility had been worrying him, but Nolan still had investments he could tap into. During his years in the military, he hadn't had much reason to spend. That didn't mean he was rich, however.

So fight dirty. "Has it occurred to you," he said softly, "that if he wins, you lose? Is that what you want? Your son going home with your ex-husband? You don't really think he's going to spend his money for you, do you?"

She flinched before regaining control. Knowing his aim had been dead-on made him once again feel like shit, but the devastating truth was that he would lose Christian if he was nice.

"You're wrong." Her voice gained strength. "We loved each other. Craig wouldn't hurt me that way."

Nolan shrugged. "Your risk."

As if his insolence had been a trigger, her eyes narrowed and she said fiercely, "Gabriel is my son. If you help me, I'll allow you to maintain a relationship with him. If you don't…?" Her turn to shrug, after which she whirled around and walked away from him.

His gaze followed her until the door closed behind her, the bell tinkling cheerfully. And then he went to the front window and kept watching as she followed the path to the inn, a hundred yards away.

That tall, slim body might look fragile, but he had a bad feeling her backbone and will both were steel. She had suffered for a very long time, but now the future that had been only a dream was within her reach.

He didn't have any doubt that she had meant her threat. Both her threats.

Nolan stayed where he was long after she vanished inside the Lookout Inn.

CHAPTER THREE

THE HOSTILITIES HAD blown up so quickly Dana hadn't had a chance to ask whether Gabriel would go straight home after school or to Mr. Gregor's business. Or whether, knowing she would be here, they'd arranged for him to hide out at a friend's.

Nolan Gregor had said, "I'm not that petty," but as she paced her room at the inn, her stomach still ached from his vicious reminder that her interests and Craig's were not the same. It was painfully true that they weren't a family anymore. He had backed off enough to allow her to make this trip alone, but Gabriel was his only son. He might insist on custody.

And what if Gabriel would be best off with him? He was most attached now to a man he saw as a father. If the woman who had stolen him really had been mentally ill, he might never have had a relationship with her that he could depend on. And, face it, however desperate Dana was to have her son, she knew she didn't have the faintest idea what a preteen boy needed, how he thought and felt. Look how poorly they'd communicated on the phone!

Yes, she would fight tooth and nail—she'd meant that—but unless she was willing to alienate her son, she needed Nolan Gregor's cooperation. There had to be a way to use his love for Gabriel to help her. First and foremost, they both wanted Gabriel happy.

But honesty compelled her to admit that her urgent need to hold her son again, to have him turning to her with love and trust, drove her so powerfully that separating that need from what was best for Gabriel would be difficult. She had no doubt the same was true for Nolan. And circumstances made it easier for him to convince himself that what he wanted was also what Gabriel wanted.

Christian.

She might have to force herself to use that name at first, but she would never, *could* never, think of her son as Christian. *Her* little boy was Gabriel, the name she'd loved, the name she'd chosen.

Nerves jumping, Dana checked her watch. Elementary school students were released at three thirty, according to the inn's front-desk clerk. It was now three forty. She had driven by the school after her confrontation with Nolan Gregor. It was barely half a mile away, so she thought Gabriel would walk or ride a bike rather than take a bus. How long would it take him? Would he come straight here, or was he so reluctant to meet her he'd dawdle as long as he could?

She pressed a hand to her stomach, churning enough that she was grateful she hadn't eaten lunch.

How petty would Nolan Gregor be?

Picturing the man who went with the deep voice didn't do anything to calm her. His sheer size had intimidated her. At five foot ten, she was tall for a woman. Her father and brother were well over six feet; Craig was, too. But they all had long, lanky builds. In contrast, Nolan Gregor's shoulders would fill a doorway. His chest was broad, his legs powerful. She didn't make the mistake of thinking he'd be lumbering and slow, like a football linebacker. In fact, instinct insisted she keep distance between them to give herself time to react, because she somehow knew if he did move, he'd be lightning fast. Remembering his mention of a military career, she wondered exactly what he'd done to develop that kind of muscle.

It didn't help that his face was…well, not handsome, exactly, but appealing, with prominent bones and a square jaw. Vivid blue eyes were a surprise considering his shaggy dark hair and dark stubble. She'd disconcerted her-

self by noticing his mouth and feeling a flicker
of warmth she hardly recognized.

No, no, no. The man mattered only because he
was her adversary at the very least. She couldn't
afford to soften toward him in any way at all.

She closed her eyes, dismissing him as she re-
focused on what mattered: Gabriel. A few deep
breaths almost calmed her. It would take her five
minutes to lock her room and make her way to
the windsurfing shop next door.

She left her handbag this time, tucking her
key in her pocket. She walked with a deliberate speed, forcing herself to exchange a pleasant smile with a couple in the elevator and then
the desk clerk. Out the door, turn left and follow the path across the lawn.

Bright sails bloomed on the broad Columbia
River. It took her a moment to see that while
some were on boats, most sent single figures in
wet suits skimming the choppy water on boards.

More deep breaths, and Dana resumed her
walk. When she saw the bike leaning against
the side of the driftwood-gray clapboard building,
her heart leaped, the beats so light and fast
she imagined herself flying across the water.

He's here.

Suddenly shaking, she literally ached, the
hunger to feel her baby in her arms almost un-
bearable.

She wasn't thirty feet from the door. It seemed impossible, unreal, that this was happening, that he was so close. *Alive.* Good at math, athletic. Every dream that had sustained her for all these years was about to come true.

What she had somehow never imagined was what would happen *after* that magical moment when she first set eyes on him, wrapped him in her arms. In her dreams, he always said, "Mom?" in a voice of wonder. Instead, during their call he'd been angry, shouting, "I *have* a mom!" In her fantasies, he never refused to believe the woman he'd called Mother had stolen him from his real mother.

Her mood shifting abruptly, she almost laughed. She had her miracle, and she was standing out here, terrified and despairing in advance?

So it wouldn't be as easy as she'd imagined. Of course it wouldn't. He wasn't the baby she remembered; *he* didn't remember her at all. He was a whole person, shaped by strangers, including a mentally ill woman who'd claimed to be his mother. She ought to be grateful to Nolan, who had apparently given him stability and a home.

Ultimately, however hostile he was now, he would have to work with her. She'd give him time, and he would recognize how little choice he had.

Dana started forward again, feeling buoyed, lighthearted, as bright as all those sails.

He's here.

"WHY DO I have to see her?" Christian whined, even though he knew the answer. Because this woman was his actual, real mother.

Even thinking that made him feel disloyal.

Uncle Nolan didn't bother to answer. "Brace yourself," he said instead. "She'll be here any second."

Uncle Nolan said she'd come by earlier and that she looked like Christian, which freaked him out. It was like if he couldn't see any resemblance, he didn't have to believe any of this was true.

The bell on the door tinkled, and his fingers bit into his palms.

Uncle Nolan's gaze went past Christian, but his expression didn't change. He had on what Christian thought of as his soldier face, emotionless, hard to read.

"Ms. Stewart," Uncle Nolan said, not exactly politely but not rudely, either.

"Mr. Gregor." The woman's voice was husky, like the women on the radio.

Shoulders stiff, Christian kept his back to her.

"Gabe—Christian," the woman said more quietly. "Please, let me see you."

Uncle Nolan's look said, *Do it.*

Taking a deep breath, Christian turned around. Seeing her felt like the shock he got sometimes touching the metal door of the freezer case in the grocery store. She did look like him, or like his mom should look. He'd never wondered why he didn't look anything like Mom, because he'd thought he must look like his father. But now—

He breathed too fast, in the grip of a panicky sense of guilt. Mom wasn't here to *tell* anyone what really happened! Maybe she'd rescued him. Maybe he hadn't been safe with his real parents. Just because this total, complete stranger said he'd been stolen—

"You're so tall," she whispered. Until now she hadn't even seemed to breathe, only stared with clear gray eyes, her lips slightly parted.

Nobody had ever looked at him like this. He squirmed.

Uncle Nolan's hand closed on his shoulder. One squeeze, and Christian settled.

"He's already in a size-nine shoe," Uncle Nolan said. "I've been thinking he won't stop growing until he's my height or taller."

"I—" Her breath sounded funny. "My father is six foot three, and my ex-husband—*your* father—" she added, not taking her eyes from Christian, "is about the same. He played guard for the Kansas Jayhawks—that's the University of Kansas."

She was trying to outdo his *real* family. No way he was going to let her.

"So?" He shrugged. "Uncle Nolan played football for Cal Berkeley. He even got drafted by the Cowboys, only he went in the army instead."

Her gaze strayed to his uncle. "Berkeley, huh?" A tiny smile might have been teasing. "Doesn't seem to go with a military career."

Uncle Nolan said calmly, "If you've read Thucydides, you know that 'the society that separates its scholars from its warriors will have its thinking done by cowards and its fighting by fools.' I subscribe to that belief."

He was *always* quoting from Thucydides, an old Greek guy.

"A historian," the woman murmured. Her eyes went back to Christian. "Could we sit down somewhere? Or go for a walk together?"

The scared feeling expanded in his chest. He looked at Uncle Nolan, who nodded. Christian saw Ms. Stewart's eyes narrow a little, but she didn't say anything.

"I guess a walk." He didn't want to be, like, face-to-face with her.

Again he felt the reassuring weight of his uncle's big hand on his shoulder as he passed.

He was trailing her to the front of the store when Uncle Nolan called, "Wait."

They both turned. Uncle Nolan wadded up Christian's hooded sweatshirt and tossed it.

"It's cold out there."

He shrugged into it, thinking if he pulled up the hood, she wouldn't be able to see his face.

"It looks like there's a trail along the river," she said.

"Yeah."

They walked in silence for a minute. He was more shambling; he really hoped none of his friends saw him. So far, nobody in town but him and Uncle Nolan knew about all this. Well, except for Dr. Santos, their family doctor, and whatever police officer had put Christian's DNA online.

He felt a spurt of anger because Uncle Nolan had done it even though he knew Christian didn't want him to.

"Why don't I tell you about your father and me?" Ms. Stewart suggested. "You have two half sisters, too. And grandparents on both sides, a couple of aunts and uncles as well as—" she seemed to have to count "—six first cousins."

Christian ignored the flash of surprise and... interest. Were any of the cousins boys close to his age?

"I had a grandma and grandpa," he said sullenly. "And I have Uncle Nolan."

"I know you did. Do. Still. More family never hurts." She paused, as if waiting for him to comment. When he didn't, she went on to tell him about growing up in Colorado Springs, where her father had been a teacher and then principal of the high school. "A couple of years ago, he became superintendent of the whole district." Her mother had stayed home when Ms. Stewart and her brother were little kids, then had gone back to work at a plant nursery. "Mom loves to garden," she said softly. "I think she might like to live somewhere without such a challenging climate, but the mountains are so beautiful they make up for a lot."

Her brother liked the mountains so much he owned his own business providing guides for climbers. "Not that different from what your uncle Nolan does," she added.

Ms. Stewart did some kind of social work with women who were having a hard time making it on their own. Kind of like Mom, he couldn't help thinking. Except Mom had been able to come home for help. She didn't need anyone but family.

"Your father is a businessman. He has an MBA—a master's degree in business administration—from Harvard. He was always good with numbers, and he seems to have a gift for guessing what people will do before they do it. He has remarried and has two daughters, so you have half sisters."

She went on talking about his father's family— his parents and a sister who was married to a guy on the Olympic luge team, that little sled that left you hanging out there when you hurtled down the icy curves. Christian remembered watching the Sochi Games with Uncle Nolan, who said those guys had to be nuts.

"Of course, he's not a blood relative, but you have plenty of talented athletes in your family tree."

He'd always thought he was like Uncle Nolan, who could do any sport and make it look easy. *I am*, he told himself now, fiercely. He didn't even know these other people.

"Will you...tell me more about yourself?" she asked hesitantly.

She had to be kidding. What was he supposed to say?

"I know you're in sixth grade." She seemed to be trying to get him started. "Are you excited about starting middle school in the fall?"

He hunched deeper in his sweatshirt. "I guess."

"And what about high school? Do you plan to play any sports?"

"I don't know," he mumbled.

"Do you have any hobbies? Collecting rocks or building a go-kart or learning to work on car engines or…" Sounded like she was running out of ideas.

Building a go-kart? Really?

Christian stopped and looked out at the river. Man, he wanted to be out there on a board instead of standing here with this woman who thought he should be her little boy when he wasn't.

"I windsurf. And I give lessons for Uncle Nolan."

"That's pretty amazing at your age." If she'd had pom-poms, she'd probably have waved them.

"Can we go back now?" he asked.

Without looking at her, he couldn't tell whether the long silence meant she was surprised, mad or hurt, but he didn't care. It was only because Uncle Nolan would be disappointed in him that he didn't leave her and run back to the shop.

"All right," she said at last.

They were halfway back when she asked, "Do you have any questions for me?"

As if a dam had broken, all of his confusion and fears rushed out, like a river current when the water was running high. He lifted his eyes to hers. "Do you think I'm going to go live with you?"

The wind had whipped color into her pale

face, but her expression made him remember Uncle Nolan's when he'd first seen all the blood that day.

"Yes," she said.

"Because I'm not! I want to stay here, with Uncle Nolan. And you can't make me go!"

He ran, sobbing, not letting himself look back.

THE AGONY WAS so great it was all she could do not to crumple to the paved path.

Dana stood stricken, watching Gabriel run from her. No, not Gabriel—Christian. The boy who was a stranger. Who loved his uncle and wanted to hate her.

No, she thought drearily, not *wanted*. *Did*. And could she really blame him? She'd turned everything he had believed about his family on end. That had to be damaging his sense of self.

His mother was no longer his mother; his uncle wasn't his uncle. He wasn't even really Christian Gregor.

Dana spotted a bench twenty feet ahead. She made it that far, grateful to sink down and bend forward, squeezing her arms around herself for warmth and protection. Thank goodness no one else was approaching. She doubted she was capable of assuming a facade.

She was bewildered, with no idea what to do. Was it even possible to get through to him?

Did she batter her head against a brick wall? Or hang around in the hopes that she had aroused enough curiosity he'd come to her?

Her earlier determination and even optimism had evaporated. For the moment, Nolan Gregor had won. Adversary? More like enemy.

She hurt so much right now she wasn't sure she was better off than she'd been before Commander Knapp's call.

No, that wasn't true—at least she'd seen Gabriel with her own eyes. She knew her baby was alive, safe, loved. Couldn't that be enough? For the first time, she let herself wonder whether planning to tear him away from the life he knew was right. Or would it be an entirely selfish act?

Maybe, if she let him stay, he'd be okay with occasional visits and phone calls. If Nolan would send pictures, copies of report cards—

The stab of pain was so acute Dana curled forward until her head almost touched her knees.

Was seeing something you wanted so desperately but couldn't have better than doing without?

How awful would those visits be? The awkward phone calls he participated in because he wasn't given a choice? It could only get worse when the hormones kicked in. And what if she gave in but Craig didn't? Would that mean he loved their son more than she did? Or that his selfishness was greater than hers? Oh, she could imagine that so easily. Craig and his parents would feel the need to see his lineage carried on through a son. She had read between the lines when he'd let her know his first daughter was born. The disappointment had been there, because he didn't have the son to replace his firstborn.

Still curled over, she asked herself whether she was any better.

Crushing disappointment and hurt had her ready to drive straight to Portland and get on an airplane, go home where she could come to terms with the hard truth—she would never have her son back.

WHEN CHRISTIAN BURST through the door, face wet with tears, Nolan excused himself to the couple who'd come in thinking about buying their own equipment instead of continuing to rent.

He followed his nephew into the office. "What happened?"

Christian swiped his face with his forearm. "She said I'd have to live with her and I told her I wouldn't."

Anger set in Nolan's chest, like fresh concrete hardening. "You have to go live with her. That's what she said?"

Skin blotchy, nose running, eyes puffy and still wet, Christian didn't look any better than he had at Marlee's funeral. "I asked, and she said yes!"

"She wanted you to pack up and go with her right away."

His face contorted. "She just said yes! But you said I didn't have to."

If he had, Nolan was beginning to think he'd made a promise he might not be able to keep. "I said I'd fight for you."

Christian just snuffled.

Nolan stepped into the doorway so he could see his customers. The man caught his eye and waved reassuringly. "We're good on our own for a while," he called, obviously sympathetic.

Nolan nodded his thanks and half sat on his desk, gazing down at the boy, who looked smaller and younger than he had in a long while.

"Did you talk at all?"

Christian lifted his head in outrage. "I told you!"

"I meant before."

"Oh." He pulled the hem of his T-shirt from beneath the hoodie and blew his nose on it, which made Nolan wince. "*She* talked. She told me about, you know, her parents and her brother and…and the guy who is supposed to be my father and all his family. Like I care," he said sulkily.

"It is kind of interesting, don't you think?" Nolan asked. "I used to wonder a lot about your dad. What he looked like, what qualities he passed on to you."

"Like?"

"You're proving to be pretty gifted at math. I can handle the books for the business, but that was never a strength of mine, and I seem to remember your m—" he cleared his throat "—Marlee flunking freshman algebra."

"She did?"

"Oh, yeah." He might have smiled if there hadn't been so many painful losses since that long-ago day. "Not sure if she stunk at it or just refused to do the work."

"She dropped out, didn't she?"

Christian knew the answer, but what he really wanted was the reassuring repetition of family history—good, bad, courageous, silly. "To my parents' disappointment, she did." Nolan heard himself say *my parents* instead of *Grandma and Grandpa* and hoped Christian hadn't noticed. "They kept thinking once she was stabilized on medications, she'd go back to school or get her GED, but it never happened."

They talked some more, with Christian gradually coming down from the emotional storm and Nolan wondering what had happened to Dana. He'd have expected her to follow Christian back here, if only to give Nolan a piece of her mind.

He kept seeing her face, luminous with hope one minute, stark white with pain the next. In turn fierce, despairing, wounded and resolute. If she'd gone back to her room at the inn, did she have anyone she could call? She hadn't worn a ring, but that didn't mean she wasn't living with a guy or at least seeing one. It sounded as if she had parents, although that was no guarantee she could talk to them. Nolan knew he'd been lucky that way. Dana would have girlfriends, surely.

Except she'd seemed so alone. If a man in her life had let her make this trip on her own, he should be shot. Family should be here for her, too. They seemed to be MIA, which enraged Nolan when he should have been glad she was vulnerable to a knockout punch. He didn't like these mixed feelings. His first and only loyalty was to Christian. How stupid was it to sympathize with the woman who wanted to take away the boy he loved?

He was frowning at a poster on the wall when Christian said, "Can I go home?"

Nolan ran his palm over his jaw as he glanced at the clock. He'd be closing in an hour.

"Yeah," he decided, "that's okay. But call me when you get there, lock the door and don't answer if anyone rings the bell. Okay?"

The rolled eyes made him smile.

"You always say that."

Nolan scooped him into a hard hug. "I won't be long."

After locking up an hour later, he jogged to his SUV. He unlocked and opened the door but didn't get in. Shit. What kind of idiot was he, to worry about his adversary? But, damn it, that was what he was doing, and he couldn't go home without finding out how devastated she was or how determined to fight with all the resources she could summon.

Which, he reminded himself, were substantial. Oregon state social services didn't even know about the situation, but Dana could change that with a single phone call. Once she filed for custody, law enforcement might get involved to ensure Nolan didn't flee with her son. Or someone might decree that until custody was determined, Christian should be placed in foster care.

Find out, he told himself, *then look for a good lawyer.*

In the lobby of the inn, he tried to appear casual when he approached the desk clerk, an occasional customer.

"Hey, can you tell me what room Dana Stewart is in? I forgot to ask her."

Only twenty-five or so, Dylan Adams said, "Third floor, but let me check." He glanced at his computer. "Three-fifteen."

"Thanks." Nolan lifted a hand and headed for the stairs before the kid could ask what he wanted from Dana or remember he wasn't supposed to give out room numbers.

But he didn't hear a peep and she sure didn't open the door. She either wasn't there or was disinclined to talk to anyone, especially him. Uneasy, he went back down.

"Did you see her going out?" he asked Dylan.

"No, sir."

If she'd checked out, the computer would have told Dylan. All Nolan could do was thank him and jog back across the lawn to the smaller parking lot beside his own business.

What if she'd gone to his house to talk to Christian again? he asked himself during the short drive. But Christian knew better than to defy a direct order from Nolan and let anyone in.

She'd probably gone out for something to eat. Keeping track of guests was not Dylan's primary function. He must go in the back or use the john once in a while.

Nolan wished he could convince himself that was what she'd done but had trouble believing it. Dana had been so hopeful. The note in her voice when she'd asked Christian to turn around so she could see his face for the first time in eleven years had gotten to Nolan.

He had a really bad feeling she was crying her eyes out back in that hotel room.

He shook his head. Face it: everyone involved could not come out of this happy. And if he had to choose—she'd be the one who ended up disappointed.

Or was that crushed? Destroyed?

Nolan groaned. A minute later, he pulled into his own driveway and turned off the engine but didn't get out. He sat there for a long time, his guts tied in a knot, his chest tight.

CHAPTER FOUR

"WHAT, YOU'RE JUST going to let this son of a bitch win?" Craig snapped.

Dana's fingers tightened on her phone. Curled up at one end of the hotel room sofa, she wished she hadn't felt obligated to call him. "I didn't say—"

He cut her off as if she weren't speaking. "A kid isn't capable of making this kind of decision. He'll have to adjust, sure. No way in hell I'm leaving him with some guy who makes his living renting surfboards."

Dana didn't recognize this cutting contempt. Was it age and financial success that had turned him into an arrogant stranger?

She knew one thing—she needed to keep him away from Gabriel, at least for now.

"The business Nolan Gregor owns is a lot more sophisticated than you're implying. Waterfront real estate right on the banks of the Columbia River has to be pricey to start with." She couldn't imagine why she was defending her enemy, but she despised Craig's withering dismissal of anyone whose income fell below—what?—half a million a year? A million? Dana had no idea, only that she was one of those little people, too. "He carries and rents equipment for windsurfing, kayaking and sailing. That's a big business here."

He snorted. "I'll fly out there and take care of this, since you won't or can't."

"No." Her anger lent power to the single word. Now the furthest thing from relaxed, she straightened and put her feet on the floor.

"What's that supposed to mean?" Oh, he was infuriated because she'd defied him. His poor wife, Dana thought.

"It means I don't have to listen to you belittling me. It means you can't ride roughshod over everyone." He said something, but it was her turn to talk right over him. "You gave up on Gabriel a long time ago. *I'm* the one who has spent a lifetime searching. I'm the one who actually cares, instead of thinking of him as some kind of prized possession." Oh, God—she was taking a leaf from her ex-husband's book, her tone scathing enough to etch metal. With an effort, she moderated it. "I didn't say I was giving up. I said there's a better way to handle this than making Gabe hate us."

"You're going to baby him along until he's fourteen? Fifteen? Ready to graduate from high

school? Guess we can count on him expecting
me to pay for his college education."

Nolan Gregor was a deeply conflicted man
who loved her son and yet had had the compassion to risk losing him by posting his DNA online. It was Craig Stewart who was the asshole,
she saw with sudden clarity.

"If you take the legal route and a judge of any
decency hears that tone of voice, he or she will
rule in favor of the good man Gabe loves." *A fe-
male judge, please—give us a woman.* "You've
changed, Craig, and not for the better."

As the silence stretched, Dana couldn't be
sure what lay behind it. Had she enraged Craig
so much he would go after Gabriel with a fleet
of high-paid attorneys, and to hell with her?
Or did some remnant remain of the man who
had blamed her, yes, but also cried with her,
held her?

"I'll give you some time," he said abruptly.
"I expect to be kept informed."

She swallowed back everything hateful she
wanted to say and settled for a too-calm "Of
course I will. Goodbye, Craig." She ended the
call without waiting for any addenda. After
which she tossed her phone to the coffee table
hard enough to make it skid across the glass
surface and fall to the carpeted floor.

Then she moaned and remembered everything she'd said.

The good man? Was that the one who'd said, "As far as I'm concerned, he's my son?" Oh, and accused her of being selfish, of putting her needs ahead of her child's?

But honesty compelled her to remember the expressions she'd seen cross that craggy face, too, the shades of emotion in his deep voice. He'd been more decent than she probably deserved. The awful thing was, she wouldn't have wanted Gabriel to be raised by a man who was now perfectly fine about handing him over. Because of Nolan, Gabe—Christian—knew he was loved. Nolan had been a rock for her son.

And she had no idea how to defeat a man like him without making her son hate her.

CHRISTIAN GAZED BESEECHINGLY across the breakfast table. "So, if she just went away, does that mean she won't try to take me?" Of course, he'd inhaled his cereal and banana before opening his mouth.

And why not? In the two days since Dana Stewart had checked out of the inn without leaving any word, Christian had asked the same damn question so many times and in so many ways that Nolan's head was about to explode.

"No," he said, going for blunt this time. He held his nephew's gaze to make sure he listened. That he really heard. Because Nolan had seen the way the woman looked at Christian. She'd gone home wounded, stymied, but they hadn't heard the last from her.

He had done some research. Dana had stayed all these years in the house from which her baby son had been abducted. It had to be too big for her. It had to hold more painful memories than good. But leaving would have meant letting go of some of those memories, and she had refused to do that.

He had no doubt her marriage had splintered over her absolute refusal to let go of one iota of her pain. Nolan could almost sympathize with the ex-husband, whose wife didn't have enough left over to love him. *Almost* being the operative word, because Nolan knew himself well enough to be sure he wouldn't have moved on any better than she had. He would have held on to the pain *and* his wife.

He knew a lot of synonyms for *stubborn*, because they'd all been thrown at him. Even in a unit of men not inclined to back down—ever— he'd been famous for his pigheadedness…to use one of the kinder descriptions.

That Dana had kept her ex-husband's last name because it was also her son's said it all.

"I'm expecting to hear from her attorney any day," he told Christian now. "Maybe Child Protective Services. She'd be within her rights to have my parenting skills and this home evaluated with a microscope. It would be really good for her case if they decide I've screwed up in some way or other."

"But you haven't!" Milk sloshed over the rim of Christian's bowl when he gave it a shove. Eyes sparking, he thrust out his chin. "I'll tell them. *Everyone* will tell them!"

Touched by the fierce defense even though he knew it was rooted in the boy's deep-seated fear of being yanked away from everything familiar, Nolan smiled. "Thank you. And you're right. I don't think a social worker will find anything to use against me. But having them look…that's a logical step in Ms. Stewart's campaign."

"If she cares about me, why hasn't she called or something?"

Studying the way those thin shoulders had hunched, Nolan felt a burst of rage. This was a kid who'd lived with enough uncertainty. Did she have a clue what she was doing to him?

But, God help him, his fury was balanced by empathy he'd rather not be feeling. No, that wasn't true; he didn't want to be the kind of man who *couldn't* see both sides, couldn't feel for a woman as wounded as Dana Stewart. And he didn't want the boy he considered his son to grow into that kind of man, either.

He replaced his coffee cup. "You shut her down pretty hard," he said, keeping the judgment out of his voice but saying what he needed to. "I know you're scared. I understand, and I think she does, too. But we have to recognize that she has suffered for a lot of years. She came out here filled with hope, to find out her kid doesn't want anything to do with her." He let that sink in, then said, "None of this is her fault, any more than it's yours or mine."

"You're saying it's Mom's."

Yeah, he was. But he softened it some. "I don't know whether she stole you or not. I'd like to think not, but if she got confused enough, it's possible. Either way, she told plenty of lies."

Instead of blowing up, as Nolan had half expected, Christian sat very still and said in a small voice, "You said she really believed I was hers."

"I'm sure she did some of the time. When she was on her meds, though…" He shook his head. "Did she really believe in her manufactured reality? I don't know."

Christian's face crumpled. "She's my mom."

Oh, hell. Nolan shoved back his chair and circled the table to wrap an arm around his nephew. "It's okay to keep loving her," he said roughly. "She'll always be your mom, in some ways."

"Why do I have to have another mom?" He was back to pleading. "It's not fair! I just want you."

Nolan squeezed his eyes shut before they could start leaking. "Here's something to think about. Right now it's just you and me." Throat clogged, he could not freakin' believe he was about to say this. Cut his own throat, why didn't he? But he said it anyway, because it was the truth. "Having more people to love you could be a good thing."

Christian wrenched away so quick his head whacked Nolan's jaw. Betrayal darkened his eyes. "You've changed your mind, haven't you? You're going to let her take me."

Tasting blood, Nolan shook his head. "No. I said I'd fight for you, and I will. But who are we fighting against, Christian? This is your mother."

"I hate her!" he spat, and raced out of the room. An instant later, the front door slammed.

"Fabulous," Nolan mumbled, swallowing the salty taste. He hoped Christian had at least taken his book bag—and was on his way to school.

DANA SAT IN front of her computer, looking through the slide show of photographs Nolan Gregor had shared before her visit. With a bottomless hunger, she started over, and over again. There he was, a toddler wearing tough-guy overalls and a red-and-white-striped shirt, his grin huge even though he seemed on the verge of falling back on his well-padded rear end. A smartly groomed boy, hair slicked down, one front tooth missing. The first day of kindergarten? Or was that too young for him to have lost a tooth?

An ache flavored with bitterness gripped her stomach. A mother should know things like that. She should have soothed her teething baby, been there to slip money under his pillow in exchange for each precious tooth lost. Other mothers knew whether their sons said *Dada* or *Mama* first. They remembered the first step, the first day of school. The first time their son stepped up to the plate and swung a bat, the first book he read all by himself.

A thousand firsts she would only hear about secondhand, if at all. So much she'd missed.

But he was alive.

Gazing at the photo taken most recently, at the tall, thin, tanned boy windsurfing, his hair sun streaked, his laughter beautiful as he soared over the water, Dana thought, *I don't have to miss another moment.*

Her eyes lost focus. Maybe she was too soft-hearted to tear her son from the man who was his security, but there was no way she would stay halfway across the country from Gabe, contenting herself with emailed photos, visits, phone calls.

Mind racing, she closed her laptop and walked slowly through her house, ending up at last in the bedroom unchanged from the day Gabriel had been stolen. Her son was no longer that baby;

the knowledge felt like truth now. Would she *want* to bring Gabe home to this house, where everything had gone wrong?

Maybe it's time to let it go. All of it.

If the mountain won't come to Muhammad, then Muhammad must go to the mountain.

She had spent eleven years fighting for her son. Of course he was afraid. Of course he loved Nolan. Of course wrenching him away wasn't the right thing to do. But that didn't mean she would give up.

So she would go to him. It wouldn't work without Nolan Gregor's cooperation—but if threats were what it took, she'd channel her jerk of an ex-husband and issue some.

Dana loved her job, but she could find a new one. She would be farther from family, but they would understand. There was hardly even any furniture she'd want to take with her. Friends, she would miss, but she'd stay in touch. Looking around, she felt odd. So light she could float away.

Laughing, she flung her arms wide and spun in place. *Lookout, Oregon, here I come.*

THREE WEEKS LATER, Nolan tracked down his ringing phone a second before it went quiet. He checked the name, then, as he waited to see if Dana would leave a message, wondered why

she'd call at this time of day. She had to know
Christian was in school.

As he'd anticipated, she hadn't given up.
Every few days, she'd called and politely asked
to speak to Christian. The conversations were
brief. Christian mumbled a few replies to questions and listened when she talked. She hadn't
said much to Nolan, who didn't like not having
a clue what her plan was.

When Nolan asked what she was telling him,
Christian looked at him without comprehension.

"I don't know. Stuff."

"Stuff."

"About her family." He shrugged. "She said
she fell out of a tree when she was, I don't remember, seven or eight and broke both her
arms." He sounded impressed. His own traumatic wound had been to his left shoulder,
which made his teacher less sympathetic to his
claim not to be able to keep up with his school-
work while he was home recuperating. Christian had gone so far as to wish Jason had had
the foresight to chop his *right* shoulder instead.
"She couldn't write or use a computer or anything, so she got out of practically *all* her school-
work."

"Dumb way to fall."

"What do you mean?"

"If you ever fall—from a horse, a cliff, even

just trip—you relax and roll with it. You don't hold both hands out to try to stop yourself."

Christian frowned. "Oh. Maybe I should practice."

Nolan lifted his eyebrows. "Throw yourself out of a few trees?"

Christian thought that was hilarious.

Increasingly wary, Nolan had begun to see Dana Stewart as a shrewd opponent, smart enough to have guessed—or possibly researched—what would appeal to an eleven-year-old boy.

But no way would a gradually softening long-distance relationship satisfy her. His worry was that she was only filling the time while the legal team she'd retained drew up the papers to sue for custody.

No message. He bounced the phone in his hand, feeling a sharp stab of anxiety. He knew he shouldn't have taken so long to find an attorney capable of standing up to a team backed by Craig Stewart's money. Nolan had asked around but not reached a decision. He didn't like putting that much trust in the hands of someone motivated by the paycheck, but he'd been a fool to give her a head start.

Wearing board shorts, flip-flops and a T-shirt that said Got Wind?, Trevor Bailey had just arrived. Trev was one of Nolan's part-timers, a student at Portland State who would be full-time for the summer. Only nineteen, he was young but had a good head on his shoulders and a passion for windsurfing.

"I need to make a call," Nolan said. "Can you take over? The guy over there is looking for a new harness."

With a nod, Trev headed that way.

Nolan didn't move from behind the counter for a minute. Then he groaned, muttered, "Crap," and went to his office. As he called her back, he rolled his shoulders.

On the second ring, she picked up. "Mr. Gregor?"

"Ms. Stewart."

"I know you must be at work, but I hoped to talk to you when Gabe—Christian—isn't around. Is this a bad time?"

"No." He cleared his throat. "This is okay, if we can keep it quick."

The silence was brief. Apparently undaunted, she said, "You must realize I want to build a relationship with my son."

Nolan stiffened at the way she said *my son.* "Yeah, I figured that out."

"Doing so long-distance is impossible."

Oh, shit. Oh—

"I have made the decision to move to Lookout."

Nolan blinked. Rarely struck dumb, he struggled to absorb what she'd just said. Move to Lookout. Not file a lawsuit. Move to his town. Become a neighbor? Or—good God—she couldn't envision moving in with him and Christian, could she?

"You make that sound easy," he said after a minute.

"Easy? No. I've had to give notice at work, will need to put my house up for sale, pack, find a new job and a new place to live in a town I've only visited once." Her tone was dry, but beneath it was pure steel. "I've concluded that you're right. Forcing Gabriel to come live with me in Colorado would be traumatic for him. But I won't quit, either. If I'm there, I can see him regularly. Attend school conferences, watch him play sports, chauffeur him to friends' houses."

He almost opened his mouth to tell her chauffeuring was rarely needed, given the size of Lookout, but stopped himself in time.

"And if he doesn't want to see you often?" he asked. "If the school balks at including a strange woman in conferences when they know me as Christian's guardian?"

"Then I prove I'm his mother and that you are not, in fact, his legal guardian." No disguise for the steel this time. "Or even related to him."

His jaw clenched so tight his teeth ached. Thanks to the DNA matching, she had him dead in her sights.

"So we're back to a court battle." He felt as grim as he sounded. "Those take a while, you know. Don't you think this move is a little premature? Not going to help if I refuse you any contact with him."

Dana hesitated. He thought he could hear her breathing.

"I don't want a court battle," she said, voice softer. "Christian's father is eager to go that route."

Was she sincere? Or was she trying to fake him out with a kind of good-cop/bad-cop thing?

"I want to become his mother without an ugly fight that will hurt Christian. I can…preempt any attempt Craig might make to sue for custody."

How altruistic of her. Despite his inner sneer, Nolan closed his eyes and let his head fall forward. He didn't like what she was suggesting—it meant making concessions that could do damage to his side if they did end up in court—but he also knew she was right. This woman wasn't going away. She might not love Christian…but she did love Gabriel.

And, yes, he might win in court, but he could just as easily lose, a result that would devastate both Christian and him. His winning would do the same to Dana—and, maybe in the long run, not be so good for Christian, either.

The only true win-win was to find a way to share the boy they both wanted to call *son*, but how was he supposed to trust her? What if Christian did warm to her, become curious about his extended family and agree to return to Colorado with her?

He pinched the bridge of his nose until cartilage creaked. If that happened... Christian would always know Nolan was here. He'd have a solid base to jump from. And wasn't that what parenting was all about, building your kid's confidence so that when the day came, he had the self-assurance to leave home?

It just might happen a lot sooner than Nolan had ever imagined. *He* wasn't ready—but neither was Christian. Ms. Stewart was looking at a long haul.

"You're selling your house." She'd said that, hadn't she?

"I am." Her composure held despite the slightest tremor.

"You're burning some bridges there."

"I'm well aware."

He gusted a sigh. "You're asking me to help you." Or was it more accurate to say she was blackmailing him into helping her become Christian's mother?

"Yes," she said, so quietly he just heard her.

He did some silent swearing, but there was only one possible answer.

"Have you looked into jobs?"

This "yes" was stronger. "I've actually found a really great one I'm well qualified for. I have a

Skype interview scheduled for Friday. I have my fingers crossed because I'd prefer not to commute to Portland, but I will if necessary."

"Are you looking to buy a house or rent?"

"I'll rent initially." No hesitation, so she hadn't suffered the delusion she'd take the bedroom across the hall from Christian's. "I…was actually hoping you might be willing to look at a few places that are possibilities."

Ballsy woman. Nolan gave a short laugh. "Yes, Ms. Stewart, I can do that. Email me the list."

"Then…you're okay with this?" The sudden display of nerves made it apparent she'd girded herself for war and was now standing on the empty field looking around in bewilderment.

"What I'd like best is for you to get on with your life and leave Christian and me to ours," he said brutally—although he wasn't so sure anymore that he meant what he was saying. "What you've suggested is second best. You hold off your ex, I'll meet you halfway, unless I find out this plan of yours amounts to a Trojan horse."

"I'm not given to subterfuge, Mr. Gregor," she said, regaining some starch. "What I've said is what I mean. I want to be part of Christian's life. I hope that, with time, he'll accept me as his mother."

"What's your ex-husband have to say about this?"

"I've asked him to back off, and he's agreed, at least for now. He does plan a visit in the not-too-distant future. You can hardly blame him."

No, Nolan couldn't. It might even be good for Christian to have parents who made plain they wanted him. Right now he'd like to go back to the way it had been, before that damn blood-typing, but long term…it wouldn't feel so great to know either of your biological parents had written you off and couldn't be bothered to connect with you.

"I hope he won't rush it. Christian already has a lot to deal with."

"That's what I told him," she agreed.

They talked for a few more minutes. He'd be the one to break the news to Christian. Then to-morrow night she would call. She was eager to send him the list of possible rentals. It occurred to him that involving Christian in the hunt for a home for his mom wouldn't be a bad thing.

"How soon are you thinking?" he asked finally.

"I should be there by the first of May."

Blown away, he said, "That's barely two weeks."

"I've already worked out a good part of my notice to my current employer. I've been packing for some time. This isn't a sudden idea. I needed to have my ducks in a row."

Discovering he was pissed, Nolan said, "You mean my cooperation was optional."

"No. You know that isn't true. I just wanted a little time for Christian—Gabriel—to become more comfortable with me."

"A piece of advice." His temper was in hand, but he didn't feel as friendly as he had a few minutes ago. "You might want to decide what name you're going to call him before you show up in person again."

Except, he thought with a jolt of surprise, throughout the conversation she had been calling her son Christian. Had she even noticed?

"I'll discuss that with him," she said with dignity. "Goodbye, Mr. Gregor."

He said goodbye as formally, shaking his head. Forget Gabriel versus Christian. The whole plan wouldn't make it off the launchpad if the two of them couldn't bring themselves to use first names.

Instead of going right back to work, Nolan stayed where he was for a minute, half sitting on his desk. Man, he felt a boatload of emotions that weren't what you'd call harmonious. The anger, he understood. The relief that she wasn't taking the legal route. The trepidation about tell-

ing Christian and the fear of losing him, Nolan
got all that, too. The whisper of anticipation…
now, that was an unwelcome surprise.

CHAPTER FIVE

AGAINST HER PARENTS' OPPOSITION, Dana decided to drive.

"A lot of empty country," her father said. "I don't like the idea of you breaking down out there."

Glad he couldn't see her rolling her eyes, she retorted, "It makes no sense to sell a two-year-old car I'm really happy with. I'd lose bucko bucks replacing it with a new one."

The surprise came when she called Nolan and Christian to let them know she was on her way.

"You're driving?" Nolan said, not hiding disapproval. "Alone?"

"You have got to be kidding me."

"About what?" He sounded clueless.

"You sound like my father."

"You won't be on interstates most of the way. Just two-lane highways through some of the most unpopulated country in the lower forty-eight, and then there are the mountain passes."

She explained again that she had a four-wheel-drive Subaru with barely twenty thousand miles on it and plenty of experience driving in snow. Which she was unlikely to need at the tail end of April. "You're being sexist."

"As a woman, you're more vulnerable if you have to depend on help from a random passing motorist."

"This isn't open to discussion. I'm leaving in the morning."

He wanted to know her route and grudgingly approved it. Like her father, he also extracted a promise that she would call each evening and at any time she ran into difficulties.

It would be nice to think his deep concern was personal, but she suspected he tended to be protective and controlling. Christian had bragged enough that Dana now knew Nolan had been in a specialized military unit. Yet he had given up that career because he believed his sister and nephew needed him.

Believed? They had needed him. After the death of Nolan's parents, she could only be grateful Gabriel hadn't been consigned to the foster-care system or left to live with a mentally ill woman. One Dana hated with every fiber of her being, a fact she would do her best to hide if and when Gabe said anything about Marlee besides a furious "I *have* a mother!"

She didn't tell anyone how much she was looking forward to the several-day drive. Alone, driving through spectacular mountain country, she could let go of the stress she'd lived with since that miraculous, life-changing phone call. The amount she'd had to accomplish these past few weeks, working full-time and spending her evenings and weekends going through everything she owned, packing and cleaning, had left her drained.

Never mind the emotional swings, exacerbated by having to say goodbye to coworkers, friends, her parents and her brother. She'd see her family again, at least, but not as often.

All that vast and, yes, empty country proved soothing. North into Wyoming, then west from Cheyenne, the names she saw on road signs and markers spoke of the Oregon Trail and cattle ranching in the Old West. Past Medicine Bow, she crossed the famously muddy Platte River. She stopped for lunch in Lookout, Wyoming, just so she could say she had. Especially since she was headed to Lookout, Oregon. There was a certain resonance.

And every night, after checking into a hotel, she dutifully called first home, then Nolan and Christian. She kind of got the feeling Christian envied her the trip. He occasionally went so far as to ask a question or two.

Dana spent the last night on the road in Pendleton, Oregon, even though she could have made it all the way. She wanted to arrive in daylight, not exhausted in the dark.

That night when she called, Nolan said, "Let me know when you get close. I'll meet you there." He had the key to the small house he and Christian had chosen. Nolan had been nice enough to email a picture of it to her.

She wanted to say, *Thanks, but I'll pick up the key at your business.* But friendly cooperation had to be the goal, and she would definitely feel friendly if he helped carry in all her stuff.

"Thank you. It'll be a relief to arrive."

"Long trip." He sounded almost gentle, or maybe she only wanted to think so. She wondered if he understood that the miles she'd driven, the country she'd passed through, were the smallest part of the seismic shift in her life.

Voices in the background when she called him the next day told her he wasn't alone. But all he said was, "See you in ten."

The last time she'd been here, she had noticed Lookout was beautiful, but only in a peripheral way. It was where her son was, which was all that mattered. This time, she took it all in. On the outskirts of town, orchards filled with fruit trees in bloom climbed gentle slopes. Snowcapped Mount Hood reared over the hilly town, appearing closer than it actually was, and brightly colored sails dotted the river, sparkling on this sunny day. And…was that an old-fashioned paddle-wheel steamship going upriver? No, it couldn't possibly be, but the illusion was wonderful.

She pulled out her computer-generated map of town and made the turns that took her from the business district uphill. The houses had a pleasantly historic feel. She knew she'd arrived when she spotted the massive SUV parked at the curb midblock. She double-checked the house number, turned into the narrow driveway that led to a single-car garage, set her brake and sagged.

Just as quickly, she pulled herself together, instinct warning her not to let Nolan see any weakness. Dana hopped out, slammed her door and pushed the tab to unlock the rear doors and hatch.

Nolan was already walking toward her, his strides long. Her stomach quivered with her awareness of his big, powerful body. She reminded herself of all her resolutions. She had to be very, very careful around this man. Reacting this way was not good.

"Hey," he said, holding out a pair of keys on a ring.

She accepted them, trying not to let her fingers touch his.

He was already studying her Subaru, packed to the gills. She had barely been able to see out the back window.

"This open? I'll grab a load."

After slinging the straps of her laptop case and purse over her shoulder, she pulled her suitcase. He carried two giant plastic totes as if they weighed nothing and waited patiently as she fumbled to get one of the keys in the door lock. Then she stood aside to let him in first.

Without a word, he crossed the small living room and disappeared through a doorway. Since she'd written Kitchen on masking tape plastered on the sides of both totes, it was no wonder he hadn't bothered to ask for instructions. And, of course, he'd toured the house before.

Hardwood floors gleamed as if they'd been recently refinished, and the interior smelled of fresh paint. Built-in shelves flanked a brick fireplace. The landlord or a previous tenant had been nice enough to leave a set of wrought-iron fireplace tools—not that she'd be lighting a fire in the foreseeable future.

The house was of an age to have double-hung sash windows and broad sills, which along with the molding were painted white in contrast to the taupe walls.

Dana dropped the laptop and purse just inside the door but pulled her suitcase down the short hall, her footsteps echoing in the absence of furniture or rugs. After glancing into the two bedrooms, she chose the slightly larger one to be hers.

Nolan appeared behind her, carrying a box on one shoulder and another under his arm. "In here?"

"Yes. Thank you."

He nodded, set them down and disappeared.

Apparently, he saw no reason to bother with extraneous words.

They passed each other going back and forth. Once he frowned and took a big tote right out of her hands, turning around to carry it into the kitchen.

"I had that," she said to his broad back, sighed and returned to her car for something he would consider suitable for the little woman to carry. She'd have been a lot more annoyed if she weren't so grateful for the help. In fact, twenty minutes after she'd pulled into the driveway, everything she'd so arduously loaded in the Subaru was now in the house, and her back didn't ache any more than it already did from the long drive.

"Thank you," she said, watching him set a lamp down in the living room. "You've been a lifesaver."

Carefully placing the shade on the lamp, he glanced at her. "You have furniture coming?"

"Yes, in theory tomorrow." She crossed her fingers.

Straightening, he loomed over her, the folded

arms and frown an excellent form of intimidation. "You can't intend to stay here tonight."

"Yes, actually, I do. I have pillows and my sleeping bag. I'll be fine."

His grunt expressed something less than satisfaction. "Why not stay at the inn again?"

Expecting him to offer his guest room was a little much, she would concede. And that was assuming he had one.

"I grew up camping and backpacking. The hard floor won't kill me for one night."

The frown stayed, but he finally inclined his head. "House look okay?"

"Very much so." She loved what she'd seen so far. It was homier than the one she'd clung to all those years only because of Gabriel. "I appreciate you finding it for me."

His expression turned sardonic. "You didn't leave me a lot of choice but to extend a helping hand."

Her heart sank. "So today's help was grudging?"

He exhaled heavily. "No. I...sympathize with you, Ms. Stewart. That's not the same as hoping everything goes so swimmingly Christian is begging to move in with you two months from now."

She nodded. This was the equivalent of them crossing swords. *En garde*. "I understand. This seemed best for Gabe."

His eyebrows rose. "You want the kid to have an identity crisis?"

"What?" Oh, heavens, they were back to the name thing. Dana made a face. "I'll try. But you have to understand that it's hard. I chose his name with love. Everything *Christian* represents, I bitterly resent."

"Yeah, I get that, too," he said gruffly, "but you're going to alienate him if you keep insisting on *Gabe*."

"Why the warning?"

The emotions shadowing his eyes betrayed inner conflict to equal hers. He'd been honest when he said he wanted her to disappear from their lives. That he'd been as kind as he had anyway made her like him. And *that* could be dangerous.

"Because I think you could be good for Christian." Seeing her surprise, he smiled faintly. "Marlee loved him, but she could never be the mother he deserved. Right now I'm the only family he has. That's not a good place to be." He paused, as if reluctant to say more, then grimaced. "I was in Afghanistan when I got word about my parents' deaths. Marlee was badly injured in the same accident. It happened Christian was at a friend's. I was lucky to be able to talk to the doctor and okay the care my sister needed, but then I had to finish up an operation." His jaw worked. "Could have gone south and left Christian all alone."

"Or with your sister."

He had to know what she was thinking—that a nine-year-old boy would have been better in foster care than trusting someone as unstable as she had apparently been. "That was a worry," he conceded. "Like I told Christian, having more people to love you isn't a bad thing."

Her eyes stung. Dana nodded, unable to speak.

With sudden brusqueness, Nolan said, "If you don't need anything else, I'd better get back."

"No, I... I'm fine. Thank you again, Mr. Gregor."

"How about if we give up and go with first names? Otherwise, we're going to sound like idiots."

Out of nowhere, a smile built. Her eyes might be damp, but she grinned. "You're right. But I think *you* started it."

He chuckled. "Pretty sure you did, but we'll let it slide. Ah, listen. Christian and I thought we'd take you out to dinner tonight, if you aren't too tired."

"I would love that. I'll have to grocery-shop this afternoon, but I don't think I can find any enthusiasm for cooking."

"We'll pick you up. Say, six?"

She smiled again, hoping he couldn't see her lip tremble. "Thank you again. I mean it."

He only nodded and left. Without, she couldn't help noticing, assuring her that she was welcome.

But otherwise...he'd been nicer than she'd expected, she had a wonderful old house instead of a cookie-cutter apartment and she'd be seeing Gabriel in just a few hours.

The tears spilled over.

"THERE ARE SO many interesting sights I could have easily taken a couple weeks for the trip instead of only three days," Dana said, smiling across the table at her son.

"Then why didn't you?" Christian's burning gaze held hers. "It's not like *we* were in any hurry for you to get here."

Nolan wanted to stomp on the kid's foot or find his ribs with an elbow. If nothing else, he'd been raised to be polite.

Dana didn't move for a few seconds. She didn't let her expression show dismay or hurt, but the glow of happiness he'd seen when she hopped in his SUV disappeared now between one blink and the next, as if his butt of a nephew had deliberately gone for the switch.

They still had menus in front of them. Nolan had chosen one of the nicer restaurants in town. The restored brick building gave it ambience, but it wasn't so fancy they would have had to dress up or a kid Christian's age would have felt uncomfortable. The menu offered some creative stuff, but also steak and seafood. On a week-night like this, they had a table by the window with a view of a marina. Once darkness settled, tiny white lights strung along the docks would come on.

He wasn't quite sure why he'd wanted to impress her. Going to the diner might have been better, or even picking up a pizza and bringing it to her rental.

"I'm sorry you feel that way," she said with the quiet dignity he couldn't help but admire. "I was excited to get here." She bent her head to study the menu with apparent calm. "I imagine the fish is a lot fresher here than in Colorado."

"Except trout," Nolan contributed.

"Yes." She smiled at him without actually meeting his eyes. "My father is an ardent fish-erman. He was disappointed that I didn't share his passion."

"Do you enjoy eating the trout?"

This smile created a tiny dimple beside her mouth. "Of course I do." She crinkled her nose. "What I don't enjoy is killing them. Or cut-ting off their heads and cleaning them. And I shouldn't say that when I'm about to order sea-food, should I?"

Nolan closed his menu. "Oh, why not? I don't hunt, and I plan to have a steak."

She opened her mouth and he just knew she

was going to ask why he didn't hunt, but then she glanced at Christian and changed her mind. "Fishing is actually kind of boring, besides. Although I don't say that in front of Dad."

Nolan smiled when he didn't feel like it. He wanted to haul Christian outside by the scruff and tell him to act like a decent human being, but the boy hadn't had any say in the decisions the adults had made. If Nolan had let him know the threat his biological father represented, he'd have soured any possibility of Christian liking the guy. And while part of him wanted to do that, it somehow seemed unfair, a point of honor he didn't quite understand.

Just part of his gut-roiling mixed emotions. Which, unfortunately, included a painful awareness of Dana Stewart's grace and beauty. A tilt of her head would catch his attention, showing him how long and slender her neck was. She had told him she was a runner, and he couldn't understand how her fine-textured skin had stayed so pale. Discovering his gaze was following the line of her throat to the hollow at the base and the V of white skin below, Nolan forced himself to look at Christian instead.

"Made up your mind?" he asked the kid, who just shrugged. Nolan let his eyebrows rise. "You don't want to eat, your privilege."

No such luck—when the waitress showed up,

Christian ordered a burger and fries plus clam chowder.

Waiting for their salads and Christian's chowder, he and Dana labored on with the conversation. Except it quickly quit being work. He was genuinely curious about her, so subjects like where she went to college held his attention. The childhood she described was pretty idyllic, with loving parents and an older brother who alternately tormented and defended her.

Nolan watched Christian out of the corner of his eye. However sullen in appearance, he had his head cocked as if he was listening, too.

"We're good friends now," Dana said of her brother. "I've officially forgiven him." The trace of amusement didn't sound forced. "I like his wife, too."

"Sounds like Marlee and me," he found himself saying, "until she hit about fifteen. That's when she started having some delusions, some really weird spells. I didn't know what to think, and I was a teenage boy, so my response was to keep my distance from her until I left for college. Not very sensitive, I'm afraid."

Christian's head had turned during this little speech. Shock overcame sullenness. "You just, like, *ignored* her?"

"More like I tried not to be around her at all," Nolan said ruefully. "Dinner table, I didn't have any choice. Otherwise, I was busy with sports and friends."

Dana's gaze had rested on Christian, but now she turned to Nolan, surprising compassion evident. "But you've spent years looking after her as an adult."

"I grew up a little and was ashamed of myself." He couldn't believe he was talking about his own long-ago failure, but he just about had to finish. How else could he combat the shame awakened by Dana's willingness to see him as a good man, despite their antagonistic goals? "I don't like to think of her bewilderment when her big brother turned his back on her."

"Did you ever tell her that?" Dana asked, a warmth in her gaze that hadn't been there until now.

"I tried. She claimed not to remember."

Christian stayed silent. Nolan wondered if he'd just acquired feet of clay. Probably, and past time.

Fortunately, their appetizers arrived, giving them something to do besides fidget and stare at each other. Nolan refrained from commenting when Christian loudly slurped his soup. He was probably hoping to earn a rebuke from one of the adults, thereby sparking a scene. Nolan's eyes met Dana's, and he had a feeling she'd made the same guess.

"I asked Craig—your dad—to email photos

of your half sisters," she said, as if Christian were being attentive and friendly. "I thought you might want to see them."

Half sisters. Damn. Nolan had yet to come to terms with that idea.

Noticing both adults were waiting for a response from him, Christian gave another of his patented "I may not be a teenager, but I can act like one" shrugs.

"How old are the girls?" Nolan asked.

"Nine and six."

He doubted she was aware of the old pain in her voice, but he heard it and understood where it came from. He didn't have to count on his fingers to figure this out. If the marriage had lasted a year after the abduction of their baby boy...that meant the SOB had managed, in just a year, to find another woman, get married *and* have another child. Quick work. Craig Stewart had moved on with a vengeance.

Nolan was surprised the guy didn't have more kids. He seemed like the kind whose ego would demand he have a son. But Nolan could hardly ask Dana about that in front of Christian.

"You ever met them?" If her ex had made a point of showing off his pretty baby girls, Nolan was damn sure going to quit shielding the guy's image for Christian.

But she shook her head. "No, he grew up

in Boston and moved back after our divorce. I haven't seen him since."

"But you stayed in touch."

"Not for long. He did let me know about his remarriage and when his first daughter was born. Mutual acquaintances mentioned the second baby. I had to call his mother to get his phone number after..." Her gaze slid to her son.

"You learned Christian was alive."

"Yes."

All he could think was, what a prince. He'd have to ask her sometime if the bastard had given her the house in the divorce or whether she'd had to buy out his half.

Their entrées arrived. As they ate, she remarked on how many sails she'd seen out on the river today. "It still seems chilly to me to be out on the water."

"Most people wear wet suits. Serious windsurfers and sailors own them. Hell, serious windsurfers go out in December."

She looked askance at him. "Is that true?"

"Oh, yeah." He grinned. "Wait'll you try it. Bet you get hooked."

Her eyes widened. So did Christian's, who then stared an accusation at his uncle. No, honorary uncle, Nolan realized, disconcerted.

He looked at Christian. "I'll let you teach her. You're good at it, patient. Just don't drown her."

Dana's chuckle was definitely weak.

Christian maintained his sullen silence until they dropped her off, when Nolan did poke him with an elbow. Then, in response to her "Good night," he mumbled, "Yeah."

Nolan waited until she'd let herself in the front door and he saw a light come on inside before he pulled away from the curb. "I wasn't proud of you tonight," he said.

"So what?" Christian vibrated with fury. "You were such a suck-up I didn't even have to be there."

Nolan's fingers flexed on the steering wheel. His jaw muscles tight, he drove a couple blocks before he could speak. "Whether you like it or not—whether either of us likes it or not—Dana is important in your life. You wouldn't *exist* without her." Christian's scoffing sound infuriated Nolan. He swerved to the curb and yanked on the emergency brake. "While you're clinging to the memory of Marlee as your mother, remember that she did something terrible. Something that does not deserve forgiveness."

Christian went off like a rocket. "You said—"

"That she could have gotten you from someone else." He'd never wanted to do this, but now he had to. He continued grimly, "Marlee started talking about being pregnant a few months before you were born. Where do you *think* she imagined she'd get a baby?"

Stunned silence.

"She might not have had her eye on *you* yet—
she probably didn't. My guess is she slipped into
a maternity ward somewhere and thought she'd
just grab a baby. But security is damn good in
hospitals these days." His rage at himself drove
this inexorable speech. How had he ever believed this bright, handsome boy who looked
nothing like Marlee was hers? If he had been,
his father would have been some street junkie.
Their newborn baby would have had problems.
"But she'd told Mom and Dad and me that she
was having a baby, so she had to find one. No,
more than that—she told us she'd had a boy. At
some point, she saw *you*, fixated on *you*."

"I won't listen!" Christian screamed, clap-
ping his hands over his ears. "I won't, I won't,
I won't!"

Throwing a Marlee-style tantrum only riled
Nolan, who raised his voice. "She didn't happen
to peek in that bedroom window. No, she'd followed you and Dana home. She'd been watching you, waiting for her chance."

Christian was sobbing now, rocking back and
forth.

Heart breaking, Nolan pulled him into an embrace the boy fought at first. Nolan just held on
until he sagged. His own cheeks were wet when
he pressed a rough kiss to Christian's head.

He wanted to stop. Damn, but he wanted to.

Yet some instinct drove him to finish it now, whatever the consequences.

"She may have believed you were hers. She was crazy enough to have decided some woman pushing you in a baby stroller had stolen you. But she was also sane enough to plot, to stalk a mother and baby, to be patient. I wanted to think she wasn't the one to take you, but I was fooling myself. She found a baby the right age, the right gender, and she took him. She claimed you and threw another woman into hell." He swallowed. "Part of me is so goddamn mad at what she did to all of us—you, me, Dana, Grandma and Grandad if they'd lived—that I couldn't have kept making allowances, kept loving her the same way. She was mentally ill. Some people would say she couldn't help herself. But what she did *wasn't* impulse. It was cruel and selfish." He was the one to rock Christian now, as much to comfort himself as anything. "And, man, I never wanted to say this to you."

They stayed like they were for a long time. So long he started to get scared. Christian could come out of this hating him, choosing to hold on tight to his memories of his flawed mommy. Seeing Nolan as a traitor who wasn't fighting for him the way he'd promised.

But his own sense of honor demanded he give Dana Stewart a fair chance. She'd listened to his accusation of selfishness, his defense of the boy he loved, and done something extraordinary. Nolan had enough regrets. If the changes she'd made in her life really were permanent, they might be able to find a way through this they could all live with.

If he were to egg on Christian, encourage his resentment—Nolan wasn't sure he could live with that. He had to give this a fair chance, even if he ended up being the loser.

CHAPTER SIX

CHRISTIAN DIDN'T SAY a word after Uncle Nolan was done, not during the short drive home, not once they were in the house. He *couldn't*. Too much was boiling inside him. He ran straight to his room, leaving his uncle at the foot of the staircase watching him.

He dived onto his bed and curled into a ball, his knees to his chest. *Don't let Uncle Nolan follow me in here. Please don't let him.* Nausea swelled until he wanted to puke, but tears threatened again, too, even though his eyes already burned and felt swollen. He'd been such a baby, crying like that.

Baby. Even thinking the word had him close to hurling.

He sucked in air through his nose, out through his mouth, over and over until the nausea subsided.

He kept hearing things Uncle Nolan said.

She found a baby the right age, the right gender, and she took him. She claimed you and threw another woman into hell.

"Mom," he whispered. "Mommy."

Cruel and selfish.

The acid in his stomach felt like it was eating him. He held himself tighter to protect his middle.

An admission crept into his head, one he didn't want to hear. She *was* selfish. Sometimes. The way she'd just disappear and not come home for weeks or even, sometimes, months. Back when Uncle Nolan was still deployed, when Christian actually lived with her, every time he walked in the door after school, he would wonder if she'd be there. And if she wasn't, whether she'd come home that day. Once he was seven or eight, he'd stay by himself for a day or two without telling anyone, in case his mom wasn't really gone, because even though Grandma and Grandpa would come right away to pick him up if he called, they would get this *look* on their faces, pain and anger and disappointment. He could never count on Mom being there even when she knew he was really excited about pitching his first game or winning an award or being in a school play. After he didn't have anyone in the audience a few times, he made sure to tell his grandparents, because they *always* came. Until they died.

When the police arrived to tell him about the accident, he'd been so scared, thinking, *But what will I do?* His mom could die, too. And if she didn't…what if she took off again? He could mostly take care of himself, but he didn't have money to buy groceries. And people would notice. If that happened, Mom would get in trouble and they might take him away to live in a foster home. It might not even be in Lookout, where all his friends were.

And then Uncle Nolan walked into the Dunbars' house where he'd been staying, swept him into a hug and said, "I'm home for good." Christian knew everything was okay then. He'd pretended to Mom that he minded not being able to live with her, but he didn't really. He *trusted* Uncle Nolan.

He used to trust Uncle Nolan.

No, he still did, except… He felt sick again. Uncle Nolan sounded so hard, so *angry*, when he talked about Mom, and it made Christian remember how mad *he'd* been sometimes, only it wasn't Mom's fault. It wasn't!

While you're clinging to the memory of Marlee as your mother, remember that she did something terrible. Something that does not deserve forgiveness.

Christian didn't know what to believe. Except he did. It just made him feel so guilty he wanted to pretend it couldn't be true. If he believed it, he'd have to be nice to that woman who claimed to be his mother. It might even mean he'd have to go live with her.

It meant…he wasn't really Christian Gregor at all. He was someone named Gabriel.

His belly cramped and he stifled a moan against his knees.

Tonight…he'd been mean to her, even when he could tell he was hurting her. Uncle Nolan had been ashamed of him.

But I don't want to be Gabriel, whoever he *is. I don't.*

THE FIRST DAY of Dana's job was a week away. The woman she was replacing had only finished her last day on Friday, just before Dana arrived in Lookout. Dana had offered to start right away, but her new boss insisted on giving her time to settle in. Time that she wasn't so sure she wanted. Being busy would be better.

Christian was in school anyway, and what was she going to do? Loiter at Wind & Waves from three o'clock on so she could greet her son with a beaming smile? She bet that would go over well.

No, she would stay away for a few days, at least. She'd pretty much thrown herself on the road in front of them. Now she had to be a little patient. See if Nolan and/or Christian made any overtures.

She laughed, a not very nice sound at all. Okay, see if *Nolan* made any overtures. The idea that he and Christian wanted to take her to dinner had been pure fiction. She could only imagine what he'd held over her son to make him agree to sit across the table from her. Too bad whatever it was hadn't been better blackmail material; Christian might have had to be polite, too.

Had the two of them exchanged high fives after they'd dropped her off? Because, wow, Christian had certainly managed to let her know how he really felt about her. Of course, he'd done that the first time they met. She'd been delusional to hope giving him time to know her might soften his instant rejection.

Not so much.

Well, news to them: she wasn't defeated that easily. Fortunately, getting settled into the house gave her plenty to do for the next few days. The moving truck had arrived midday, the two men unloading her furniture and heaps of boxes with startling speed. She'd had to leap aside to avoid getting run over a couple of times.

Now she had a sofa, a TV, a coffee table and a bed. A dining room table and chairs. She also had those mountains of boxes. Her next task was to find her linens, her socks and underwear, the multiple-device charger for her iPod, laptop and phone. She wanted her books on the shelves, her dishes in the cupboards.

Sighing, she went back to work in the kitchen, where she'd begun this morning. Empty totes were piled next to the refrigerator. Finding her coffeemaker and toaster hadn't been optional. Those, she'd dug out last night.

She had unpacked every box labeled Kitchen and was wondering what to do with tablecloths and place mats and cloth napkins when her doorbell rang. Her stupid microwave didn't have a clock. Maybe a neighbor had noticed someone new had moved in.

In faded jeans, a Denver Broncos sweatshirt and sneakers, her hair straggling out of a ponytail, she didn't look her best, but anyone would understand. Moving was hard work.

She opened the door, a smile forming, and found her son on her doorstep. His bicycle lay on its side on her ragged front lawn. Her gaze went back to the boy with shaggy blond hair, jeans and a Wind & Waves hooded sweatshirt, a blue backpack slung over his shoulder. Nolan was nowhere in sight. Disbelieving, Dana looked both ways to be sure.

She caught herself an instant before she said, "Gabriel." However much she hated using the name given to him after his abduction, she had to for now, or alienate him further.

"Christian. Does...your uncle know where you are?"

"Not exactly." He squirmed. "But he won't worry about me or anything."

"Um...come in." She backed up. "Why won't he worry about you?"

"'Cuz I said I was going to a friend's house and I'd see him at home." He shrugged. "He doesn't care what I do after school."

She sincerely hoped that wasn't true, even if this was a small, relatively safe town. She closed the front door and saw him gape at the mess.

"How'd your stuff get here?"

He was talking to her. Why? She didn't dare get excited.

"Moving truck."

"Oh. That's a cool TV."

"I'm glad you approve."

He kept standing there. He twitched, he shuffled his feet, he opened his mouth and closed it. Dana wouldn't have been surprised if he had bolted for the door without saying whatever he'd come to say.

But at last he blurted, "Uncle Nolan was mad at me."

Kudos for courage, she thought. "Because you were rude yesterday."

Christian drew up his shoulders like a turtle. "Um, yeah."

"Why were you rude? Did you think I'd pack up and go back to Colorado?"

He sneaked a desperate look at her with eyes the same shade as Craig's. "I don't know. I just..." His throat worked, but he didn't finish.

Taking pity on him, she said, "You wish everything could go back to the way it was before."

Now she was exulting. He was here. He hadn't exactly apologized, but that was really what this was about.

"I guess so." He was mumbling, but that was okay.

Dana leaned against the back of the sofa. "I don't. Finding you, at least knowing you were alive and well, was everything to me. Maybe too much." It could be this was a mistake, but she didn't think so. "My husband—your dad— did a better job of moving on with his life. I've learned since then a lot of parents react the way I did when a child is abducted or lost. It's as if…your life stops. How can you go on without knowing? As terrible as it sounds, being able to bury your child has to be better than never knowing. So I won't apologize for anything I've said or done since I found out about you."

He'd watched her throughout this speech, his lips pinched.

"What I am sorry for is that it's been such a shock to you. I was so happy I didn't let myself realize how you'd feel."

He lifted one shoulder.

She wondered suddenly, painfully, whether he would smell like her Gabriel if he let her hug him. The thought stole her breath.

Don't blow this. She forced herself to smile. "So, do you like to read?"

He looked at her like she was nuts.

"Most of those boxes—" she waved toward one of the mountain peaks "—are full of books."

"Really?"

Laughing at his incredulity, she said, "Really. I'm a huge reader, and I like to own books. I use the library, too—" Wait. "There *is* a library in town, isn't there?"

"Well, yeah. They have lots of computers. I think you can get books from other libraries, too, like Parkdale."

"So it's a county-wide library system."

"I don't know." He cast what she took as a longing glance toward the front door. "I guess."

She had a flashback: her brother coming home from school and going straight to the refrigerator. He was always starving.

Inspiration struck. "Are you hungry? Do you want something to eat or drink?"

He hesitated, but her lure succeeded. Dana was able to offer soda, which she occasionally drank, and a selection of cookies as well as a sandwich. She was glad she'd found the bakery on River Street and let herself be tempted by the goodies.

As Christian opened a cola, she wondered if she should have asked whether Nolan allowed him to have caffeine. Then he dived into the sandwich she made. While he was still wolfing that, she set out the cookies.

Underhanded tactics, but if the way to a man's heart was through his stomach, the strategy had to work even better for a nearly teenage boy.

Her phone rang while she was sitting across from him with a cup of coffee. If it had to do with work— No, her ex-husband was the caller. She tried not to let Christian see the tension that knotted muscles in her neck.

Ignore or answer?

It wasn't fair that she was here, feeding their son, and Craig hadn't even heard his voice. She couldn't reconcile it with her conscience to *not* answer.

"Craig."

"You promised to stay in touch."

How like him to go straight to an accusation. "I only arrived in Lookout yesterday," she pointed out.

"Well? Have you seen him?"

Recognizing the strain in his voice, she closed her eyes on a wave of guilt. "Yes. The three of us had dinner last night."

"Just like that? Gregor isn't trying to keep him away from you?"

"No." Oh, Lord—did she have to tell him she was with their son right now? Christian had set down the remnants of his sandwich and was watching her, renewed wariness in his expression. Could he hear both sides of the conversation? "I'm...actually with him right now." Ignoring Craig's exclamation, she pressed the phone against her thigh. "Christian, I'm talking to my ex-husband. Your father. Will you talk to him? I think he'd love it if you would say hello."

Panic flared, but after a second he swallowed and nodded.

She lifted the phone to her ear again. "Would you like to talk to him?"

There was a tiny pause. "You know I would," he said.

"Then here he is."

She handed over the phone and started to push back her chair. "If you'd like me to give you some privacy..."

Christian shook his head frantically. Sandy hair flopped over his forehead.

Dana heard the rumble of Craig's voice but couldn't make out words.

"Uh, yeah," was Christian's first response, followed by, "I guess," and her personal favorite, "I don't know."

She couldn't yet accurately read her own son's rapidly shifting expressions. All she could do was wait tensely and hope Craig didn't blow it by demanding too much, too soon.

Like she'd done during that first visit.

Although she wasn't sure why she cared. On a wash of more guilt, she knew that wasn't true;

back then Craig had grieved just as she had. She had never felt the same about him again after he had also lashed out at her, but in other ways he'd been a rock. People mourn differently. How many times had she read that, been told the same? Men were more likely to take refuge from grief in anger. Craig had loved their baby boy, too.

Christian mumbled something even she couldn't make out and thrust the phone at her. She took it.

"Craig?"

"I take it he doesn't want me to come out there."

"I don't know." She winced at the echo of their son's favorite response. "I think he has a lot to deal with, Craig. Can we talk about this later?"

He grumbled and growled but eventually agreed that he could wait. Call over, she set the phone on the table and looked at Christian.

"What did you think?"

All the animation had left his face. He ducked his head. "I don't know."

"Have a cookie." She pushed the plate toward him.

He ate two, guzzled the rest of his cola and said he had to go. Dana swallowed her protest and walked him to the door. "Thank you for visiting," she said.

He slipped his other arm through a strap

so that his pack rested between his shoulder blades, picked up his bike and pushed it across the lawn. When she called goodbye, he hesitated at the sidewalk, turning his head. "I guess I'll see you."

Not until she felt the sting in her sinuses as she watched him pedal away did she realize how much sadness underlay her exhilaration.

She had always known his body might be found someday, that her only resolution would be having the opportunity to bury her little boy. What nobody ever said was that finding your miracle also meant being confronted with how much you'd lost.

Her son could just as well be some random neighborhood boy, reluctantly compelled to be polite to this strange adult.

He's not your baby anymore. How right Nolan had been.

"So ONCE SHE had you alone, she made you talk to your father." Newly awakened anger in Nolan's blood reached a simmer.

Christian hunched in that disconcerting way he had taken up since the revelation about his background had been sprung on him. Hair that shouldn't have been long enough somehow succeeded in veiling his expression. "Well, not like *made*."

Nolan's teeth ground together. Damn that

woman. He'd trusted her. The deal was, he co-operated, she held off her ex. Instead, the second she got Christian alone, she'd pressed him to talk to the bastard.

Of course, Craig Stewart hadn't actually threatened Nolan directly. Who knew how much of what she'd told him was true? Her ex-husband's supposed determination to sue for custody could have been nothing but a tool she'd used to worm her way in.

"You do your homework." Nolan turned off the oven. "I won't be gone long. Dinner will only take half an hour or so when I get home."

"Wait." Christian jumped up, the straight-back kitchen chair rocking. "You're not going to her house, are you?"

"She broke her word to me. Yeah. I intend to talk to Ms. Stewart." Dana was a nice woman; Ms. Stewart, who knew what she was? He sure as hell didn't.

"But it wasn't like that!" Christian cried.

"Homework." Nolan grabbed his keys and wallet out of the basket on the counter and stalked out the door.

The drive took less than five minutes. He could get anywhere in Lookout in under five minutes. His once-large world had shrunk in many ways.

He slammed to a stop in front of her small

house, killed the engine and strode to the front porch, where he leaned on the bell.

Dana opened the door almost immediately, looking rumpled and relaxed in a way he hadn't yet seen. A snug T-shirt and skinny jeans let him see every curve. Had she maybe put on weight since her first appearance in town?

Didn't matter.

"Nolan." She peered past him. "Is Christian with you?"

"No. I came to talk to you."

Her face tightened. The happiness, or maybe only peace, evaporated, leaving her skin stretched tight over her cheekbones and her eyes big and wary.

"All right," she said slowly, and let him in.

Still feeling the slow burn, he stopped in the middle of the living room, cluttered with boxes, and faced her. "I thought we had an understanding."

Her expression was now icy cool. "I thought we did, too."

"And yet the minute you get Christian alone, you have him talking to your ex. The guy *you* told me is pushing to go to court. Who is looking for any nugget of information he can use to persuade a judge Christian can't be left with me."

She simply didn't react, which infuriated him further. Hyped on adrenaline, his body was combat ready. He leaned toward her. "So either you're colluding with him to go behind my back, or you were playing me. And that tells me *he* isn't the threat."

Anger sparked in her gray eyes. Folding her arms was the only giveaway that his aggressive body language might have caused her to feel defensive. "Craig is Gabriel's father. Neither you nor I has the right to deny him the chance to talk to his son. The son who was abducted from us by *your* sister." Her voice sizzled by the end.

"You and I both know you can't prove that. We don't know how Marlee ended up with *Christian*." He leaned on the name, furious to have been driven to defend Marlee's indefensible acts.

Strung tight, Dana appeared too thin again. He'd swear he saw ghosts in her eyes. "I suppose you'll blame me next. If I hadn't left the window open, none of this ever would have happened."

Pissed to the max, he came closer than he wanted to saying something unforgivable like, *Seems you think I should.* Whatever she'd done today, she didn't deserve that kind of blow.

"I hope you know I'll never say anything like that."

Looking brittle, she backed a couple of steps toward the front door. "I have my differences with my ex-husband, but he loved our baby boy, too." She spoke coolly. "He deserved a chance to hear his voice. What I told you was that I'd persuade Craig to allow us a chance to work out a plan without involving lawyers. I did *not* promise not to allow Gabriel to speak to his father. And when he's in my home, he's my son."

Nolan saw red, as she'd no doubt intended. "Then I guess he won't be spending time with you unsupervised, will he?"

For a moment, she said nothing, her face so lacking expression he expected it to crack. Then she opened the front door and said, "You need to leave."

"With pleasure," he snapped, walking out. His shoulder brushed her, knocking her momentarily off balance. He hadn't meant to do that and hesitated, about to turn and apologize when the door closed quietly and he heard the dead bolt engage. Angry at himself as well as her now, he muttered an obscenity and returned to his truck, where he shoved the key in the ignition but didn't turn it.

She was right. Goddamn it, she was right. Nothing had been said about whether Christian could talk to his dad on the phone. It was the idea she'd pressured him that had enraged Nolan—and the fear that Craig Stewart would be cold-blooded enough to try to lure an eleven-year-old boy into saying something that would put a weapon into the son of a bitch's hands.

Nolan sat unmoving for a long time. The

blinds had already been drawn, and as far as he could tell, she never parted them to sneak a look out. He felt sure she wouldn't let him in again. He was still on edge from the flood of adrenaline, his fingers tight on the steering wheel as if he were strangling it.

Way to go, he congratulated himself. *Now what?*

Swearing some more, he fired up the engine and drove home.

Distraught, Christian met him at the door. "Did you get mad at her? Why did you get mad at her?"

"Because she shouldn't have encouraged you to talk to him when I wasn't there." He explained his fear that Craig Stewart would mine Christian for some detail that the attorneys could spin into poison.

The accusation on the boy's face remained. "But she didn't. I *tried* to tell you. He called while I was there. I don't think she wanted to let me talk to him, but she asked me and I said okay."

Nolan didn't so much as breathe. Oh, man.

Wound tight, Christian cried, "And he didn't ask me anything like that. He just talked about how happy he was when he heard I was okay, and how he looked forward to getting to know me, and how he'd call another time so my sisters could say hi 'cuz they were so excited to meet me." His voice grew smaller. "*You* were the one who said we should be nice. Then you didn't even listen to me!"

Nolan dropped into a chair and bent forward, elbows on his knees, his fingers tangled in his hair. Among the guys, he'd always been known as rock steady, the last one to shoot off his mouth or throw a fist. So what had happened?

He'd panicked, was what had happened. He could never set aside the deep-down, sickening fear that he'd lose Christian. Twenty-four/seven, it stayed with him. Anxiety filled his dreams. First thing when he awakened, he felt the rock in his stomach. Last thing at night, he lay calculating how long he could hold off these people who had a claim to Christian that he couldn't match. His only remaining mission in life was to keep his nephew safe, and he didn't know if he could. He'd been primed to blow.

He gave his hair a last yank and lifted his head, meeting the boy's eyes. "You're right. I went off the deep end for no good reason. I'll make it right with Dana. I promise."

"Were you really awful?"

Now there was a question he didn't want to answer. He did, anyway. "Yeah." He cleared his throat. "I didn't give her much of a chance."

The brown eyes he'd always believed came from the boy's father stayed anxious. "I kind of said I shouldn't have been rude last night, and she said it was okay. Then she made a sandwich for me and gave me some really good cookies and asked whether you'd be worried about where I was." The speech surprised Nolan. Christian still talked to him sometimes, but he hung out with his friends more, and they played either video games or sports.

"I was a jackass. You don't have to tell me again."

Christian's grin popped out, letting Nolan know he'd said the right thing. "Is that swearing?"

"Probably." Nolan smiled ruefully. "Actually, it's an animal."

"So can I say *ass*?"

"Depends on the context." Seeing the kid's mouth open, Nolan said, "And don't ask. You know what that means."

"I'm hungry," the boy announced.

Nolan shook his head. "You just finished telling me about the sandwich and cookies you ate."

"And a Coke, too," Christian said with satisfaction. Nolan let him have soda when they ate out but didn't buy it for home.

"So how can you be hungry?"

"I just am."

"Fine. You can cut up the asparagus."

"Do I hafta eat—"

Reassured by the standard-issue protest, Nolan said, "Yes," shutting down any further argument.

Rising to his feet, he gave Christian a gentle, re-assuring bump with his shoulder—their version of a hug.

And he winced at the recollection of his bad-tempered display at Dana's house.

CHAPTER SEVEN

DRAGGING HERSELF OUT of bed the next day, Dana's mood reminded her unpleasantly of all the mornings before the miraculous phone call.

She wrinkled her nose at the thought. How ridiculous. Then she hadn't even wanted to open her eyes. Today she felt a little low, that was all. The pep talk got her into the shower, dressed and to the kitchen.

The scene with Nolan had erupted out of nowhere and wasn't fun. So what? Nothing—*nothing*—would ever be as bad as imagining her baby boy tortured, dead in a shallow grave, scrabbling for food in a filthy apartment while his abductor was out scoring a hit. Oh, she'd thought of every possibility and then some.

Instead, Gabriel had been loved. Raised to be a boy who felt guilty because he'd been ungracious to her. Guilty enough, despite his mixed emotions about her, to apologize.

He'd been right here, eating food she'd given him. He was skinny, energetic, bright eyed and surprisingly sure of himself, considering the turmoil he had lived through the past few years. Whatever happened, whether she ever set eyes on him again, she had this much.

She poured herself a cup of coffee and announced, "Nolan Gregor can go leap off a tall bridge." There were a couple of bridges available in Portland that would do just fine. "So there!"

At least she'd stood up to him yesterday. He'd ruined her evening, but then, wasn't that what he intended?

Uncertainty gave the hand lifting the coffee cup to her mouth a faint tremor. So, okay, she was a little worried. And to think *he* was the one who'd persuaded her that staying friendly was best for Gabriel's sake. Christian's sake.

She gave her head a small shake. She was confusing even herself.

Tempted to drive down to Wind & Waves, march up to its proprietor and say, *What the hell?*, Dana decided to wait twenty-four hours. Give tempers time to cool. Well, *his* temper; hers was righteous.

Back to unpacking.

She marched to her bedroom and opened one of the tall boxes that held her work wardrobe on hangers suspended from a narrow rod. She began transferring them to the closet. Not a wrinkle to be seen. Amazing.

The doorbell rang.

Dana had quit hoping for a friendly neighbor. Since she knew exactly two people in Lookout and one of them was presently in school, that left...Nolan Gregor.

Or maybe someone serving her with a summons from him.

Deeply reluctant to face either scenario, she groaned and headed for the front door, anyway. Avoidance was useless.

Her caller was, in fact, Nolan. Wearing camouflage cargo pants and a coordinating tan T-shirt, he might have just wandered by from a base in Afghanistan. Too bad she couldn't help noticing how that T-shirt stretched across broad shoulders and powerful pectoral muscles, and even those sacky pants reminded her how very male he was.

"Mr. Gregor. I see you dressed for battle," she said drily.

"What?" He frowned and looked down at himself. A flash of discomfort showed on his face. "I just grabbed from my drawer."

She arched an eyebrow. "The subconscious has a way of speaking."

"I wear stuff left from my army days. That's all."

"Okay." She continued to block the opening. "Was there something you forgot to say last night?"

"Yeah." His stance was military, too, feet far

enough apart to make him appear braced. But his very blue eyes held regret. "I'm sorry."

"You're sorry." The echo was senseless but all she could come up with.

"Can I come in?"

Dana thought about it while he waited with apparently unending patience. "Fine." She held open the door and stepped back. He passed her, stopping a few feet into the living room. Close, in fact, to where he'd stood yesterday while he blasted her. His posture remained military formal. Or was it firing-line formal? "What are you sorry about?" she asked.

"That I was a jerk. That I didn't give Christian a chance to tell me what really happened before I lit out of the house. That I was…unreasonable." He seemed to choke on that one but continued, anyway. "That I bumped you on my way out." The wrinkles on his forehead deepened. "I was being an ass, but that part was an accident."

It was a heck of an apology. Dana's anger dissolved. That didn't mean she felt the tentative trust and even liking she had before, but this very inconvenient attraction seemed to be here to stay.

"Thank you for saying that," she said finally. "I take it Christian told you Craig was the one to call, not me."

"Yes."

"And that made a difference?"

He was smart enough to look cautious. "Your point?"

"My point is that there wasn't any reason I *shouldn't* have called Craig to give him a chance to hear his son's voice for the first time in eleven years. We're divorced. He—" She shook her head. No, she wouldn't say that Craig had abandoned her in her grief. That wasn't any of this man's business. "At the moment, he's behaving decently."

Matching knots formed to each side of Nolan's jaw. "And I'm not?"

"I didn't say that."

"The implication was loud and clear."

Dana didn't bother to comment.

He chewed on his pride for a minute, then bent his head. "Okay. I'll suck it up and take that."

She sighed, knowing she had to relent. "Do you have time for a cup of coffee?"

"Will you call me by my first name again?"

She turned and headed for the kitchen, tossing over her shoulder, "You should take what you can get."

His low, rough laugh heated the coal of sexual awareness instead of warming her heart. Wonderful.

As she poured coffee, he said, "When I got home, Christian reamed me a new one. I tell you that since you deserve a moment of triumph."

She set both cups on the table, then looked at him. "Is that what this is about? You screwed up yesterday, so I win? But, hey, you have more time with him, so you're sure to have me beat in no time?"

"No." His pained expression appeared genuine. He pulled out a chair but waited like a gentleman for her to sit first. "Okay. I've thought in terms of winning and losing. I can't deny it. For a big part of my life, losing could be fatal. You can't tell me *you* aren't afraid of losing, too."

Dana's mouth twisted. "No. Of course I am. To lose him again would be...terrible. Never as bad as it was, because I'd know he's safe and loved. But it would mean he doesn't love *me*. If that makes me sound selfish..."

"No, blast it." Scowling, Nolan startled her by reaching across the table and covering her hand with his.

Startled, she looked down at that big hand, so much darker than hers. It was the first time they'd touched, at least voluntarily. She was absurdly conscious of his warmth, the dip of his palm, even the calluses on his fingers.

After a second, she realized he was still talking.

"I have the same fears. He's all I have." His expression clouded and the frown deepened even as he took his hand back. He hadn't liked admitting that.

Dana would have sympathized, except she was *glad* he suffered the same terror as she did. It gave them something close to equal weight on this emotional seesaw. Thinking that, she felt how chilled her hand suddenly was. She tucked it beneath the table on her lap.

"That's…partly why I'm here, you know," she admitted haltingly. "Because I do understand."

His gaze pinned hers. "How badly have I screwed up?"

"Are you asking if I called an attorney this morning?" She saw on his face that was exactly what he'd feared. "No. I didn't call to give Craig an earful, either. I was mad, but I expected us to have ups and downs. We have too much at stake to behave well all the time."

Suddenly he was laughing again. "I think I could like you if—"

Abruptly, he shuttered his laugh. Dana couldn't look away from him. The air she drew in was too thin.

"—I wasn't your worst nightmare." Her voice came out thin, too.

He was the one to look away. "We have each other by the short hairs."

"How nicely put."

Nolan picked up his mug, only to cradle it in his big hands. "Guess we have to trust each other, to a point."

"I thought we'd already agreed on that." So she was being a bitch; he deserved it.

"Yeah." He cleared his throat. "Did I say how sorry I am?"

Her mouth curved. "Yes, Nolan, quite adequately, thank you."

They smiled at each other until she felt her cheeks warming.

"You want to hang out at Wind & Waves part of the day Saturday?" he asked. "Christian usually works with me. He can handle the cash register, give advice, set people up with equipment. I suspect they all think he's a young-looking fifteen or so. He'd enjoy showing off for you."

She might have to kill Craig if he ever disparaged Nolan's business in Christian's hearing. "That sounds like fun. Why don't I bring a lunch? Unless you have something you usually do."

"Skip lunch? Order something in?" His mouth quirked. "Drop some coins in the snack machine?"

Dana rolled her eyes. "I can do better than that."

Voice low, husky, he said, "I'm sure you can."

THINKING IT WAS sort of weird having her here and sort of not, Christian kept a close eye on Dana Saturday. She was superenthusiastic, which made him wonder if she was faking it.

The store was quiet when he came back in from setting up a customer with a windsurfing rental package. Nolan waved him over to where he was rearranging wet suits by size. They had to do that all the time. People pulled stuff off the shelf, then dumped it back wherever.

Nolan nodded toward Dana, chatting with a woman who was holding up T-shirts to herself. Wind & Waves sold shirts with the shop's own logo, of course, but also a few popular ones that had to do with windsurfing. Christian's friends practically fell down laughing every time they saw the one that said Got Wind?.

"So, what do you think?" Nolan asked.

"You mean about her?"

Nolan shrugged. "And her being here. Do you mind that I suggested it?"

Christian hadn't liked it at first, but… "She's okay. I mean, lunch was good."

At first he wasn't sure he wanted to eat what she brought. Instead of sandwiches, she'd made something she called pita pockets. She warmed them in the break room microwave. They were full of rice and beans and veggies and were spicy. She'd made pumpkin bread, too, and brought a tub of cream cheese to spread on it.

Even with Amir working today, it had been too busy for them all to eat together. Dana sat with Christian for a while, asking questions

about the business while he ate. Then he saw
her and Uncle Nolan eating together later.

"Did you tell her you liked her food?"

Christian shuffled his feet. "Not really."

Nolan clapped him on the back. "You should."

For a minute, neither of them said anything,
although Christian could tell that Uncle Nolan
was watching, too, as she threw back her head
and laughed at something the other woman said.

"Mom never liked it here. I mean, at the store."

Nolan looked at him with an expression Christian didn't totally understand. "No. She didn't."

"How come?" It just burst out. Christian had
never asked. It felt like something Uncle Nolan
didn't want him to know.

"Huh." Uncle Nolan got broody looking. "She
was never interested in windsurfing."

Or any other water sport. Christian nodded.

"But I think it had more to do with me."

He stared at his uncle in astonishment. "But…
she loved you!"

"Yeah. Maybe." Nolan moved his shoulders in
that way he did when he was feeling tight. "She
didn't love that I took you from her."

Christian had known that, of course. Nolan
wouldn't bad-mouth her, but she had yelled about
him sometimes.

"I was kind of living with Grandma and
Grandpa, anyway."

"Yeah, but she could tell herself they were

just taking care of you when she was gone. I put a heavy boot on that little illusion."

Christian would never forget what Uncle Nolan had said. *You'll be living with me from now on.* He had felt a flood of relief so powerful, he'd almost cried.

"Dana sort of looks like she's having fun," he heard himself say.

One corner of Nolan's mouth quirked. "She does."

"I get confused about her."

His uncle laid his arm across Christian's shoulders. Not like a hug. Christian really liked when he did that. "I understand," Nolan said. "I'm of two minds about her myself."

"I wanted to hate her," Christian confessed. He'd told himself he was glad when she just went away after that first meeting. Really glad.

"Yeah." Something dark in his voice made Christian wonder if Uncle Nolan *did* hate her. Only…his expression when he watched her didn't look like hate, although Christian couldn't figure out what he was thinking.

"But…it felt sort of good when she said she was moving here."

Uncle Nolan nodded as if that made perfect sense. "Having your real mother shrug and decide she couldn't be bothered to change her life for you wouldn't feel so good."

Christian agreed, even though he thought it

might be more than that. Like, she made him feel stuff. He didn't even know what to call any of it yet.

The customer Dana had been helping carried what looked like two T-shirts and a sweatshirt to the checkout counter. Nolan dropped his arm from Christian's shoulders and took a step, but Dana smiled and waved to let him know she'd take care of it.

Earlier they'd discovered she knew how to operate a cash register. As long as the items were clearly labeled, she could ring them up. She'd helped Christian get a kayak into the water, too, plus the woman renting it couldn't figure out how to buckle into her life vest. If Dana didn't know how, she figured it out really quick and kept the customer from feeling stupid. That was one of Uncle Nolan's Rules for Business: help customers feel smart and competent. The rules were all like that. He phrased them positively. That's what he said. He didn't use the words *no* or *never*, except for in a couple rules that had to do with safety.

By the end of the day, when Uncle Nolan ordered Christian to turn the sign to Closed, Dana looked really different than she had when she arrived at noon. She'd gone back out to the beach with him a bunch of times to help renters with Hobie Cats or windsurfing boards. Since they had to go into the water, she ended up rolling her khaki pants to her knees. Her pants had gotten wet anyway, and he could tell they were stiff now.

Her hair had started loose and shiny. He'd seen her pull it into a ponytail to keep it out of her way, and now hairs were straggling out. Her cheeks and nose were pink from the sun and her lips looked chapped. Uncle Nolan noticed at the same time and handed her a tube of lip stuff.

He was grinning. He held up his hand and Christian smacked it. When he turned to Dana, she did, too, but awkwardly, as if she'd never done it before.

"Hot damn," Uncle Nolan said. "We did some good business today." His smile for Dana was teasing. "And had free help, too." He turned it on Christian. "*Lots* of free help."

"Yeah!" They joked about this practically every weekend. "When are you going to start paying me?"

"When you're legal." He wrapped his hand around the back of Christian's neck and gave it a squeeze. "Right now I'd get arrested for violating child-labor laws if the authorities knew I was paying you under the table."

"Are you really?" Dana's eyes widened.

"Yep." Uncle Nolan knew to have a little pause before the punch line. "It's called an allowance."

She giggled. "Well, he deserves to be paid." She smiled at Christian. "He's a good worker."

All loose now, she didn't seem as fake as she had when she arrived. She didn't look all that much older than Molly, the high school girl who stayed with Christian when Uncle Nolan had to be out at night. Like when he went to see that woman. The one he thought Christian didn't know about.

Jason said Christian should watch out, that Uncle Nolan would probably marry her and she might not like having someone else's kid living with them. But Christian knew his uncle would never marry anyone who didn't want him, too. If he even *thought* about marrying her, he'd bring her home first, or take Christian with them sometimes when they went out, but he never did.

Except…now Christian had all this other stuff to think about. Like, what if they made him go live with Dana or the father he'd talked to on the phone? Would Uncle Nolan get married then? Something else that gave Christian a stomachache. He didn't want anything else to change.

If he could stay with Uncle Nolan, he didn't mind Dana being around. She wasn't awful—in fact, today she'd been kind of cool. She was like a friend of Nolan's hanging around. But thinking of her as his mother? Even the idea made him feel like he'd swallowed a baseball.

NOLAN INSISTED ON taking them out for pizza. Determined to soak up every minute she had with Christian, Dana accepted even though she'd been disturbingly aware of Nolan all day and really needed a time-out to talk some sense into herself.

"Are we celebrating something?" she asked as they walked out to their vehicles. Did she dare ask Christian if he'd like to ride with her? No, she decided; he was being too careful to keep Nolan's bulk between them.

"Today's take beat any day we had in May last year, and we're still in the first week of the month." His voice was rich with satisfaction. "Windsurfing is big business here in the Columbia River Gorge. Every town along this stretch of the river has a place that sells the same kind of equipment I do and offers rentals, too, but either the sport is gaining even more in popularity, or enthusiasts are choosing Wind & Waves. After the winter slowdown, I worried. Looks like I didn't have to."

"You bought an existing business, you said." After hearing her brother's stories about his guide business, Dana really was curious about Wind & Waves.

Nolan nodded. "It gave me some stock to

begin with and ensured I didn't have a competitor right here in town. I'd have put them out of business anyway—they didn't have enough square footage, which meant limited stock, and the location downtown had problems, starting with a lack of adequate parking. Moving the business to the shore gives us a big boost. I got the idea of teaming up with the inn from a store that did the same in Hood River. They have a deal with a Best Western that gives them a private beach like we have."

She unlocked her door. "Stealing ideas. Tut-tut."

The humor in his eyes made her pulse bounce. "In the military, if you can't learn from your enemy, you're toast. Now, I wouldn't go so far as to call my competitors along the Gorge enemies, but…"

Dana was laughing when she backed out of her parking spot to follow the big SUV to Nolan's and Christian's favorite pizza parlor.

She parked to find man and boy already out of the SUV and waiting for her. Christian stayed quiet as they walked in, however, and once they put in an order, begged Nolan for money to play video games.

Dana watched him go to the small arcade room, some of her pleasure evaporating. "Has he had enough of me today?"

"He's not much for talking."

She believed it was more than that, except it was true he hadn't had much to say even as they worked side by side. Maybe the day hadn't been as successful as she'd believed.

Seeing she'd made Nolan uncomfortable, she decided not to challenge him. "You were right. He could just about run the place."

His subtle relaxation told her she'd made the right choice. "He's a smart kid."

"Is that a compliment?"

Sprawled on his side of the booth, his knees occasionally brushing hers, he smiled. "Could be."

"Will you tell me about your sister?"

That wiped out the smile. "To give you some more ammunition?"

"No!" Of course that was what he'd think. "Never mind. I just thought…" Dana trailed off, turning her head as if she was interested in a family walking in. The boy, about four or five, had a shock of blond hair. Even now, the sight of him gave her a sharp pain. She'd missed so much. She would never know Gabriel at that age.

"Then why?" Nolan asked.

She turned back to see his gaze had followed hers and settled briefly on the little boy before returning to her. There was understanding in his eyes that made her feel a little angry to be so easily read.

Nonetheless, she answered honestly. "She was part of his life. In his eyes, I'm trying to replace her."

A struggle showed on his face. "I don't want to disparage her to you," he said finally.

"I didn't ask that."

"You know she died a month after I discovered from Christian's blood test that he couldn't be her son."

"Yes." She hadn't asked how. It was horrible to admit, but she'd been glad. She had no idea what she'd have said or done if she'd had to come face-to-face with that woman.

"I killed her," Nolan said with such bleakness she sucked in a breath.

After gaping, she had to reshape her lips to form a word. "What?"

"It's more accurate to say she killed herself. I drove her to it."

"How?"

"I wanted answers and was determined that, by God, she'd give them."

Unsettled by his self-loathing, Dana tried to think of what to say. "You were shocked."

The dislike on his face made her want to shrivel. Instead, she lifted her chin and held his gaze.

"All she did was scream, 'He's mine! It's not true. He's mine!' over and over. How could I accuse her of something like that? It was lies. She remembered every minute of her pregnancy, from puking to labor. Why wouldn't I believe her? I suggested her baby could have been switched in the hospital with another little boy."

"You gave her an out," Dana said flatly.

"It seemed a possibility. But she insisted that couldn't have happened. She said he was born with more hair than any of the babies, that everybody commented on it. And it was so blond."

Her heart cramped at the memory of the pale fuzz Gabriel had actually been born with. "She didn't see him until he was eight months old. By then, his hair had grown."

He was watching the door to the arcade room, not her.

"What if her baby died?" Why she felt any pity for the woman who had stolen her Gabriel, she couldn't imagine, but she of all people knew what losing your baby could do to you. "And... she convinced herself he hadn't, that Gabriel *was* hers."

He grunted. "Now who's offering an out?"

"I'm not—"

"She was never pregnant."

"What?" Dana whispered again.

"Because she committed suicide, they did an autopsy." His eyes met hers, and she wished they hadn't. "I asked the pathologist whether she had ever been pregnant. I was told she'd never carried a baby to term or even close. She lied."

"I—"

"Enough," he said, his voice so cold it could raise goose bumps. "Here comes Christian."

Christian. Not Gabriel. Jarred, Dana resented the reminder.

He stopped at the table, looking curiously at them. "Didn't you hear our number?"

"No." Nolan slid out. "You get the plates and a knife—I'll grab the pizza."

Left alone, Dana stared, dry-eyed, toward the back of the restaurant, where there was a glassed-in room, probably for private parties. She wondered how many times Christian had celebrated with his friends in that room. The end of soccer season, baseball, other activities. Not just friends—family.

What had Marlee been like at those parties? A mom, like any other? Or had her craziness been obvious to everyone? Had she embarrassed Christian?

Dana turned her head to watch the two returning to the table, an ease and trust between them that gave her a bittersweet feeling. Oddly, it brought her back from the dark well of hatred. This—today—was a gift. She'd wasted too much of her life in grief and bitterness. No more.

She only wished she truly believed herself.

CHAPTER EIGHT

SUNDAY MORNING, NOLAN was checking the status of an order on his computer when his phone rang. He took it from his pocket, saw the name and muttered an imprecation.

He hadn't seen Ellie in weeks. Not since Christian's biological mother called to announce she was moving to Lookout. He'd been a little preoccupied since then. Stressed, too. Both fine excuses, except the truth was, he hadn't even thought about her.

But that wasn't fair to Ellie, even if all they had was an occasional meal and jump into bed, not a relationship. Unfortunately, he knew she'd have liked it to become so.

A whole lot passed with lightning speed through his mind while the phone continued to ring.

His sudden attraction to a too-skinny blonde woman with long legs and dove-gray eyes that betrayed her every emotion was bound to pass. Wouldn't it? Think of the complications.

Answer the phone, he told himself. *Put Ellie off.*

He tapped his thumb on the screen and said, "Hey."

"Nolan. Did I get you at a busy time? We haven't talked for a while, so…" She let her sentence trail off suggestively.

"I've been pretty busy," he said, thoughts still churning. Keep Ellie in reserve? Man, that sounded cold-blooded. Plan a date with her and hope he'd be in the mood? He winced. Or should he end it now?

"Business good?" she asked.

"Crazy good. Plus, Christian has had some things going on." He hesitated.

Dana wouldn't settle for anything but a real relationship. He wasn't opposed to one with the right woman, but…Christian's mother? The woman who held the power to destroy him in her slender hands?

"Well, if you can get away…" Ellie said uncertainly, in her soft voice.

"Not in the near future," he said, then grimaced. Keeping her hanging was a crappy thing to do. He sighed. "Ellie, I've met someone. Nothing has happened with her yet, but I'd feel like a crud seeing you when I'm thinking about another woman. I'm sorry. I like you too much not to be honest with you."

Silence answered him. He knew he'd hurt her, even though he'd never made a single promise or hinted at future possibilities.

"Well," she said. "Thank you for telling me. I...wish you the best, Nolan." And then she was gone, not even giving him a chance to say goodbye.

She'd been dignified and gracious—leaving him feeling...not so good about himself.

MONDAY MORNING, DANA walked in the door of her new workplace, an agency called Helping Hand. She felt an unsurprising mix of apprehension and excitement. The huge hug the receptionist gave her the minute she introduced herself warmed her.

"Oh, we've been so excited about you!" the very young woman exclaimed. She wore a nose ring and had bright purple streaks in her pixie-short brown hair. She introduced herself as Greer French. Dana liked her right away.

Greer let her drop her purse in the office that would be hers, then led her to a conference room, where she was soon joined by two other women Dana had met via Skype during the interview. Jessica Overton, likely in her forties, was the director, and Meghan Getchel, no more than midtwenties, was the other social worker.

Dana already knew that Helping Hand had opened its door ten months before. From the brochures and lists of programs, she suspected the agency was in an exploratory stage, stretching its muscles, learning what worked and what didn't. For Dana, the job had appealed in part because she'd be able to shape programs and areas of focus, not just deal with individual clients.

She'd also worried about the scope of their promises, given the modest list of staff members and even more modest funding.

"It's wonderful to be here," she said, smiling at the other two women. Greer had returned to the ringing phones.

"We're so pleased to have someone with your experience," Jessica said frankly. "We were shorthanded even when Kendra was with us. I didn't want her starting any kind of ongoing program that she wouldn't be around to complete."

Dana figured her predecessor had accepted the job with Helping Hand because it was better than nothing on her résumé. When she'd had a more tempting offer, she'd taken it.

Both women studied Dana expectantly. She'd been somewhat evasive about her reason for moving to Lookout. With her education and years of experience, this job was a step down. She'd taken a significant cut in pay, too, although salaries in this kind of social work never qualified as generous.

After a deep breath, she began. "I'd have moved to Lookout whether you offered me the position or not. I felt confident I could find a job in Portland, although I preferred not to have the commute." She told them in as few words as possible about Gabriel and the miraculous discovery that he was alive, well and living in a small town on the Columbia Gorge. "So, you see…"

"Oh, my," Jessica said. She might have been blinking away a tear. "How extraordinary. How wonderful for you!"

"We have a ways to go," Dana admitted. "He's at a difficult age to have his world upended, but his current guardian, the man he thought was his uncle, is being cooperative."

Jessica sobered. "And if your son reaches a point where he's ready to live with you? Do you envision staying?"

"I think that's a long time away. And…" Strangely, she'd never thought this through. "Yes," she heard herself say. "If I'm happy here, I don't see why not. It would be good for him to stay in the same school system with his friends. And…having his uncle nearby."

Jessica nodded with relief. They got down to brass tacks.

Dana was drawn into admitting her concern that Helping Hand was overextended. "Looking at your materials, I suspect you're duplicating resources that exist elsewhere. I know you want every opportunity to be available right here in Lookout, but the drive to Hood River and even

The Dalles isn't long enough to prevent most people from taking advantage of what's already being offered."

She'd been really impressed with a local publication called Parenting in the Gorge that listed classes, play groups, library story times, places that offered after-hours health care, and resources for teen mothers and Spanish speakers. Some of what Helping Hand did filled holes, in her opinion, while some could be dropped in favor of a more finely tuned focus.

The focus, she learned, was the problem. Jessica had originally intended to serve primarily struggling single mothers, as A Woman's Lifeline did in Colorado.

"But, you know, there are single fathers, too," Jessica said ruefully. "And dysfunctional two-parent families, including those being court-monitored. And then there's the challenge of raising a child when you're extremely low income. So many of the parents we see are just so *young*."

Dana thought of Lucy and her little blond boy, Phoenix. When she had called to say goodbye, as she'd done with several favorite clients, she'd given Lucy her cell number, in case she needed advice or just wanted to share a triumph or disappointment. She hoped for updates.

"It's true," she agreed. "If only teenagers understood what an unplanned pregnancy would mean to their lives."

To her surprise, Jessica proved to be the rare individual who was eager to hear everything Dana had to say while showing no signs of becoming self-defensive. In fact, she and Meghan had already been worried about low attendance at some classes.

Dana explained more about the primary role A Woman's Lifeline had set: making women aware of every possible resource and helping them weave together those opportunities into a safety net.

In the end, Jessica asked her to spend this first week making contact with other agencies, government and private, and coming up with a list of what needs couldn't already be met. Meghan professed herself eager to look over Dana's shoulder as time allowed; she'd finished her master's degree in social work only the previous spring, with this her first job after an internship.

Excited to have this chance, Dana settled into her new office, a whole lot more bare-bones than her last one, and began making calls to set up appointments to meet with people at a dozen other nonprofits in the county. And she started making notes—lots of notes.

It wasn't until she left for home that her mood dimmed.

No, she hadn't expected to hear from Nolan or Christian every single day. She had to make a life separate from them, too. But…somehow, after Saturday, she'd thought Nolan might call.

Maybe Saturday hadn't been as successful as she'd believed. Maybe Nolan and Christian had struggled to be polite and breathed a sigh of relief after they parted outside the pizza parlor. She had a painful instant of imagining them exchanging high fives for a second time.

I'm going to be positive, remember?

Anyway, she was just being paranoid. It *was* a good day. Christian had relaxed around her, and just as Nolan had said, he'd enjoyed being the authority to her newbie status at Wind & Waves. He hadn't been very talkative at dinner, but he wasn't sullen, either.

If there was a bad moment, it had come when she had asked Nolan about his sister. She'd known it was a hot button. She could have begun satisfying her curiosity *and* been more tactful if she'd asked instead about Nolan's parents, who'd also played a big role in Christian's life.

Next time.

And, oh, she hated having no idea when that would be.

She had a free evening now and needed to buy a new lawn mower. Her old and increasingly cranky one hadn't been worth putting on the moving truck. The plan seemed sensi-

ble and an excellent distraction. Plus, the tiny
lawn at her rental was starting to look ragged
after just a week of inattention. Forget the local
hardware store, where if she ran into Nolan,
she'd look like a stalker. No, she'd head for the
Home Depot in The Dalles and eat out there,
too. She'd spent eleven years alone. She knew
how to function on her own.

ONCE HE HAD let himself think about the possibility, however remote, of starting something
with Dana, Nolan couldn't *stop* thinking about
it.

There would be pitfalls aplenty.

And, face it, he didn't really know her, not
yet.

He'd already speculated about whether she'd
gone to bed with a man since her marriage
ended. He'd bet no, although he almost hoped he
was wrong. He'd rather not think of her bearing
an open wound for all those years, refusing to
allow herself even the simple pleasure of good
sex. But he knew better, having seen surprise in
her extraordinary eyes only because she'd felt a
flash of awareness of him as a man.

Yeah, he knew she was as attracted to him as
he was to her. That was part of why he couldn't
stop thinking about how it would be, taking her
to bed.

One of the pitfalls was her thinking he was coming on to her as a backdoor route to keep Christian—and for good reason. There were complications, sure, so many he pictured a roll of barbed-wire fencing. But think how convenient it would be if they got married. Her bastard of an ex-husband wouldn't have a prayer of wresting custody from them.

The satisfaction Nolan felt had flashing yellow warning lights.

So a marriage between them would be very convenient. Did that have to be a drawback?

He'd test the waters, he decided. The two of them needed to get to know each other better, no matter what. He could start with that as a goal, see where it went.

Nolan grimaced at how hard he'd worked to justify the phone call he was about to make.

Dana answered on the third ring. "Nolan." She sounded pleasant, neither annoyed at the several-day silence nor excited to hear from him.

"I'm hoping you will have dinner with me tomorrow night."

Her "Just you?" sounded cautious.

"One of Christian's friends turns twelve tomorrow," he explained. "The birthday party isn't until this weekend, a sleepover." Another chance to spend time with her apart from Christian.

"But his big present is an Xbox One. He doesn't know it yet, but his mother called me to ask if Christian could go home with Jason tomorrow, stay for dinner, a family celebration and the chance to set up the new system and give it a dry run. Jason is his best friend," he added.

"This is Jason the ax wielder?"

He laughed. "Yes, but his level of maturity is pretty standard. He's a good kid. I'm pretty sure he'll be a lot more careful after that incident."

"One would hope," Dana said tartly. Her caution reasserted itself. "So…is there a reason you want to talk to me alone?"

"Nothing bad. I really just thought it would be a good idea for us to spend some time together. I, uh, shut you down when you asked about Marlee. That wasn't fair. We probably both have questions."

After a small pause, she said, "Thank you. Tomorrow night is fine."

They agreed on a time. He set down his phone feeling relief and a bubbling excitement. A high school kid who'd finally worked up the courage to ask out the girl of his dreams. And she'd said yes!

Down, boy. They'd talk, that was all. Eat a good meal without a sulky preteen quashing any chance of genuine conversation.

Try for nonadversarial, he told himself ruefully. Then see where they could go from there.

ONCE SHE SAW NOLAN, wearing a polo shirt and khakis, Dana wished she'd dressed down a little. But when he said, "You look great," his expression seemed genuinely appreciative. So all she did was thank him, lock her front door and let him escort her to his SUV.

"I thought we'd try someplace I wouldn't take Christian," he said once they were on the way. "It's a wine bar and bistro. Don't know if you're into wine…"

"I enjoy a glass now and again, but I'm no connoisseur," she admitted.

Nolan chuckled. "I'm not, either. Tell you the truth, I hardly ever have booze at home. Didn't much when I was serving, either. The guys gave me a hard time. I was the One-Beer Wonder." His smile widened. "And they never figured out why I could clear the pool table every time."

Laughing, Dana said, "Then they deserved to lose their stakes."

"So I told them," he said smugly.

The Lookout Wine Bar & Bistro wasn't waterfront, but it occupied the second story of an old brick building high enough up the hill to allow a view of city lights and the river. Brick interior walls and open beams gave the space a rustic look. At one end, flames crackled in a fireplace big enough to roast an ox. Nolan had apparently made reservations that nabbed them a table by a window. Glancing around, Dana saw attire from jeans to dressy.

After they'd ordered, for what had to be a minute they only looked at each other.

His dark hair was always ruffled, as if it had some wave, or perhaps he couldn't keep from shoving his fingers into it. In the dim light, his eyes were the deep blue of twilight. She guessed he might have gone home and shaved for a second time, because he didn't have the stubble she had noticed Saturday evening when they parted.

He was a big man, with those huge shoulders and powerful forearms, lightly dusted with dark hair. Big hands, too, and strong bone structure in his face. No, she still wouldn't call him handsome, but that didn't seem to matter. Strong was sexy.

Dana had a sudden insight: Craig *was* handsome. Model handsome, able to use his looks to charm people. He'd always made her heart and body quicken, until that shocking instant when she understood that he blamed her for the abduction. And after, as soon as a few weeks later, when he grew impatient because she couldn't respond to him in bed.

That kind of handsome would never appeal to her again.

She fixated on Nolan's mouth, softer now than when they were in the middle of one of their standoffs. Her gaze lingered until she realized that mouth was curving.

Praying her face hadn't betrayed her thoughts, she spoke quickly.

"Does Christian know we're having dinner tonight?"

"Sure. He didn't seem to mind."

She nodded. "You said we both have questions. What are yours?"

Small lines formed between his eyebrows. "I was surprised you showed up alone, that first visit. I assume that means you weren't dating anyone seriously, but are you not close to your family?"

Whatever she'd expected, it wasn't that. Why would he care?

"I am close to my parents and brother." Dana found herself hesitating. "They wanted to come. They all offered. I just…" She looked out the window over rooftops to the broad river. What had to be powerful currents weren't apparent from this distance. At six thirty in the evening, it was still daylight, sunset an hour and a half away.

"You just…" he prodded.

"I suppose I've become more of a loner since… you know." She turned back to him, to find herself the object of his complete attention. Sometimes his intensity was banked, but not now. When he nodded his understanding, she continued, "I see my family, I love them, and I know they worry about me. But I've gotten used to doing things alone. They've learned to respect that."

He frowned. "Respect? To hell with that. If I'd been one of them, I'd have bought a second airline ticket and come along whether you liked it or not."

Dana was unexpectedly amused. "Then I'm lucky we're not family."

His frown deepened...or something else caused him to feel troubled. She couldn't decide. For a moment his fingers drummed on the table.

Finally, he said, "In a manner of speaking, we are now."

Wow. She blinked. That was a thought. He was Dad, and she was Mom. In a manner of speaking.

"I...suppose so." She pondered that. "Does that mean you won't listen when I express my preferences?"

A grin caught her off guard, humor in his eyes. "I'll listen."

She couldn't help but chuckle, too. "But you'll do whatever you want, anyway."

His face sobered, and she had another of those moments when she had no idea what he was thinking. "Want?" he said slowly. "Probably not. What I think you need? That's different."

"What I *need* is to spend time with my son."
If she sounded sharp, who cared?

"I told you before, pushing will backfire."

"Have I pushed?" she shot back.

"Since you announced you were moving to
Lookout, you mean?"

They stared at each other, hostilities momentarily renewed.

Then he sighed. "No, you've been patient.
He'll come around, Dana. He...talks about you,
a little."

A little. Wasn't that heartwarming? But she
said, "Good or bad?"

"Uncertain, but more positive lately." He hesitated. "He's struggling with what you mean to
him, but he admitted that he was glad that you
hadn't given up on him."

Around a lump in her throat, she said, "Thank
you for telling me that."

Nolan nodded.

Their salads and the bottle of wine he'd ordered arrived. The balsamic dressing on her
salad was good, the wine even better. It crossed
her mind that she might not have shared Craig's
taste in wine.

"Your parents planning a visit?" Nolan asked,
sounding casual.

"Yes, when I say it's okay. There's no point
in them coming if Christian isn't interested."

"This is a pretty time of year here, though."

"It is." She smiled at him. "Still too chilly to make windsurfing look fun."

He laughed. "Water stays cold year round. And the gusts right now are exhilarating."

"Do you ever have a chance to go out?" she asked.

He made a grumbly sound. "Not very often. The more successful Wind & Waves gets, the less time for recreation I have. Plus, there's Christian."

"And now me."

"You haven't taken a lot of my time yet." Unreadable emotion crossed his face. "I imagine that'll change."

"Why? I could take Christian off your hands sometimes and free you up."

"Somehow, I don't think that's the way it'll happen."

Was that *amusement* crinkling the skin at the corners of his eyes? She studied him suspiciously. Why would what he'd just said amuse him?

"I can never tell what you're thinking," she complained.

He laughed. "Good."

Once their entrées arrived, he started talking about his family without her having to ask. His dad had owned a service station and automobile repair shop. His mother worked for an insurance agent.

"I can rebuild an engine but had zero interest in doing that kind of work for forty years. I was the first in the family to go to college. Mom was a sharp lady. She should have gotten an education, but I don't think her parents encouraged her. She grew up on a ranch in a town that's a dot on the map near La Grande, in eastern Oregon. She met my father at a rodeo he'd gone to with some friends." Smiling, he shook his head. "Not sure what he was doing there, since I doubt he ever threw his leg over a horse's back in his life. Mom took a big chance and ran away to marry him."

His gentle affection didn't surprise Dana. This was a man who put family first. He had re-shaped his life for the sake of his troubled sister and the boy he'd believed to be his sister's son.

"Christian must miss them."

Nolan took a swallow of wine. "Yeah." He cleared the roughness from his voice. "They were always there for him. They were his parents, as much or more than Marlee was."

"I wish I could have met them. Thanked them."

He contemplated her for a minute. "They'd have liked you."

"I… That's nice of you to say."

With a crooked smile, he said, "I like you."

"Oh."

He laughed again. "You're supposed to say,

'I thought I'd hate you, but turns out I like you, too.'"

Chuckling, she said, "What you said."

She let him persuade her to order dessert. Both had berry cobbler à la mode, which was amazing. She'd better find a good place to run soon, or she'd be in trouble. Her appreciation for food had sprung back to life.

She was savoring a bite when Nolan said, a little gruffly, "You do have a right to know about Marlee. None of us would be where we are if it weren't for her."

"No." If Gabriel had never been taken, Dana had to wonder what her life would have been like. Would she and Craig have stayed happily married, had another baby? Maybe he'd never have become as ruthless as he sounded now. Or maybe they'd have been long divorced. Who knew?

"She was a sweet, sassy little girl," Nolan began, his tone odd, as if he hadn't let himself think about her like this in a long time. He must carry his share of anger. "Thinking back, she was always a little different."

Looking out the window, as if he was seeing the past, he described a girl who'd insisted on wearing clothing that never matched and grew even more eccentric when she reached

her teenage years. She'd had friends, until the
real strangeness emerged in her midteens.

"She was never the student I was. Her interests jumped from one thing to another, never
lasting long. The school recommended she be
tested for attention deficit disorder, but I guess
that label didn't fit her. Later, of course, we
knew why."

Marlee had always been creative, he said.
"The art teacher loved her. She designed a mural
for the wall of the gymnasium that's still there."
Nolan's eyes focused on Dana. "You might want
to go see it. It's this explosion of color and joy
and—" he seemed to think about it "—maybe
some shadows we should have noticed."

His fingers contracted, not quite into a fist.
Dana almost reached for his hand, the impulse
taking her by surprise. She didn't do a lot of
touching anymore. She was probably the last
person from whom he'd accept comfort, anyway.

"It would be so hard as a parent to accept
that your dreams for your child would never be
fulfilled." She kept her voice quiet, in keeping
with his mood.

"Yeah." Suddenly he rubbed a hand over his
face. "Yeah, it hit Mom and Dad hard. She had
gotten into drugs by high school. She might
have been self-medicating, even if she didn't

know that's what she was doing. A lot of mentally ill people living on the street use booze and drugs to drown out confusion and anxiety and, in Marlee's case, voices."

Startled, Dana said, "She really heard voices?"

"So she said." His tone had become wry. "We were never sure. The voices had a way of telling her to do what she wanted to do anyway, which made Mom and Dad suspicious."

"I can see that, but…"

Nolan nodded. "She was diagnosed as schizophrenic, and the medications did help. When she was willing to take them."

"I've had clients who seemed to be doing so well, until one day…" She spread her hands.

"That was Marlee. The frustrating thing was, she could be so lovable. Her vulnerability was right out there. It made people want to take care of her. But then she'd get to feeling trapped, and she couldn't bear it, so she'd bolt. Disappear. Sometimes just for a few days, sometimes for weeks or months. She'd call now and again, even email sometimes when she'd find a roost where she had access to a computer." Regret deepened lines in his craggy face. "She'd been gone for almost a year when she showed up with Christian. I think once she got her hands on him, she realized she didn't have a clue. My parents attributed her clumsiness with him to her mental illness. It didn't occur to any of us that she might have only had him a matter of days. That he didn't know her, and she didn't know him."

Anger swelled in Dana, but Nolan's openness and, yes, his regret, kept the crest from being as high or as violent. She couldn't blame his parents or him. How could they have guessed the dreadful truth?

"The birthday she gave was off by less than a month." The words just popped out of her mouth. It had bothered her terribly when she realized her son had celebrated every birthday for eleven years on the wrong day. A sudden fear stabbed her like a thorn. "Is he… Will he accept his real birthday?" It was only a little over two months away. He'd been born in July, not August as he had believed.

"We haven't talked about that yet. Celebrating on his real birthday will mean telling all his friends the truth."

Reeling from the blow, she whispered, "You mean…he hasn't?" *Nobody* here in town but Nolan and Christian knew? Well, and her co-workers, but she hadn't told them the name he was going by.

"That's…one of the things he doesn't seem ready to do yet." Pity softened Nolan's often stern face.

"If he hasn't told anyone—" she faltered "—he has no way to explain me."

Silence.

Hurt congealed into something harder. "How can he be seen with me if he can't explain me?"

"He'll get there," Nolan said, in the deep voice that made her want to believe anything he said.

But this…she suddenly didn't believe.

She met his eyes. "Will he?"

CHAPTER NINE

DANA HADN'T HEARD from either Christian or Nolan by the time she arrived home Friday after work. She decided she'd do the calling.

When Nolan answered, she said briskly, "Hi, this is Dana. May I speak to Christian?"

"Dana. I'll have to go find him."

He didn't sound annoyed, but neither was he glad to hear from her. Wednesday evening, she'd almost thought he might kiss her good-night. Wishful thinking— No, no! They had achieved some closeness, that was all. Well, until he spoiled it by telling her that he and Christian weren't yet owning up to her existence.

"Uh, hi."

"Hi, Christian. I hope you had a good week at school." She cringed. Like any self-respecting kid would feel anything but incredulity at a remark like that.

Silence. Then a mumbled "It was okay."

"I actually called to find out if you'd like a very, very part-time job. I bought a lawn mower this week, but I really hate mowing. If you're interested, I'll pay you—" She managed a laugh. "Under the table, of course. It could be a good weekend—"

He sliced her off. "I work for Uncle Nolan on the weekend."

"I see."

"I guess I could do it after school some day."

"But I wouldn't be home to let you into the garage or—" She didn't finish. He wouldn't appreciate knowing she felt she ought to be supervising, given his age and the fact that the job involved sharp blades.

He didn't say anything.

"I… Let me think about this."

"Okay. Well, bye." And he was gone.

A small sound escaped her, one she didn't recognize. She'd been sitting on the sofa; now she lifted her feet to the cushion, wrapped her arms around her lower legs and rested her forehead on her knees. She stayed that way for long minutes, wishing she could disappear.

Eventually, common sense pointed out that this was a setback, that's all. A minor one, at that. Christian resented her attempt to intrude on his time with Nolan. And had she really expected a boy his age to willingly chat on the phone?

Dana's body gradually loosened. She ought to think about dinner, but her newly awakened appetite was missing again. So—a salad. She could do that.

If Craig calls, what do I tell him?

She could lie.

When her phone chose that moment to ring, she jolted. *Please, not Craig*, she begged. The number was her parents'.

"Dad," she said after her father identified himself. Tears threatened. She remembered what Nolan had said. *If I'd been one of them, I'd have come along whether you liked it or not.* A small part of her wanted to say, *Daddy, I wish you were here. Please come.*

The rest of her wanted to hide her bout of self-pity.

She burbled about how exciting her new job was, telling him how much she liked her co-workers and how Meghan had asked her to come along on the Hood River Railroad excursion next weekend. Oh, and how cute her house was and how she'd already bought a new lawn mower and gotten it running although she hadn't actually mowed yet.

Her father made encouraging noises. Not until she wound down did he say quietly, "Gabriel?"

She hadn't heard or thought that name in too long. The burning in her chest intensified. "Last week was good." She had to swallow a couple of times to strengthen her voice. "He… I told you about him coming to see me, didn't I?"

"You did," he said, just as gently.

She described spending the day at Wind & Waves and what fun she'd had. Told him about going out for pizza afterward. "This week, I haven't seen him at all."

"Either of them?"

"Nolan took me to dinner one night. I think we're—" what? "—achieving an understanding." Yes, that worked.

"And yet he's kept Gabriel away from you." Her father's anger came rarely, but she heard it now.

"I don't think it's him," she admitted. "I think it's Chris—Gabe. He's not so sure he wants another mother."

"You're not *another*. You're *his* mother."

"It's hard for him."

He sighed. "I do know that." After a pause, he said, "Your mother and I are really looking forward to seeing him."

"I know. Right now—" she hated to say this but had to "—I'm not sure you *would* see him. Let's give it a few weeks. Wouldn't it be better for you to take time off once school has let out anyway?"

"Maybe. All right. I love you, you know."

She smiled with difficulty, suddenly aware

her cheeks were wet. "I know. And you know I love you."

"None of us say it often enough." She could hear his smile in his voice. "Your mom is grabbing for the phone."

Hearing the muffled protest and her father's laugh, her own smile became real.

"WHAT WAS THAT all about?" Uncle Nolan asked with what sounded like mild curiosity, lowering his newspaper.

Christian stared at him. Why was he even pretending he hadn't listened to every word?

"She wants me to mow her lawn. On weekends. I told her no."

"She offer to pay you?"

Christian shrugged.

"Might be nice to pick up a few extra bucks."

"I said I'd do it after school. She didn't like that."

Nolan didn't say anything. Since the accident with the ax, he didn't let Christian use anything sharp or mechanized when he wasn't home, which made Christian mad. He and Jason had been playing around, and they shouldn't have. So that meant he wasn't trustworthy forever?

"What do you say we invite her to join us again tomorrow? She was a big help last week."

After last Saturday, Christian had thought maybe it would be cool if she came again, someday. But it didn't have to be every week, did it? "We don't need her."

Uncle Nolan's eyebrows went up. "No, we don't. But she moved out here so she could spend some time with you. Seems like lately you've resisted my every suggestion."

Still standing, Christian curled his hands into fists. "So now I have to see her even if I don't want to?"

"She's a part of your life." His uncle suddenly sounded hard. "You need to accept that."

Christian didn't know why he felt so mad, just that he did. "You said you'd fight for me."

Uncle Nolan pushed the newspaper aside and clasped his hands behind his neck, his gaze steady. "You're still living with me, aren't you?"

"Maybe you wish I wasn't!" It burst out of him, like…like steam out of the teapot when the water boiled. He *was* boiling. "Or maybe you *like* her. You think she's going to be your *girlfriend* instead of Ellie?"

His uncle didn't move. "What do you know about Ellie?"

"Do you think I'm *stupid*?"

"No." He sounded tired. "I think you sound like a brat. I've done nothing to deserve having you talk to me like this. Ellie is none of your business. I will say, she's not my girlfriend. That's all you need to know."

"Quinn says she's your fu—"

Nolan was on his feet so fast the word died unborn. Christian shuffled backward.

"You will *not* use that word. Do you hear me?"

He didn't even recognize this man, eyes narrowed, mouth thinned. Scared and mad and almost crying, Christian yelled, "Yes!"

"Quinn is not welcome in this house until I say otherwise."

Christian opened and closed his mouth.

"Go to your room." Sounding disgusted, Uncle Nolan turned away as if Christian wasn't worth his time. He folded the newspaper and started for the kitchen.

Christian couldn't seem to move. He was frozen. "But...tomorrow..." He was practically whispering.

Uncle Nolan stopped, his back to Christian. "Right now you're not acting like the kid I know and love. I'm hoping he'll reappear tomorrow morning. I don't want to see you until then." And then he kept walking.

Christian tore up the stairs.

IN THE KITCHEN, Nolan flattened both hands on the wall and let his head fall forward. Damn it. He didn't let his temper loose often. He'd come a lot closer than he liked just now. He had no idea whether he'd handled that well, in a way a boy could respect, or whether he'd screwed up royally.

Or whether the call he was about to make would be a monster mistake.

Dana's "Hello" was careful. As it so often was, and for good reason.

"It's Nolan," he said. "I'm sorry—"

She cut him off. "No. You're not responsible for how he responds to me." Pause, and then more slowly, "At least, I hope not."

Her implication that he was influencing Christian against her should have made him mad, but it didn't. How could she *not* wonder, especially given this week's backsliding on Christian's part?

"You and I have a deal. I'm doing my best to uphold my end."

He strained for any sound in the long silence, even a breath.

"Thank you," she said then, so softly he barely heard.

"Ah… Is there any chance you'd like to hang out with us at Wind & Waves again? Say, Sunday?" That would give him a day to prepare his bratty—and, yes, wounded and bewildered—kid.

"Is this another invitation from you and Christian?"

Nolan winced at her dry tone. He hesitated a little too long.

"I thought so. Thank you, but no. Good night, Nolan."

And, damn, she was gone. Nolan closed his eyes. Now what?

SHE'D MOWED HER own lawn.

At a stop in front of Dana's rental on Saturday evening, Nolan cranked the steering wheel to ensure his SUV didn't roll down the steep hill before killing the engine.

He gritted his teeth at the sight of the smooth, short grass. No, it wasn't a big job, and, yes, she was in good physical condition. It was the principle of the thing that took a nibble out of his heart.

What am I doing here?

He didn't have a good answer but grabbed the food he'd brought and got out, anyway. A moment later, he rang her doorbell. Waiting, he didn't let himself glance toward the front window. If she peeked out and then decided to pretend she wasn't home, he'd rather be left thinking she wasn't here.

But the door did open. Dana was scruffier than usual in faded jeans with grass stains around the hems, an old T-shirt that molded to her breasts and slim torso, and a blue bandanna that held back her hair. He liked her this way, just as he'd liked seeing her wet and wild-haired after helping out at Wind & Waves.

It occurred to him that he probably looked a little ragged, too, since he hadn't gone home to shower after work.

She studied the bag in his hand before raising her gaze to meet his. "I take it this is in lieu of the fun time I was supposed to have with you and my son?"

He grimaced. "You could say that."

"I did." She sighed. "Fine." And stood back.

Doubting himself, he still stepped over the threshold. "I hope you haven't eaten."

"No." She led the way to the kitchen. "I suppose Christian is at the official birthday party for his ax-wielding friend."

"Yes, and spending the night."

"You sure there won't be any bloodshed?"

He chuckled. "Oh, yeah. Jason's dad came down hard on the kid. I suspect he thinks about it every time he so much as picks up a pair of scissors."

"I suppose I ought to be grateful for what he did," she said, sounding thoughtful. She opened the refrigerator. "What would you like to drink?"

They both went for soda. As he opened the half-dozen takeout boxes of Chinese food, she brought plates, silverware and napkins to the table.

"Why grateful?" Then he got it and winced. "Because otherwise we might not have known."

"It could have been years before he had reason to find out his blood type. And then, if he was an adult, he would have been unlikely to understand the significance."

"Do you ever have moments when you wish you *hadn't* found him?" Nolan asked.

She kept her head bent, as though deeply pondering whether she'd help herself to spicy pork with bell peppers or cashew chicken. When she finally looked up, she still hadn't succeeded in burying all of her pain. Nolan had never seen eyes as expressive as hers.

"No." Her voice was small and husky. "No, never."

Throat thickening, he said, "I'm sorry." He had to say that too often to her.

She shook her head. It took everything he had to make himself stay on his side of the table. He wanted to touch her. He wanted to hold her. He even thought she needed to be held, but he was unlikely to be the man whose arms she would want around her. Not yet, anyway. He refused to believe he couldn't change how she felt about him.

Clear now and disconcertingly sharp, her eyes met his. "Why are you here?"

"Because, once again, Christian was a shit to you." At least this was partial honesty. "I understand his turmoil and I know you do, too. That doesn't mean I can excuse the way he's been acting. I damn near kept him home from Jason's party, but…"

When he hesitated, she finished, "Trying to compel him to be nice to me might have him digging in his heels even deeper."

"That's what I figured." Nolan nodded at the food. "It's getting cold."

She started with a couple of spring rolls, and they ate in silence for a few minutes. "What will you do with him come summer?"

"Encourage him to spend as much time as possible with me at work. He does teach some lessons, and a couple of his friends are as into windsurfing as he is, so they spend time out on the river."

In the act of dishing up sweet-and-sour prawns, Dana stopped with her hand suspended above the box. "Is that…safe?"

"You mean him being out there without adult supervision?"

"Well, yes."

"He doesn't go alone. They always wear life vests." Some rules, there was no give, and this was one of them. If he ever found out Christian left off the PFD, the kid wouldn't be going out again. Period. "Weekends, nice summer days, there's always a crowd out there. The locals and the regulars all know him. They keep an eye on each other, anyway. Is the sport a hundred per-cent safe? No, but what is?"

She wrinkled her nose but didn't argue.

"A commuter driving the freeway to work in any major metropolitan area is probably in more danger than a skydiver or a BASE jumper," he pointed out. "Never mind a windsurfer."

Dana lifted her eyebrows at that, and he smiled crookedly.

"Okay, maybe not the BASE jumper."

"You haven't done that, have you?"

"Nope. Jumping out of airplanes, sure. It was part of the job." He hesitated. "Not my favorite part."

Amusement softening her face, she said, "Bet you never said so then."

He smiled. "Big tough army ranger? Not a chance."

The ripple of her laughter stirred thoughts about what her fingers would feel like, touching him delicately. And not so delicately.

Whatever his expression showed made her stare, humor gone and pupils dilating. They looked at each other for longer than was comfortable.

She was the one to wrench her gaze away. He made himself take a bite and chew mechanically. Had he just scared her? Or had he seen a hint of yearning to match his?

"Why did you go into the military?" she asked suddenly. "Was it a family tradition, or...?"

Conversation. Not his strength, but he could do this.

"Not family tradition, although my dad did serve in Vietnam. Involuntarily. He was drafted. Given his memories, Dad wasn't happy with my decision." Nolan had been too young then to understand that his parents would live in a state of suspended fear for months and years at a time when he was deployed. Waiting for that knock on the door, opening it to find an army chaplain in full uniform there to give them the worst news.

"I can understand that," Dana said, nodding. "I…have to admit I hope Christian won't decide to follow in your footsteps, not that way."

Nolan hadn't really thought about it before. Now that he did, he hoped the same. The only regrets he had about his military service were the impact on his parents and the years of Christian's life he'd missed. He'd had good times and bad. Made lifelong friends. He was proud of his service. But modern warfare had gotten increasingly vicious, lacking any traditional battlefield or sense of decency and humanity. Soldiers in Iraq or Afghanistan never knew who carried a bomb, which stretch of road was mined, what shadow atop a roof hid a sniper. The stress was unrelenting. No, he didn't want that for Christian.

He told Dana so and, pushed by gentle questions from her, kept talking. He shared some of the good, told funny and heartwarming stories about his buddies, and even told her some of the bad—but not the worst. Not about the nightmarish moments that would never leave him.

In turn, she told him her brother had been career army until he came back from his second deployment in Afghanistan and decided he'd had enough.

"I don't know if he has PTSD, exactly," she said, "but he spent a lot of time alone in the mountains for a while. Soaking up the peace and grandeur, I guess."

"Needing to be free of noise and movement and the demands of other people."

"You…don't wish you could have done the same?"

He shook his head. "I'm a guy who needs a mission, I guess you could say. I tend to focus on a goal and not deviate. Sometimes that's a strength, but I force myself to be conscious that sometimes the plan really should change." Now, why had he told her that? "I wasn't ready to retire from the military, but, see, I had a mission."

"Taking care of your sister and Christian."

"Yep."

Dana's brows knit as she studied him, looking deep. "But then your sister died."

He didn't say a word. Wasn't sure he could. Nolan was well aware he hadn't begun to deal with his sense of failure and of guilt.

"Now I'm sorry," she murmured.

He dipped his head and concentrated on putting away another helping of the Szechuan beef. He'd come over here tonight to soften the blow Christian had struck and maybe to get a sense of whether his latest plan had any chance of succeeding. But laying bare the agony he'd locked behind high walls? No.

Eventually, she poured coffee and offered cookies from the bakery downtown. He had a feeling she took one only to encourage him to eat some. She nibbled on the edges and crumbled the rest of it. Maybe she was a closet eater, but he thought it likelier she was keeping goodies on hand in case Christian showed up again.

How many stale cookies had she thrown out this week?

They kept talking. She told him about her new job. As a former officer, he understood her current focus. Even generals were prone to imagining troops on the ground could accomplish too much, thereby guaranteeing they failed at the core goals.

"Core goals," she mused. "That's a good way to put it." Her face brightened. "I'm lucky because the director had already realized there was a problem and is open to change and to ideas that don't necessarily come from her. If you knew how rare that is…"

He grunted, recalling a particular colonel. "Oh, I know, all right."

"One irony is that I'll be teaching some parenting classes. I've done it before, but—" her smile twisted "—I've become a teeny bit aware how unqualified I am."

"I can't believe that's true." The instinct to defend her came so fast he realized it had become a default. Didn't matter that she was dissing herself. He couldn't let her. "In your years in the profession, you must have seen a lot of parenting, from great to terrible."

"That's true, of course—"

A *but* was coming. He cut her off before she could say it. "Good teaching requires distance. You know what you've observed. The last thing the struggling people who come to your classes need is for you to let your own turmoil impact what you have to say."

For a long, quiet moment, she only studied him. At last, she gave a small nod. "Thank you."

"You're welcome." He caught a glimpse over her shoulder of her wall clock, jarred to realize he'd been here two hours, and too much of the time, it had been his mouth flapping. He couldn't remember the last time that had happened. "I'd better get going."

Her mouth curved. "In case you have to respond to a frantic call reporting bloodshed."

Nolan laughed. "Can't let that go, can you?"

"Have you?"

"No." He patted his pocket. "Believe me, I'm keeping the phone close. I've never been that scared before."

Of course, she understood. He didn't have to ask to know the most frightening moment of her life: when she stepped into her baby's bedroom and saw an empty crib and a wide-open window.

She encouraged him to take the leftovers home. Obviously, she'd already noticed the amount of food Christian could put away. As big a man as Nolan was, the kid could outeat him.

On her doormat, he turned back. "Hang in there, Dana."

"I'm not going anywhere."

He didn't like knowing how alone she must feel. "Good."

The penetrating way she looked at him always made him twitchy, as if he had something to hide. Or maybe just a new dose of guilt at how this was playing out.

"I don't understand you," she confessed.

He stood half a step below her, allowing their eyes to meet straight on. His gaze lowered to her mouth. He wouldn't even have to bend his head...

"That's because I have this problem," he said huskily. "My first loyalty needs to be to Christian. But you're stirring a lot up in me. Right now—" his voice became ragged "—I want to kiss you."

Once again, her pupils flickered, large and then tiny. Her lips parted as if she thought she should say something but had no idea what.

He took a chance and caressed her cheek with his knuckles, ending with a stroke of his thumb over her lower lip. "So what do you think?"

"I—" Her tongue touched her lip right where his thumb had been. "I don't know."

This time he slid his hand around her nape, squeezing gently. He bent slowly, watching for a rejection. Instead, she seemed to sway toward him and her eyes closed. He could tell she was holding her breath. He thought he was, too. Why else would he already feel light-headed?

Her lips beneath his were as soft as he'd expected. He brushed his mouth over hers, nibbled a little, then lifted his head to see her expression.

Her lashes swept up at the exact moment her chest rose and fell. "Oh," she whispered.

"Oh?"

"It...felt nice."

He smiled. "It did. I'd like to do it again. And more."

"More?" She looked stunned.

"Good night, Dana." He didn't want to go but knew he had to. Right now he had a tactical advantage. He'd be a fool to relinquish it. Giving her something to think about was enough.

Walking toward the street, Nolan heard the door close quietly behind him.

Unfortunately, he'd given himself something to think about, too. He shouldn't be so aroused from a kiss so chaste, but he had to lower himself carefully behind the wheel of his SUV.

Nice? Not the way he would have described that kiss. Maybe he'd been wrong not to push it a little.

No, she had a quality of innocence that made him doubt she often kissed men passionately. The idea that she might not have had sex in eleven years worried him even though he found he didn't like the idea of her in bed with another man. Had she met a single one who understood what she had gone through? Saw her shadows, guessed at the vast empty place inside her? Or had the men she met seen only a beautiful woman, lonely enough to be vulnerable?

He swore softly. He was an idiot to think *he* really understood her. Considering his original intention had been to fight dirty, he should be wondering if he wasn't being manipulated. He was so damn torn now Christian's anger and accusations were justified.

Sleep wouldn't come easily tonight, for a lot of reasons.

CHAPTER TEN

HE'D KISSED HER. He'd have liked to do more.

She'd have liked that, too.

Dana stood staring at her front door. She heard the engine outside fire up, followed by the subdued roar as he drove away.

Why had he kissed her? Was it possible Nolan really *was* attracted to her? That…he had genuinely come to be conflicted about the battle they were waging for Christian's affections?

Gabriel's. In the privacy of her own mind, he should be Gabe. *Her* Gabe.

Except…he wasn't. She realized she was wringing her hands in distress because she thought about her own son as Christian. A name given to him by the crazy woman who'd stolen him.

Calmed by the necessary reminder, Dana returned to the kitchen. Cleanup took no time at all.

He kissed me. The memory sang to her. It had been so long. She had been so lonely, without knowing she missed physical affection. Sex.

But the numbness had worn off, either because she'd found Gabriel—or because she'd set eyes on Nolan Gregor.

Grabbing the local newspaper she had been about to read when the doorbell rang, Dana analyzed her initial reaction to Nolan and had to admit that she'd been rocked. Then she'd believed it was all about Christian—Gabriel—damn it, Christian. Because she was going to see him. The tall man with the massive shoulders and sharp blue eyes, he was both her adversary and her fairy godfather. If he hadn't put Christian's DNA online, she never would have known. She would have lived her entire life not knowing.

Now…she couldn't let him toy with her. Except what could he possibly believe he'd gain by coaxing her into some kind of relationship? He had to know she wouldn't be overcome enough to sign a document blindly, say, giving up parental rights. Even if she was that stupid, without her to hold him back, Craig would immediately sue for custody.

The hopeful thought sneaked into her head: maybe Nolan really *was* drawn to her.

Sitting at the kitchen table, Dana felt weightless for an instant. If she could have one miracle, what was to say she couldn't have two?

Because one in a lifetime was more than most people had? Reality brought her down hard.

JANICE KAY JOHNSON 197

Probably all Nolan intended was to distract her from noticing how little she'd seen her son. Convincing her he sympathized so she wouldn't push.

Unfortunately, that made a whole lot more sense.

Heaviness settled in her chest as she picked up the paper, a weekly, appropriately named *The Lookout*. She'd grabbed last week's edition at the grocery store, then decided to subscribe. The focus was entirely on *very* local news, from high school baseball scores to students who'd received scholarships and what colleges they would attend. Now she read about a fund-raiser for the family of a woman in a coma in intensive care who had been hit by a car. Another car accident, this one involving two teenagers, one from Lookout, the other from The Dalles. Experts commented on laws involving young drivers. She reached the middle of the paper, where her eye was caught by a calendar of upcoming school events. Most were at the high school or middle school. But there—

Sixth-grade open house, celebrating family, to be held Monday night. Lookout had two elementary schools, but this was Christian's. Student projects, it said. Public welcome.

Dana read the single line over and over. What did that mean, *student projects*? Something they were showing off? If so, Christian had no interest in *her* seeing whatever it was he'd done. Because he wasn't celebrating his biological family.

Of course his project had to do with the Gregors. Otherwise, he would have talked to her about it. Otherwise, he'd have had to admit to teacher and friends the whole sorry tale. He might have had to acknowledge her.

Nolan, who had just left, hadn't so much as mentioned the open house. Christian's choice hurt. Nolan's part in this enraged her. So now she knew. If she heard about the open house, she was meant to remember his sympathy, his promise to advocate for her, his friendliness, his kiss. And stay home.

Hands cold, Dana folded the paper so that the school events schedule showed and left it on the table.

She'd have to think about this.

"Hey." Nolan rested a hand on Christian's shoulder as they walked across the parking lot, joining a stream of other parents and kids entering the school. "Don't worry. You did a great job on your project."

"I don't know. Wait'll you see Ryan's. His great-grandfather smuggled Jews out of Denmark during World War II."

Nolan chuckled. "Fair enough. I can't top that. But, you know, your grade depends on the quality of your presentation and research, not on how awesome your ancestor was."

"His is cool. I bet he gets an A." He grinned. "Bet I do, too."

"I like confidence." Nolan gave a last squeeze before letting his hand drop from the boy's shoulder. He didn't want to embarrass the kid.

He hoped Christian didn't guess how dark his mood was. Dana would see tonight as a betrayal. When the assignment first came up, Nolan had suggested Christian use the chance to explore the history of this new family. He'd met furious resistance. At the time, he'd been feeling a whole lot of resistance, too, so he hadn't argued.

Now? He was still flattered that Christian had done his project about his army-ranger uncle who had spent years fighting terrorism. But Nolan also had a crawling sense of shame, because he hadn't told Dana about this thing tonight or about the decision Christian made and why.

Chances were, she'd never hear about it. Why would she? And the hard truth was, acceptance had to come from Christian. Nolan couldn't coerce it.

"There's Jason!" Christian exclaimed, veering toward his best friend.

Following, Nolan greeted the parents, people he really liked. Jason's father grinned. "I was excited about tonight. He pried his fingers off the game controls."

Nolan laughed. "Tell me you aren't letting him play the violent ones." And Christian when he was there.

"Mature and Adults Only are banned," Ben assured him. "Sooner or later, he'll borrow 'Halo' or 'Resident Evil' from a friend and have the surprise of finding out that I meant it when I said I'd take the system away for a month with the first offense, three months for the second."

"Forever for the third?"

"And do it with pleasure." He gave Nolan a mock scowl. "You know you're undermining my attempt to raise a pacifist son. He starts talking about how heroic spec ops soldiers are…"

"Heroic? A pretty word for an ugly business." As the two chattering boys rushed ahead to join other friends, Nolan said, "You'll let me know if Christian is the one to sneak a banned game in."

"Oh, yeah." They'd made it into the classroom, and Ben's head turned as he took in the various projects, displayed either in poster form or using trifold setups resting on tables. "I'm impressed."

"So am I."

Christian dropped back to say, "Ryan's is right here."

He'd been right; Ryan had done a nice job, including some family photos and ones he'd printed from online articles or copied from books.

Nolan congratulated Ryan, part of Christian's circle, and Ryan's parents. Then he and Christian wandered, meeting up with more friends. Nolan was talking to the Aceros, whose son Tomás was another of Christian's best buds, when by some sixth sense he glanced toward the classroom door. A woman had just entered.

He tensed in alarm. Oh, hell. This wasn't going to be pretty. Crowding out the shame was a jolt of anger. What was she thinking? He'd just told her that Christian had yet to admit even to his closest friends that Marlee wasn't really his mother. So what? Dana had decided to put him on the spot? She imagined she could *force* him to acknowledge her publicly?

"Excuse me," Nolan said to Juanita Acero, and moved swiftly to separate Christian from the two boys he'd been hanging with. "Dana is here," he murmured. "By the door."

"What?" Christian whirled to see her. "Did you tell her?"

"No. One of her coworkers may have a kid your age. Or she saw the listing in the paper."

"What should I do?" Christian asked, his panic obvious.

She'd seen them. For seconds that lasted too long, her eyes held Nolan's. He saw pride, embarrassment and determination. Her body language was stiff. As he watched, she stepped aside to allow a group to pass her.

"I don't know," Nolan admitted.

All but vibrating with anxiety, Christian exclaimed, "I don't want her here!"

"Should I try to head her off?"

"Yes!"

Nolan didn't love being the bad guy, but his anger propelled him across the classroom.

Long before he reached her, she had turned away and begun checking out the student projects. She didn't give them the time he had, but then, she didn't know the kids who had created them, either.

In the crowded, noisy room, with students calling to each other, parents socializing and exclaiming over individual projects, she held herself aloof, as if she thought she were alone.

She was studying a poster about a covered-wagon journey, sketchily done, when Nolan reached her.

"What are you doing here?" he asked, voice low.

Dana didn't even look at him. "I had the impression the public was invited."

"You had to know how Christian would feel about you showing up."

"It would appear," she said, cool as a cu-

cumber, "that I'll only learn anything about his life by becoming an observer. That's what I'm doing."

"Sure it is," he said grimly. "You thought he'd have to accept your presence, didn't you? At least introduce you, even if he doesn't say *mom*." His anger spiked. "Or did you plan to introduce yourself? Chat with other parents, tell them how excited you are about your son's project?"

She had moved on to the next poster, but now she went completely still. She was looking straight ahead, but Nolan doubted she saw what was right in front of her. He waited.

"No," she said quietly. "I wouldn't do that to him." She turned her head, letting him see eyes brimming with pain, color painting her cheeks. "I just…wanted to see. Give myself—" She stopped and shook her head. "I shouldn't have come. Tell him I'm sorry." She whirled too suddenly, blundering into another woman. "I'm sorry," she said again. "So sorry." And was out the door.

Nolan went after her.

Late arrivals and people leaving made the hall too populated for him to say anything. She was the only person hurrying. Not quite running, but close. She'd have lost him if not for his long strides.

She was rushing across the parking lot when he caught up enough to call, "Dana."

She hesitated between one step and the next, then kept going.

"Damn it, Dana!"

She reached her car, unlocking and wrenching open the door. Nolan made himself halt some ten feet from her. A quick glance told him there was nobody in the vicinity.

"What did you want to give yourself?" he asked her quietly.

He'd feared she was crying, but the face she turned to him was carved in marble. Only the turbulence in her eyes and the white-knuckled grip she had on the top of the car door betrayed any emotion.

"A memory," she said. "That's all I wanted." Then she was in the car, slamming the door. While he stood frozen, she backed out and drove away.

Nolan watched her go, feeling like the scum of the earth. He knew suddenly that he hadn't entirely let himself understand.

This was a woman who had missed everything. She'd never been able to hang finger paintings on the refrigerator or the Santa with a cotton-ball beard made in first grade. No Mother's Day card drawn with stick figures and lopsided letters saying I LOVE YOU, MOMMY.

No spelling tests with an "A—Excellent!" at the top. She had never seen a single school assignment or project her son had done.

She'd just wanted to *see*. And he hadn't even let her get as far as Christian's masterpiece lauding his "uncle" Nolan.

Nolan let his head drop back and looked up at the sky, starting to deepen toward twilight. He felt too much for a woman who'd lost everything. Tangled with it was a kind of panic, even desperation, because he knew *he'd* lost something tonight that he might not be able to get back.

That maybe he didn't deserve to get back.

HER DOORBELL RANG an hour later. Dana ignored it. Then her phone rang. Nolan's number. She muted it and ignored the buzz a minute later that told her he had left a message.

She shouldn't have gone. She'd *known* she shouldn't. Now she'd ruined everything.

Huddling on the sofa wrapped in a fleece throw, she felt her mouth twist. Just what was it she'd ruined? The warm, loving relationship she had been tentatively building with her child? Get real. There'd been nothing to ruin.

Right this minute, she wished she hadn't moved. The decision had been so impulsive. She'd been willing to do anything, anything at all, to be near Gabriel. Now here she was, over a thousand miles from her friends and family. Entirely isolated.

Because I believed in Nolan Gregor's sense of honor.

No, that wasn't true. She'd made the decision before she called to discuss the move with him. She'd pretty well blackmailed him into agreeing to her deal. Maybe he'd been upholding his end; there was no way for her to know. He'd said himself, his first loyalty was to Christian.

Yes, but he'd also said— No, she thought sadly. He'd *implied* that he had mixed feelings. She'd snapped up the implication like a trout with a juicy fly.

Her phone rang again. This time the number was her brother's, but she couldn't talk to him without crying. He'd want to take the next flight so he could beat the crap out of Nolan. She relished the picture until she remembered how much bigger Nolan was.

Peter left a message, too.

Feeling so drained she staggered when she first stood up, Dana made her way to her bedroom, turning off lights as she went. She took a shower, staying under the hot water until it started to run tepid.

Just think, she had to go to work bright and early tomorrow. Back to planning the series of parenting talks. She laughed at the irony, the sound foreign to her ears.

Dana simply didn't know where she would go from here. She was too tired, too hollowed out, to think reasonably. Oddly enough, she was sure she could sleep. She could close her eyes and fall into a deep, dark well. The idea held a lot of appeal.

Tomorrow…well, tomorrow was another day. *Me and Scarlett O'Hara.*

She crawled into bed and turned out the light.

IT WAS THE longest goddamn day of work Nolan could remember, and that included some spent crouched for hour upon unending hour in the scant shade of barren rocks in hundred-and-ten-degree heat, weapon cradled in his arms, as he watched the entrance to a cave for the slightest movement.

He didn't try to call again. Dana wouldn't answer. This morning, a chastened Christian had said, "What if I call her?"

"From my phone?"

"Oh." He looked down, letting hair fall over his forehead.

Time for a haircut, Nolan had thought absently.

Then Christian burst out, "Do you think she'll go back to Colorado?"

Nolan let out a harsh breath, one expelled as forcefully as if he'd taken a blow, and said the same thing he had last night. "I don't know."

The boy's brown eyes were wild. "I didn't mean—"

Nolan made himself spend some time reassuring Christian, who had youth and one hell of a lot of tumult in his life to excuse him. Nolan's best efforts hadn't made Christian look any happier when he left for school, pushing his bike out of the garage.

The interminable day was also a profitable one, for a Tuesday. They'd been having a streak of sunshine, and people were cutting out of work to spend a day on the water. Standing knee-deep after helping some renters get moving, feeling the tug of current, Nolan couldn't remember the last time *he'd* taken a board out. Maybe that was what he needed. As always, he balked at the idea of paying someone to take his place while he had fun.

Fifteen minutes after school let out, Christian dumped his bike outside and hurried in, gaze going right to Nolan.

He shook his head. "Go on in back and do your homework."

At five thirty the last rental was returned by a young couple whose sunburns had Nolan wincing. He'd warned them about the effect of the rays bouncing off the water, but because it was only mid-May and not the heat of summer, they apparently hadn't believed him. He handed the woman a bottle of aloe-vera gel.

"This'll help. It's on the house."

She smiled weakly. "Thank you."

It took Nolan a few minutes to rinse off the boards, sails and harnesses and lay them out to dry. Then he rubbed a hand over his raspy jaw and let himself in the back door, where Christian hovered.

"Time to go home."

"But...can't we go see...her?"

"Dana?" Nolan sighed. "I'm not sure how welcome we'd be, Christian."

The boy's chin tilted stubbornly. "But...I have to say I'm sorry."

"Yeah. Okay."

"Could we take her a pizza or, I don't know, burgers?"

Good idea or terrible? Who knew? "Why not?" he said with a shrug. "It'll give us a dinner if she kicks us out."

Burgers and fries, they decided, which required only a quick detour.

Ten minutes later, they arrived at Dana's house. No way to tell if she was home, since Nolan assumed she parked in the garage.

They trudged in silence up to the small porch. Nolan held the bag of food; Christian rang the bell.

After what had to be a minute, the door opened. Dana stood there, wearing black leggings, knee-high black boots and a thigh-length white knit shirt, the fabric draping to emphasize every curve.

"Christian. Nolan."

Christian appeared tongue-tied. Nolan cleared his throat. "We came to—"

"Hear my apology?" Her eyebrows arched. "I'm sorry. I intruded where I hadn't been invited. I know how awkward that must have been for you. I really am sorry."

Nolan frowned. "We're the ones who owe you an apology."

Her lips curved, but her eyes remained... blank. "You know that isn't true. Now, if you'll excuse me..."

"We were hoping you'd share our dinner." Nolan hoisted the bag.

"That's kind of you, but I'm afraid I have other plans." She produced another smile. "Enjoy your meal."

The door was almost closed when Christian cried, "Wait!"

After a pause, she opened it partway again. "Yes?"

"It's my fault!" he said passionately. "When my teacher assigned the project, I was still mad." His throat worked. "Then…I couldn't tell you. I just couldn't," he finished, his voice dying to a near whisper at the end.

"Christian," Dana said softly, "I do understand. Like I told your uncle, all I wanted was to see your project. I thought I'd gone late enough that you two wouldn't still be there. And I meant it when I said I shouldn't have gone. Okay?"

He nodded, the distress on his face not lessening.

She nodded, too, and closed the door in their faces.

Neither of them moved for a minute. That had gone about as well as Nolan had expected. Dana had hidden her hurt, apologized gracefully and left him feeling like something she'd scraped off her shoe. Had she even looked at him? He didn't think so.

"Well, bud, what say we go home and eat?"

Christian's shoulders sagged, but he nodded and turned to the SUV, Nolan following behind.

Buckled in, the food on the backseat, Christian said, "Do you think she really has other plans?"

No. Although she'd looked sexy enough, was there any chance she had a date? The roiling in Nolan's belly felt more like a vicious eddy now, the kind that could suck you down.

"I think she felt too uncomfortable to pretend

to have a good time with us," he said truthfully, accelerating away from the curb.

"Will she stay mad at me?" Christian asked in a small voice.

Nolan shook his head, reaching out to ruffle the boy's hair. "With you? No."

With me? Oh, yeah. Although what she felt for him right now was a lot more complicated than mad.

CHAPTER ELEVEN

DANA HAD DELETED the message Nolan left Monday without listening to it. But she listened to the one he left Wednesday after their visit.

It was terse. "Christian would really like to see you. Since you're working now and he can't come by after school, would it be okay if I drop him off for an hour tonight or tomorrow night?"

She had just come out of a meeting with Jessica and Meghan, where she'd shared some of her conclusions on programs that didn't serve a large enough population or duplicated the efforts of other agencies. Alone in her small office, she returned his call, half hoping she would be able to leave a message.

No such luck.

"Dana?"

Even his deep voice sent a shiver through her, which today made her feel foolish.

"Tonight would be fine, if Christian wants to come by," she said pleasantly. "Shall we say seven?"

"Sounds good." He was quiet for a moment. "Are you ever going to speak to me again?"

"Aren't we speaking right now?"

"You know what I mean."

"I took your...friendliness at face value, which was clearly a mistake. I'm here to get to know my son. I let myself be distracted."

"I've never been dishonest with you."

Surprised at how heated he sounded, she retorted, "An omission can be as dishonest as a lie."

"Damn it, Dana—"

She closed her eyes. "No, I shouldn't have said that. All I know is, you're in Christian's corner. I thought..." She shook her head, even though he wouldn't see. "Never mind. It doesn't matter."

"It does," he said intensely.

"I'd hoped we could all have the same goal, but I don't think we do. So let's just leave it, shall we, Nolan?" At a knock on her door she said, "I'm at work and need to go. I'll expect Christian this evening unless I hear otherwise." Setting down the phone, she called, "Come in."

Meghan poked her head in. "Hi, it's just me. I had a few questions, if you have time."

Dana made herself smile despite the knot in her stomach. "Of course. Sit down."

I'm seeing Christian tonight. So why aren't I excited?

Because he was probably coming under duress? Or, at best, because he felt guilty?

Her feelings had nothing to do with the fact that she *wouldn't* be seeing Nolan.

My choice. One I'd be smart to keep making.

EVEN AS CHRISTIAN rang the doorbell, he cast a pleading look over his shoulder at Uncle Nolan, waiting in the SUV at the curb. When Christian had begged him to come in, too, he'd shaken his head.

He heard the sound of the lock being turned, and then the door opened. Dana smiled and said, "Come on in." She waved at Uncle Nolan. By the time they were inside, he was driving away.

"I assume you had dinner?"

He nodded, relaxing a little. She was being nice, like she had the time he came by after school.

"Do you have room for a cinnamon roll?" She wrinkled her nose. "I shouldn't have bought them, but temptation overcame me."

He had a weird moment. Something about that expression made him realize that he did kind of look like her. Maybe…a lot like her.

Would everyone guess if they saw him with her?

"Um, yeah, cool," he got out.

They sat at the kitchen table again, both drinking milk. She nibbled on half a cinnamon roll—Christian could kind of see why, since they were *huge*—while he had one to himself.

She repeated her apology, promising not to put him on the spot again.

Feeling a cramping in his chest, he flattened some icing on the plate with his fork. "No, I should have said you could come. It's just..." He took a deep breath. "I was embarrassed. You know. Because I did my project on Uncle Nolan."

"I would have understood," she said quietly. "You're proud of him. That's okay."

"I always wanted—" He stopped, ducking his head again.

"To be like him?"

Christian nodded.

"You probably *will* be like him in some ways, you know. He raised you. That may have more impact on how you turn out, what interests you, what you're good at, than your genes do."

He lifted his head. "You really think so?"

Her smile made him feel good. "Yes, I do. Plus...the Gregors have a lot in common with my family. We tend to be tall, for example. Athletic. We're good students. Those things are all true of Nolan, too."

"Mom wasn't." He heard himself. "I mean..."

"I know what you mean. And— Well, I haven't even seen a picture of her. Was she short?"

"Kind of medium," he said. "Not as tall as you."

Dana nodded. "It sounds like she may not have done well in school, but that doesn't mean she wasn't smart. Her mental illness could have made it hard for her to focus or remember why finishing something was important. It obviously got in the way of her working well with other students."

"I used to worry—" He sneaked a look at her.

"What did you worry about?"

"That, I don't know, I might end up like her. Sick in the head. I went online," he said in a rush, "and schizophrenia can be inherited."

"I know that's true sometimes," she said gently. "But not always. Is there anyone else in the family you know of who was mentally ill?"

He shook his head. "Uncle Nolan says no."

"Well, hey!" She laughed, but kind of softly. "At least you can forget that worry. My grandfather died of heart disease when he was only in his early sixties, so my dad worries a lot about his heart, but you're a long ways from having to think about that."

He grinned. "Yeah." Sixties *was* old.

"I have some photo albums, if you'd like to see pictures of my family," she said, sounding a little nervous.

His family, was what she meant.

"Do you have a picture of you at my age?"

She made a funny face. "Probably. I looked like a giraffe."

He laughed. "There's a girl like that in my class. I'm taller than her, but hardly any of the other guys are. And she's got arms like sticks."

"That was me."

She went off and came back with several photo albums, plunking them down on the table. "No, I won't make you look at every picture," she said, laughing.

She put an album in front of him. "This one, Mom put together for me. When I was eleven…" She started to flip through.

Christian stopped her. "No, that's… Wow." He went back to the beginning, seeing her as a newborn in her mother's arms in the hospital. She didn't look that much like her mother. As he slowly turned pages, he saw that she took more after her father, who… He stopped and stared at one photo.

"You look a lot like your grandfather," she said softly. "And my brother, too."

He stayed mostly quiet, but he kept turning pages until he finished this album, with her in college graduation robes. *My mother.* Then he reached for another album, and another. She pointed out his uncle and aunt, and he saw their children growing up. *My cousins.* Yet another album held pictures from her wedding, so he saw his dad, too, and grandparents on that side and an aunt. And there was the uncle who'd been on the Olympic luge team.

It was completely bizarre, but he couldn't quit looking. It was like…this whole history. *His* history, in a way. Like photo albums Grandma and Grandad had had, but he was actually related to these people.

Christian didn't even know what he felt. It got so he could hardly breathe. For a minute he was afraid he might cry, but he couldn't even do that.

Finally, he closed the last album and just sat there.

"I thought," Dana said, "that I'd take out some pictures and get them copied. Make you an album. You could put it away, in case you're interested later."

He nodded.

"Good." She smiled and piled them up. "It's already after eight. I'll bet your uncle will be here anytime."

"He's not really my uncle."

She hadn't touched him before, but now she did, squeezing his shoulder very quickly, kind of like Uncle Nolan did. "I think he always will be," she said, not as if she minded.

Now his eyes did sting, so he kept his face turned away until he was sure he wouldn't start sobbing or something.

Watching Dana put their plates in the dishwasher, Christian said, "It wasn't his fault, you know."

She turned to look at him. "That I didn't know about the open house, you mean?"

"That, and—" he shrugged, feeling awkward and dorky "—me not wanting to see you. He kept saying you're part of my life, but… I don't know. I had to sort of think about it."

She smiled, but crooked. "I swore I'd be patient." Her eyes looked wet, although no tears fell. "And then I wasn't. I promise I'll do better."

"I wish you weren't mad at Uncle Nolan!" He swallowed hard. His voice came out small and shaky. "It's fun when we're all together."

He thought she was crying a little now. "You're telling me I should quit sulking, huh?"

"Just… I've been mad at him because he was kind of on your side. And now *you're* mad at him."

She swiped the back of her hand over one eye, then the other. "Okay. You're right. I thought… Oh, it doesn't matter. You can tell him he's officially forgiven."

"Cool." He tipped his head, hearing an engine out front. "I bet that's him. I guess I better go."

"Yes." This time her smile was real.

She walked him to the door and opened it, surprising Uncle Nolan, who had a foot on the first porch step. She politely thanked him for coming and Uncle Nolan for driving him over and said, "Good night."

When they got in the SUV, Uncle Nolan looked at him.

"She showed me pictures. Of her growing up and her parents and brother and...and my father and *his* family." Christian stared ahead through the windshield. "I look like them. Dana's dad and brother. And even her, when she was my age."

"That's to be expected." Uncle Nolan sounded kind.

Christian turned to him. "But she said I might grow up to be like you anyway, 'cause you raised me and that's as important as, you know, genes."

"Did she," he said under his breath, not asking a question.

"And she said to say that she's gotten over being mad at you. Because I explained it was all me."

Uncle Nolan's face changed. Christian couldn't tell what he was thinking, except he was really glad. "Thank you," he said.

Christian nodded. "I was thinking."

His uncle cocked an eyebrow.

"That she might like to see pictures of me, too. You know, when I was little."

"You're a good kid. We'll have her over and let her look all she wants. Then we'll make up an album for her. Okay?"

Christian drew a breath. It filled his lungs, as if they'd expanded. For a minute he felt light-headed. "I bet she'd like that."

"I bet she would, too."

"HEY, HAVE YOU ever tried wave jumping?" Jeff Yantis was a local who competed internationally in freestyle and big-air windsurfing, especially popular in the Hood River area. In big air, competitors went for the highest jump or maneuver. Yantis had endorsement deals with several board and sail manufacturers, making his a familiar face throughout the sport. He was the classic surfer dude: skin tanned and leathery, shaggy hair bleached nearly white by the sun, electric-blue eyes.

"I did some during R & R when I was military," Nolan said. "It was fun. Oahu and Africa."

"Africa?"

"Namibia." He had no intention of explaining why he'd been in the vicinity.

"Awesome," Jeff declared. "The speed-sailing record was set there."

"Yep." The bell on the door tinkled. Nolan was more interested in who was coming in than he was in Jeff, who loved talking about his own exploits.

One of his part-timers met the two women who entered, and Nolan returned his attention to Jeff, who was likable enough, as well as a good customer. He talked up Wind & Waves in a way that had boosted business, too.

Rhapsodizing about this new experience, he made wave jumping sound like skateboarding only using giant waves as ramps, which wasn't a bad comparison. Apparently, Jeff had been lucky enough to be on Maui when massive swells made huge aerial moves possible. He was demonstrating how he had twisted his body while performing two rotations when the bell over the door tinkled again.

Nolan's adrenaline rush at seeing Dana probably compared with Jeff's while he was pulling off the Crazy Pete. He smiled when she spotted him.

"Jeff, sorry to interrupt, but my lunch date is here."

The guy turned to look, then grinned. "Hot lady."

"She is."

"Listen, I got to be going, anyway. I'll be away for a few weeks—Australia—but when I get back, I'll stop by. I've heard about a new board, different comp—"

Nolan quit listening midword and forgot to say goodbye. Instead, he watched Dana approach. "Hey."

"Hi." Dana appeared shy, but she lifted

the white paper bag she carried in one hand. "Lunch, as promised."

She'd called that morning and asked if she could come by. Nolan jumped on her offer to bring lunch.

He signaled toward the back, and today's assistant nodded and waved. Nolan led Dana through the store, stopping to pick up drinks from a small fridge in the break room, and out the back door to a patio with a table, chairs and a big umbrella.

"Is this warm weather normal for May?" she asked, sitting at the table.

"No. Don't worry. Rain is bound to come."

She chuckled. "I suppose I'll have to get used to rain if I stay in Lookout."

If. Not the word he wanted to hear.

Nolan pulled out a chair, too, and watched as she produced deli sandwiches and potato salad in small cardboard containers.

"Looks good," he said, reaching for a sandwich.

Sounding tentative, she said, "I know you probably can't spare much time, but I thought—"

"I'm the boss. After you called, I arranged staffing to give me as long as I want."

Her face didn't relax as much as he'd have liked. "Mostly, I wanted to tell you the same thing I told Christian. I'm—"

He interrupted again, with no compunction.

"If this is an apology, skip it. Once is enough. And we screwed up, too."

She blinked. "Well…okay."

"This is going to be a short lunch if that's all you have to say." He let some humor inflect his voice.

"I had hoped to eat," Dana said tartly.

He nodded at the untouched food. "Then eat."

They both started with potato salad, silence holding for a couple minutes. Dana looked out at the river, relatively placid with mild winds, and Nolan watched her.

Damn, she was pretty. For a woman of her height, her bone structure was fine, almost delicate. Her cheekbones were sharp rather than rounded, her often stubborn jaw so defined his fingers itched to trace it. A high, slightly curving forehead gave her an appearance of vulnerability that he doubted had been true before her son was stolen. He found himself wondering if he'd have been as intrigued by the happier, less complicated woman she had been.

Maybe not. Aside from the tragedies that had winnowed his family down to two, he had seen and done too much in the service to feel comfortable revealing much to people whose lives had been safe, who saw the world in black and white.

He wanted to know Dana.

She turned luminous gray eyes on him at that

moment. "Can we go back to…I don't know, being friendly?"

To risk or not to risk. He mentally tossed the dice. "I liked it when we were more than friendly."

She kept studying him, a hint of warmth in her cheeks. "You admitted how goal oriented you are. Was that kiss a way of softening me up? Deflecting me from *my* goal?"

He wanted to take offense but couldn't. He did have a goal, or at least the desire to explore the idea of how the three of them would work as a family. In the shorter term, though…

"I'm attracted to you," he said, answering her blunt question with a blunt answer. "I had the impression it might be mutual."

Her gaze slid away but returned to meet his. "Going anywhere with that attraction would complicate things."

It would, but he asked anyway, "How?"

"At least one of us will end up hurt. How can that help but taint our effort to be civil for Christian's sake?"

Disconcerted, he repeated, "At least one of us *will* end up hurt? There's a positive way of looking at the future."

She set down the half sandwich she'd just picked up. "I haven't thought positive in a very long time."

Frowning, he said, "I have the impression

you spent a lot of years believing fiercely that you'd find Christian, alive and well. Isn't that positive?"

"I tried very hard to convince myself that he was alive." She offered a small, crooked smile. "It's not quite the same thing."

"No." He tacked a different direction. "Your parents are still married."

"Yes. They have a good marriage. But do you know how rare that is?" She gave her head a quick shake. "Anyway, that's marriage. More casual relationships? What tiny percent last more than a few weeks or months?"

"You're seriously negative." And, yeah, that was a surprise. "I hope you express a more positive attitude for your clients."

"Of course I do!" she exclaimed. "I'm not—" A lot passed through those eyes before she said slowly, "Maybe I am negative."

Nolan laid it on the line. "Do you want to live alone? Forever?"

"I...had hoped to live with Gabe—Christian." But tiny lines furrowed her usually smooth forehead.

"He'll be twelve soon. Six years from now, he'll be packing for college."

Dana's body quivered. Then she searched his face. "That doesn't bother you?"

"Yeah," he said gruffly. "Of course it does. But I want him to go eagerly, not looking over his shoulder and worrying about me. When the day comes…?" He turned his gaze to the river. He knew he didn't have to finish his sentence.

"Have you ever been married?" Dana asked, sounding tentative.

He shook his head, taking her interest as a good sign. "Career military do marry, but it's a hard road for the spouse that stays behind. Can't say I met anyone I could be serious about, anyway. And since I came home, I've had a lot on my plate."

Getting the business relocated and running would have been enough on its own, but he'd also had to deal with Marlee's wild mood swings and disappearances and Christian's grief after losing the grandparents who'd been his bedrock. Never mind the aftermath of the ax incident. The wonder was how the kid had remained as stable as he was.

He could tell Dana's thoughts paralleled his. She kept looking at him, her gaze clear.

"All right." She hesitated only momentarily. "Then let me ask you something."

"Okay." He tried not to betray how wary he suddenly felt.

"Are you interested in…in marriage? Having a family?" She tipped her chin up, speaking frankly despite her anxious blush. "Do you see that as a possibility for the two of us? Or is being 'more than friendly' just sex?"

Knocked off balance, Nolan tried to figure out the right answer. If there was a right one.

"I wasn't asking for 'just' sex," he said. He wished he could tell her he had begun every relationship open to greater possibilities, but that was a lie. For the most part, since graduating from college, sex *had* been his only goal. He had tried not to hurt women, most of whom, he hoped, had gotten exactly what they wanted, too. "You're right. That would be a lousy idea, given our situation."

She nibbled on her lower lip, distracting him. *He* wanted to be the one doing that.

"I can't claim to be in love with you. I don't know you well enough yet." Inexplicable panic built up in his chest. Because...he knew her a whole lot better than would be usual from the time they'd spent together. "But to answer your question... Yes. I do want marriage and a family." Until this moment, he hadn't realized how much. It made him feel defenseless, not his favorite state of being. This had to be said, though. "And I do see that as a possibility for you and me. You...make me think things I never have before."

The truth of that shook him, until he reminded himself that marriage and family *was* the plan. For Christian's sake. For all their sakes. He liked Dana. He liked how she interacted with Christian. He wanted to spare her pain, make her happy—natural, given the protective part of his personality. He thought he could live with her.

And he wanted her. Damn, did he want her. Even thinking about her in his bed was enough to arouse him uncomfortably. Good thing they were on opposite sides of the table.

She hadn't so much as blinked in a long time. He was about to slap her on the back, make sure she was still breathing, when she murmured, "How can I believe you?"

"I won't lie to you." Misdirect, maybe, he thought, feeling a pang of guilt. He'd omit. But flat-out lie? No.

"How do you think Christian would feel about seeing us...together?"

"I can't be sure," he admitted. Christian could love the idea or hate it. These days, he was hard to predict. "I think ultimately he'd go for it."

"He might feel threatened if he imagines your loyalties are...divided."

"He's started to accept that you'll be part of his life."

"But he still wants you in his corner."

Considering the kid's occasional volatility, that was one way to put it. "We take it slow."

"Immunize him?" she asked so politely he had to grin.

"Something like that."

Dana looked down at her mostly untouched lunch. "I have to think about this."

His body tensed. If he let her think too much, she'd circle around to being sure hooking up with him was a bad idea. He needed to sweep her away. Remind her she was a woman, and a lonely one. Offer her refuge in his arms.

"This seems so—" she frowned a little "—cold. As if we're laying out a plan."

Plan? Last word he could let cross her mind. And *cold?* That one he wouldn't swallow.

He sat forward so fast the table rocked. Flattening both hands on the surface, he leaned forward and let her see his teeth. "When I'm thinking about you, I'm not cold." She shrank back, but he didn't let himself worry about it. "You don't seem all that cold to me, either. I've seen your temper. And don't tell me you didn't feel the heat when I kissed you."

She stared, eyes dark and turbulent. The air felt charged. His breathing sounded as if he'd just finished a hard sprint.

"I...didn't mean..."

The obscenity he growled caused her to wince. Nolan forced himself to sit back. Damn it, what was *wrong* with him? Rubbing a hand over his face, he scrabbled for his usually rock-steady control. "I overreacted," he admitted, wishing he knew why. The rasp in his voice told him he didn't have it together yet.

"I wasn't meaning to insult you."

"I know you weren't." He rolled his shoulders. "You're the one who asked my intentions. If my laying them out sounded cold-blooded to you, I can't help that."

"I've never seen you as cold." The hand he could see curled into a knot loosened, knotted again. "You have too much temper for that."

Her deliberate echo of what he'd said roused a whiff of amusement, bringing him down like nothing else could. Had she been teasing him?

Yeah, he decided, seeing the way she'd firmed her mouth as if to combat a smile. That was a good sign, right? And her hand had opened and relaxed.

"Why don't you do your thinking while we get to know each other better?" he suggested. "How about dinner tomorrow night? And maybe you could spend at least part of Saturday working here with us."

"I actually have plans Saturday."

Like she'd had plans when he and Christian showed up on her doorstep with burgers and fries? He'd let himself keep believing he and Christian were the only two people she knew in town, but she had to be getting to know her coworkers, at the very least.

"What kind of plans?" he asked, hoping he sounded more casual than he felt. What if she'd gotten far enough with some guy to be dating?

"A woman I work with is new in Lookout, too," Dana said, seeming oblivious to his instant fury. "This is her first job out of grad school. She suggested we take the Hood River Railroad excursion. It sounded like fun."

As if a plug had been pulled, the testosterone-induced combativeness drained away. "I've never been on it, but it's a popular tourist attraction. I hear it's a good way to take in some scenery."

"Would Sunday be okay?" she asked uncertainly. "I mean, to spend time with you and Christian?"

"Sure." Disliking this roller coaster of emotions, he had to ask. "Is that a no about tomorrow night?"

"Oh." She smiled. "No. I mean, it was a yes. If you think Christian will be okay with it."

"Yeah. I'll let him spend the night at Jason's. Christian doesn't have a gaming system at home. I didn't want him to get addicted."

Dana laughed, a ripple of sound that stirred the tiny hairs on his body. "Present the irresistible…"

"And he won't so much as wonder what I'm doing." An empty house. Matching her smile, Nolan regretted with every fiber of his being that it was way too soon to suggest she come home with him.

CHAPTER TWELVE

TWO WEEKS LATER, Dana was happy enough to sail aloft in an iridescent bubble.

She laughed, since at the moment she stood thigh-deep in cold river water. Her job was to help launch the biggest sailboat Wind & Waves offered for rent. All the sailboats and some of the kayaks were made by Hobie. Nolan had called this one a T2. Molded out of something that felt like plastic, it was a catamaran that Christian told her was sixteen feet long.

She, Christian and the couple taking it out had skidded it into the water. Dana now helped steady it as the apparently experienced couple tinkered with lines.

The man hoisted himself up onto one of the two parallel hulls and stepped carefully onto the frame between them so he could reach the mast. At whatever he was doing, the sail unfurled enough to make the boat buck. Dana held on, even as the current tugged at her enough to make her feel unstable.

"Okay, Brie," the guy said.

Blond hair captured in a ponytail, his companion wore a skintight black-and-purple wet suit, the kind that stopped short of her knees. She swung a leg over the near hull, looking like a gymnast mounting a balance beam.

The Hobie fought harder, trying to swing with the current, or maybe the wind. Dana didn't know, only that her fingers were slipping.

The man snapped a short, sharp expletive. The boat leaped forward and Dana lost her hold entirely. Christian was yelling something, but she couldn't make it out. All she could see was the boat swinging hard toward her. She tried to step back, but between the depth of water and the current, she felt like she was trying to move in molasses.

With a wham, the back of the near hull hit her. She barely pulled in a breath before going *splat*.

BUSY AS THE store was, Nolan was drawn out to the patio to watch the launch. Often the group could handle it themselves. He didn't let anyone take a piece of equipment out unless he could verify they had the experience needed. The T2 was a safe boat, good for families, and the wide stance kept heeling to a minimum. Still, the thing weighed close to four hundred pounds, which made it unwieldy as hell until it was flying in front of the wind.

Watching, he smiled. Dana had thrown herself into working at Wind & Waves. He bet most people she helped hadn't a clue that she had never windsurfed *or* sailed, not the way she talked knowledgeably about harnesses, boards and foot straps, mimicking what she'd heard the regular staff telling customers. She didn't seem to mind getting wet, either. Coming back inside, she'd shiver and laugh at the same time, towel herself off and be behind the cash register two minutes later.

This time…he wished Christian had put himself in front and let her stay in the shallower water. Unlike the sailors, she wasn't wearing a PFD. She'd done this before without displaying any nerves, but he didn't like the way the catamaran was moving. He stiffened, shading his eyes with one hand.

And then the damn thing yawed so suddenly she didn't have time to get out of the way. It sent her flying, out deeper where the current was stronger.

On a burst of fear, he started running. She'd surface any second, swim back to shore. Laugh to see him tearing to the rescue.

The boat pulled away, both sailors staring back. Christian threw himself forward into the water, even though he wasn't wearing a vest, either.

THE INSTANT THE water closed over Dana's head, she panicked. The boat was going to hit her again. Run right over her. If she was trapped under it... Her flailing arms and legs proved useless against the power of the current. She opened her eyes, but in the murk she couldn't tell up from down.

A hand closed around her ankle. Her panic intensified. She kicked out, but the grip tightened. The pressure in her chest built, and she knew she'd have to exhale—and then she wouldn't be able to help *inhaling*. Filling her lungs with water.

But then the hand on her ankle was doing more than holding her—it was pulling her steadily backward. She was too terrified to do anything but struggle. Water trickled into her sinuses, stinging. In a violent rush, all the air in her lungs escaped. Suddenly she was breathing water, her body trying to convulse.

And more hands closed around her leg, then her waist, and lifted her out of the river. She saw Nolan's face, skin stretched tight over the bones. Christian, soaking wet, crawling onto the beach.

Nolan laid her down on her side, and she choked on the water trying to come back up. Over and over, Dana coughed and retched, until finally she went limp. She was breathing air. Thank God, thank God.

Nolan's big hand moved soothingly on her back. "Tell me you're all right," he demanded. Then, in a different tone, "Call 911, Trevor."

"No." She pushed the one word out and made herself roll over, not sure she could have if Nolan hadn't helped. "I'm okay." The voice was small and scratchy, barely above a whisper. "No ambulance."

"You're sure?" He focused such intensity on her she couldn't look away from his face.

Dana coughed again and slumped back to the sand. "Yes."

He'd been crouched on his haunches but now fell to his knees. "All right. Damn. Trev, can you run and get us a couple of towels?"

A male voice answered.

"Christian?" Nolan said.

"I'm fine, Uncle Nolan."

She turned her head. Christian was soaked, too, even his hair dripping. It must have been him who'd dived after her, grabbed her ankle. And Nolan, wet to his chest, had pulled them both out.

"I'm sorry." She squeezed her eyes shut. "I panicked. I couldn't think. It wasn't even that deep."

"It was plenty deep." Nolan's voice was grim. "The drop-off there is sharp. You shouldn't have been as far out as you were without wearing a vest."

"It's my fault." Christian rose to his feet, his cargo shorts and T-shirt plastered to his long, skinny body. I thought—"

"That she could swim." Nolan scowled at her. "Why didn't you tell us?"

"Because I can!" She pressed her lips together. "In a pool. And…I'm sort of intermediate."

"Sort of intermediate."

Dana pushed herself to a sitting position. "I had a bad experience. I didn't like lessons."

Nolan's chin dropped to his chest. He muttered under his breath. She was pretty sure she didn't want to hear what he was saying.

Face contorted, Christian said in a high, thin voice, "I almost got you killed."

"No!" Dana held out a hand to him. "It's not your fault. It's mine! I wanted—"

Man and boy stared at her. "What did you want?" Nolan asked, gentle compared to his earlier adrenaline-driven anger.

"I wanted to impress you." Hot tears blurred her eyes when she looked at her son. "If I'd told you I'm not very good around water, you wouldn't have let me help." Despite her raw throat, words rushed out. "I know I was stupid."

"You wanted to impress *me*?" Christian's voice cracked, the last word going bass deep.

She pulled her knees up, nodded and rested her forehead on them.

"Okay." Nolan squeezed her nape. "No one is hurt. We just need to calm down."

A hysterical laugh bubbled in Dana's throat. Yep, that's all they needed to do.

He thanked Trevor, the younger of the two men who'd been working today, and a moment later wrapped a thick towel around her shoulders. Dana hadn't realized she was shivering until she felt the comfort of that rough terry-cloth.

"Hey." Nolan had moved in front of her. Squatting, he speared her with those bright blue eyes. "You up to standing?"

She nodded, took his hand and let him pull her to her feet. She didn't want to look at Christian. "Ugh," she said, plucking at her canvas shorts as she began the plod up the grassy slope to the building. "I need to go home."

"We can find you something to wear," Nolan said.

"I need a hot shower. Christian…?" She looked around, not finding him.

"He went ahead while you had your face buried."

Would he ever speak to her again?

She had to enter the back of the business to grab her purse and flip-flops. Not wanting to drip on the floor, she went back out and circled the building, Nolan at her side.

"You sure you're okay to drive?" he asked.

"Yes. You know it isn't far."

She had her car door open when his hand on her arm stopped her from getting in.

"Will you look at me?"

Dana reluctantly met his eyes.

"You've withdrawn." And clearly, he didn't like it.

"I feel like an idiot. Plus, my lungs and throat are burning and my stomach muscles hurt." She felt weird overall and suspected she might be a little bit in shock. She'd been so happy…and then *boom*. She was drowning. Her eleven-year-old son had had to put himself at risk to haul her out.

"You'll meet us for pizza once we close?"

Feeling pitiful, she asked, "Is that a good idea?"

He smiled, murmured, "Of course it is," and kissed her lightly on the nose. "Soak in a hot bath."

Dana wrinkled her nose at him. "I think I might have had enough immersion in water for one day."

At least she had the satisfaction of seeing him laughing as he walked away.

"SPIT IT OUT," Uncle Nolan said. He rested a forearm on the steering wheel and turned in his seat to look at Christian.

"Dana's probably waiting." He hated trying

to figure out what to say to her. His forehead wrinkled at the thought. She might just pretend nothing happened. He'd seen her swallow something she'd been about to say often enough.

"She can wait."

Christian looked straight ahead, at the Lookout Inn. "It's just…you know. What she said."

"About wanting to impress you?"

Christian shrugged, keeping his face averted. He felt so mixed up he didn't want to know what Uncle Nolan was thinking.

"Why does that surprise you?" he asked, in that calm way he had.

"Because she's a grown-up!" Christian cried. "I'm just a kid." He tugged at the seat belt, sliding it out farther, letting it slip back, over and over.

It was quiet long enough he almost did turn his head, but then Uncle Nolan said, "Usually parents get mad at their kids, have fun with them, snap at them, encourage them. The whole gamut." His shoulders moved. "But underneath, there's this mutual security. The love is taken for granted."

Christian frowned at that. As tangled up as his feelings were for his mom, he had loved her and he knew she loved him. She couldn't help the stuff she did that hurt him.

"Dana doesn't have that luxury," Uncle Nolan continued. "I think she believed it would be there. As if love was locked in from birth. But that's not how it happened. You didn't want to acknowledge her. Things are getting easier, but she's a nice lady to you, not your mother. I imagine she's trying really hard to be so great you'll decide you want to brag to everyone that she's your mom."

"You think she's been *faking*?" he heard himself ask.

"No." Uncle Nolan put a hand on his shoulder and gave a little squeeze. "I think she's been having a lot of fun with us. Maybe…letting herself believe it would happen. But also not wanting to admit to any weaknesses."

"Like being scared around water."

Uncle Nolan took his hand back. "You going to hold it against her?"

"Of course not," he said indignantly. "Today *was* my fault. I shouldn't have let her get out so deep when I knew she hadn't even sailed or kayaked or anything."

"Yeah, I should have wondered, too," his uncle agreed. "If we'd known she isn't a very good swimmer but she insisted on helping out, we could have strapped her into a vest."

Christian nodded. "Do you think she'll want to come back? I mean, to Wind & Waves?"

"I hope so. She's a quick learner and a harder worker than anyone I pay."

Hearing the smile in his voice, Christian relaxed. "You just want more free help."

"You got it." Uncle Nolan fired up the engine and backed out.

"She said she'd meet us, right?"

"She did."

"Okay." He still didn't know what he was going to say, because now he felt kind of ashamed that he hadn't told anyone they were related. Not because there was anything wrong with Dana. It just…made him feel bad. It was like saying he'd forget all about Mom. Besides, everybody would talk about him, like they had when they knew he had to go back and forth to his grandparents' house because his mother was so weird. He could be *proud* of Uncle Nolan.

Unsettled, he had the thought that at least Dana wouldn't embarrass him by talking too loudly or not dressing right, and he bet she would show up when she said she would, too.

He hunched his shoulders. What she'd be was different from Mom.

"MY BAD EXPERIENCE," Dana echoed. Of course Nolan had asked, waiting until they'd ordered and taken their drinks to a booth. "My parents had rented a cabin on a lake. I was…I don't know, maybe six? Anyway, Peter and I had this rubber raft. I was supposed to wear a vest, and I didn't. The raft sprang a leak and started to sink. I went under. I guess Peter screamed. Dad ran out, dived in and got me." Aware that Nolan and Christian were both listening attentively, she made a face. "We probably weren't very far from shore. Anyway, I took lessons after that, but once I could make it from one end of the pool to the other, I thought that was good enough."

Nolan groaned.

She stuck out her tongue at him. "It's not like I've spent lots of time around large bodies of water."

"Until you moved to this small town that happens to cling to the edge of the Columbia River."

"Fine. I should have told you."

"Uncle Nolan says you should wear a vest when you help launch a boat," Christian surprised her by saying.

"Maybe I should just stay away from the water." For a dark instant, she was going under again, helpless against the power of the current, feeling her lungs screaming with the need for air. Shaking off the memory took serious effort. "Somehow, I didn't realize that wading could be dangerous."

Nolan set down his glass of beer. "The catamaran you were launching is a good-sized boat. Most of what you've helped with aren't heavy enough to knock you over. And with you in that deep, I wouldn't call it wading."

"Okay. Still."

"That's our number." Christian sprang up so fast Nolan's lips twitched.

"Is he starving?" Dana asked, startled by the hasty departure.

"And desperate to escape our conversation." Nolan smiled. "Boys his age and any subject that ventures into emotion? Not so good."

"No wonder girls the same age are so disappointed in boys. By twelve and thirteen, girls are *drenched* in emotion."

Nolan laughed, the skin beside his eyes crinkling. "I didn't quit thinking girls were scary until I was in high school. I had a girlfriend in eighth grade—sort of—but if she'd insisted we talk about feelings, I'd have been gone."

Dana rolled her eyes. "From the complaints I hear, grown men aren't much better."

One eyebrow rose to a peak. "That's because we're cold-blooded."

She hoped she wasn't blushing. "You know what I meant."

"Yeah—" His gaze went past her. "You mind getting plates, too?"

Christian deposited the gigantic pizza on the table. "I couldn't carry both at the same time." He was back in only moments.

He inhaled the first slice while Dana was using her knife and fork to eat tidily. As he reached for a second piece, he said out of the blue, "You could take lessons."

She stared at him. "You mean swimming? Me?"

"Well…yeah."

"We do have a pool in town," Nolan agreed. "There might be adult lessons."

"Or—" Christian's face had turned red "—maybe I could teach you."

Knowing she had to hide the surge of joy, Dana said, "I'm not sure if I'd be more humiliated with you or some sixteen-year-old that probably teaches the adult class."

"What can be more humiliating than almost drowning and having to admit you don't know how to swim?" Nolan asked drily.

Silenced for a moment, she said, "You have a point." She looked at Christian. "Thank you for offering. I guess if we could do it evenings…" She didn't say, *What if one of your friends sees you with me?*

Still blushing, he bobbed his head.

"Nolan," a surprised voice said.

Nolan raised a hand. "Ken."

A man and woman, both probably in their midthirties, approached their table. The woman smiled and greeted Christian, then looked inquiringly at Dana.

If she knew Christian, chances were good

she had a son or daughter his age. Or she and her husband were friends of Nolan's, not just customers.

Dana hurried to fill a silence that felt like a minefield. "I'm new in Lookout, working for Helping Hand. I took an unintentional dunk in the river today, and Nolan and Christian insisted on feeding the woman they'd hauled out by one ankle."

Both the strangers laughed. "Lissa likes to admire the river from afar," the man said, dodging when his wife poked him with an elbow. "No intention of joining me sailing. I'm Ken Dorsey. One of our kids is in Christian's class this year."

"And was in fourth grade and…" His wife paused to think.

"First," her husband supplied. "Or was it kindergarten?"

There was motion under the table. Dana thought Nolan might have kicked Christian, who said reluctantly, "First."

The adults chatted for a minute, the couple wanting to know where Dana had moved from, the husband just happening to have a business card in his shirt pocket to hand her. Since she did need to have an insurance agent closer than Denver, she told him she'd be calling. Finally, they went to the counter to order.

Nobody said anything for a minute. The tension was visible on Nolan's face. Christian kept his head down.

Dana threw out a placid remark. "They seemed nice."

Christian mumbled something she didn't hear.

"Excuse me?"

"She's a girl. The kid in my class."

"Oh." She'd have smiled if she weren't dealing with Nolan's and Christian's obvious discomfiture with her identity. "Not a friend, then."

"They used to be," Nolan said abruptly. "Didn't she come to your birthday party once?"

"Maybe." He shrugged. "When I was a little kid."

"You might end up friends again," Dana said, sounding so upbeat she disgusted herself.

They managed to regain some kind of flow, enough so Dana was able to quit feeling so self-conscious.

What she carried home was an ache she knew she'd better become accustomed to. Christian's willingness to give her swim lessons had to be extraordinary for a boy his age. But the other moment, when she'd seen alarm escalating into panic because *somebody* was going to have to introduce Dana, had served as a counterweight.

As she prepared for bed, she tried to convince herself that he might start to trust her more because she'd handled the situation without embarrassing explanations. But staring at herself in the mirror, Dana acknowledged another truth: the more often he and Nolan introduced her as a friend, the harder it would become for them to tell people she was really Christian's mother.

Craig…he would have said brusquely, *I'm Christian's father.* Which meant she had to keep fending him off. But…how could she even let her parents come out for a visit, when Christian probably wouldn't want to be seen with them?

The answer, of course, was that she couldn't.

"THAT'S THE ALBUM of pictures Grandma and Grandad made for me," Christian said, plopping it next to Dana on the sofa.

Nolan had suggested having her over for dinner Monday night, partly wanting to get them all past the twin disasters of Saturday and partly for a more basic reason: he wanted to see her.

He'd called her Sunday, catching her out shopping, sounding distracted although she agreed to dinner tonight. He couldn't think of a good excuse to call a second time, which left him restless and frustrated.

Sunday's rain had made business slow, and Mondays and Tuesdays, Wind & Waves was closed. Later in June, once schools had let out, he'd go to a seven-day-a-week schedule with more staff, but the rest of the year, the reduced traffic wasn't enough to justify the extra cost. Filling his days off wasn't usually a problem.

The old house needed work, the lawn had to be mowed weekly and he did the usual errands. When the weather was good, he'd be out on the river or, occasionally, hiking or cycling.

Today he'd added a couple miles to his morning run, after which he'd grocery-shopped and cleaned house—he didn't want Dana thinking it was a pit—but he stayed restive. He hadn't been able to get her alone as often as he'd have liked the past two weeks. Lunch a couple of times and dinner twice. Restaurants and picnic tables at either the park or outside Wind & Waves didn't offer much privacy. He'd kissed her goodbye each time, but lightly.

He wanted more.

More meant he had to tell Christian about the developing relationship.

Calmer because she was here now, he waited until she laid the album on her lap and opened it to lower himself to the cushion beside her, his thigh touching hers. She could have edged away—but didn't. On her other side, Christian said, his voice stifled, "I look like I did in your pictures."

Nolan's gaze went to the first page and the photos his parents must have taken as soon as Marlee showed up with her eight-month-old "son." These could have been taken within days of the abduction.

He remembered everyone's surprise. Brown

eyes with white-blond hair? Neither matched the coloring of anyone else in the family. Medium height, Marlee had been curvy, her hair darker than Nolan's, her eyes more of a blue-gray. Christian had been long and skinny even then. Mom and Dad had had a lot of questions about Christian's father. Marlee's answer? "I don't want to talk about him." They'd all been gullible enough to assume that was because the baby's biological father had been some random hookup. If she'd been stoned, she might not even remember him.

Even now, Nolan understood why none of them had asked themselves if there were other possibilities. His goofy, annoying sister, who'd trailed him around for years, plotting to steal a baby and actually going through with it?

He gave his head a shake he hoped Dana didn't notice.

The second page had a photo of Marlee holding the baby, grinning at him. Tellingly, Christian strained away from her. Dana stayed quiet, although she touched the tip of her finger to her infant son.

By the time they reached kindergarten, tears ran down her face.

"Ignore me," she said, sniffling and laughing. "It's just…seeing you growing up."

Nolan brought her a wad of tissues.

Christian recovered from his alarm at the

tears and answered questions with animation, telling her where they'd been when each picture was taken, what they'd been doing. Once his expression became flat when he said, "I don't think Mom was around."

He didn't repeat that, but he didn't have to. Marlee was only occasionally in photos. Nolan had been mad as hell when he found out she took off and left her kid alone, starting from when he was only five or six.

"Only for a day!" she'd cried when he confronted her. Overnight, was what she meant. And she really believed that was okay?

Watching Christian grow up in the pages of the album, Nolan felt the simmer of his anger build toward a rolling boil. Why *hadn't* Mom and Dad demanded guardianship? Why had they left Christian at risk for so long?

But he knew. Marlee was their daughter, precious and fragile. Seeing her descent into mental illness had damaged them. Their effervescent, smart, sweet, if also sometimes wild, daughter using drugs, screaming at invisible people, letting her hair become filthy and tangled... Every time she appeared stable, they would let themselves hope. This time she'd stay on her meds. Surely she would be able to see how much her beautiful son needed her.

Yeah, and where was I?
Living his own life. He couldn't even blame

himself; Marlee and Christian *did* have his parents, who wouldn't have wanted him to became caretaker for his sister and her child.

Birthday parties came and went—kids sitting around the table watching as tall, skinny Christian blew out his candles. His hair darkened as the years went by. There was Nolan setting the cake in front of him for his ninth birthday. He'd been home for a flying visit, not knowing that his parents would be killed only nine months later.

"That's Jenna Dorsey." Christian pointed with disfavor at a freckled redheaded girl.

"The people at the restaurant?" Dana bent her head to study the picture, her frown suddenly clearing. "I saw her at the school when I went to the open house. She was giggling with some other girls. She's really pretty."

Nolan had a suspicion that Christian thought so, too. Now all he did was mumble, "She's okay."

Dana looked at Nolan. He grinned as he nodded an answer to her wordless question.

A suppressed smile created a tiny dimple in her cheek he'd never noticed before.

She flipped the next page to find herself at the end, her dismay obvious. "You must have more."

"I think we went digital from then on," Nolan said. "Christian, why don't you grab the laptop."

His parents had kept using the same camera,

having those photos developed the old-fashioned way, long after most people had switched to digital cameras and then smartphones. Nolan had given his mom an iPhone for a birthday to replace her old flip phone. It took her a while to get into it, but once she did, wherever he was in the world, he could count on opening his email to find pictures. He wasn't sure how many other features on the phone she'd ever figured out, but she loved the high-quality photos she could take so easily. Nolan felt his eyes sting at the memory of her delight. His parents had been in only their early sixties, and in good health. They should have been here now.

More grimly, he thought, *To stand by their daughter's grave? To have to face what she'd done? To meet their grandson's real mother?*

He gave his head another tiny shake. They were good people. They'd have grieved but also greeted Dana with open arms.

Sandwiched on the sofa between Nolan and Christian, Dana kept murmuring the right things as her son told her about the friends who appeared in these later pictures. Once, she said, "Wait. Jason? Isn't he the ax murderer?"

Christian flushed. "We were just kidding around. It was an accident."

Dana slid an arm around him as naturally as if she'd done it a thousand times, gave him a quick hug and took her arm back before he could become self-conscious. "I'm just teasing."

The timer went off in the kitchen, and she insisted on helping Nolan get dinner on the table. While they ate, Christian talked more than he had in a long while. She heard about how gross his wound had been and how *his* scar was more spectacular than *any* of Uncle Nolan's. Friends, teachers, Jason's amazing gaming system, even a slightly shy admission that "some of the guys" liked girls. He and another friend, Dieter, had taken to shooting hoops after school. They thought they'd go out for basketball when they were freshmen. "Because we're both tall."

She didn't remind him that his father had played college ball. She didn't have to. Nolan had a feeling that learning about his father's prowess had had something to do with Christian becoming more interested in the sport.

This boy Nolan thought of as his son wanted to follow in another man's footsteps. His father's.

Nolan wasn't proud of the pang he felt.

CHAPTER THIRTEEN

"Your ex called Christian last night." Nolan's tone suggested this was only a mildly interesting tidbit. He crumpled his sandwich wrapper.

He and Dana sat, as they did at least once a week, on the covered patio behind Wind & Waves. She brought lunch when she came to him, while he supplied it when they picnicked at a small community park with a playground and tall trees a block from her office.

His news didn't surprise Dana, but it did make her mad. With a sigh, she let it go, knowing even annoyance was irrational. Craig had as much right to build a relationship with Christian as she did. The surprise was that he'd held off this long.

"Did Christian talk to him?"

Nolan might not have betrayed any emotion with his voice, but the hard line of his jaw and the glitter in his blue eyes did. "Yes. Or, at least, he listened and mumbled a few words."

"Did Craig get mad?"

"Not sure." Nolan turned his head, his gaze seemingly following a scarlet sail forming a

perfect arch to lift a windsurfer in leaps that
defied gravity. "When I asked, Christian just
shrugged."

Nolan didn't have to tell her he hadn't liked
that. He obviously felt it was his right to protect her son—a right, she had to admit, he had
earned. But it was equally possible he'd felt re-
jected. As Christian's father—a man—Craig
might seem even more the enemy to Nolan than
she did.

Yes, that made sense. Nolan had said *your ex.*
He hadn't used Craig's name. And he'd waited
until they'd finished lunch to mention the call.

"I wondered why I hadn't heard from him
this week," she said.

Nolan tapped a beat on the wrought-iron table,
then frowned at his fingers. They immediately
went still. "Your parents?"

"They're more understanding than Craig is."
Although they weren't thrilled about having to
wait to visit.

"Let's talk about something else," Nolan said
abruptly.

"Actually—" Dana glanced at her watch "—I
need to get going. I have an appointment at one."

Not arguing, he helped gather their trash and
walked her to her car. When she reached for the
door, Nolan's hands closed on her shoulders,
turning her to face him. Suddenly he was close
enough for her to feel his body heat.

"Friday night?" he murmured.

Dana nodded, then clutched at her courage. "Why don't I cook dinner instead of us going out?"

A flare in his eyes sent a quiver through her. "Good," he said roughly. "I'll palm Christian off on a friend."

Her son. The reason she had moved halfway across the country. At this moment, she couldn't summon the tiniest desire to include him Friday. Dana lifted her hand to Nolan's jaw, the sandpaper sensation against her fingertips blurring her thoughts.

"Won't he wonder?" Nolan had sent Christian to friends' houses three—or was it four?— Friday nights in a row.

"I'll have to talk to him." He stepped closer, pressing her against the car. His left hand flattened on the window, caging her in, while he tipped her chin up with the right. "I'm really looking forward to kissing you without an audience."

She tried to turn her head. "Do we have—"

"Doesn't matter." His mouth captured hers, the kiss demanding, lacking the patience he'd given her so far.

Dana instinctively rose on tiptoe, throwing her arms around his neck and arching against him. A clattering sound had to be her keys hitting the asphalt. She wanted to melt—and she wanted to climb him, too. His tongue drove into her mouth, aggressive and hungry. When she stroked it with hers, he shuddered.

The next instant, he groaned and ripped his mouth away. He was breathing hard and fast, his gaze heated. "Bad timing."

She made a tiny sound of protest. Dropping back to her heels, she rested her face against Nolan's strong chest. *Audience*, she remembered. In fact, if she wasn't mistaken, a car had just pulled into a close spot. He must have heard it coming.

"Bad location."

"Yeah. Damn."

They separated, her reluctance reflected on his face. As he greeted someone, Dana stayed tucked behind his big body. When the footsteps receded, she sighed and bent to find the keys.

Unfortunately, crouching brought her to eye level with the ridge that made loose-fitting cargo pants not so loose. The ache between her thighs intensified. Even as she fumbled with the keys, Dana tipped her head back to find him watching her with a hunger that sent heat running across his cheekbones and his hands fisting at his sides.

That was the picture she carried with her as she drove away, leaving him standing in the parking lot watching her go.

WEDNESDAY EVENING, CHRISTIAN set the frying pan in the rack to dry. He had KP duty tonight. Just as he grabbed the dishtowel to wipe his hands, his uncle came into the kitchen.

"You have much homework left?"

"I'm done." He'd hurried, because Ryan had slipped him a movie that Uncle Nolan would have probably banned. He intended to take the DVD to his bedroom, where he could watch it on his laptop with the sound low.

"There's something I've been wanting to talk to you about," his uncle said, sounding deadly serious.

Christian froze. Was this going to be like the last time, when he found out Mom couldn't be his mother?

"What?" His voice squeaked, which he hated.

"Nothing bad." Uncle Nolan leaned back against the counter. "I need you to know I've been seeing Dana."

Seeing. Christian frowned. Of course he'd been seeing— Wait. "You mean…" He couldn't even say it.

"I do mean." His uncle crossed his arms loosely, posture relaxed, which didn't fool Christian for a minute. "She's a beautiful woman."

"She's my mother!"

"That's right. She is."

"I thought she was here because of me," he

blurted, then felt himself flush. That sounded like he was jealous.

"She is." Uncle Nolan stayed serious, but his voice had softened. "She and I have talked about this. We know we have to stay friends for your sake, no matter what."

"If you break up…" Tension screamed through him.

Uncle Nolan nodded. "But I don't plan for that to happen." There was steel in his voice.

Christian stared. This was so weird. "What about Ellie?"

"You never did explain how you know about her."

"I hear things," he said sullenly.

"You eavesdrop when you think I'm not telling you stuff that I should."

He didn't say anything.

Uncle Nolan shook his head. "Ellie wasn't any of your business. I never intended her to impact your life. Dana is different, which is why I *am* telling you."

Christian threw the dishtowel onto the counter in a furious movement. "You're supposed to be on *my* side."

"I am. Always."

"But what if she decides to take me—" He stopped, understanding coming with a *pop*, like a lightbulb in a cartoon. "You think if you

marry her, even my…my father won't be able
to take me."

Uncle Nolan had the same look on his face
that he did when he didn't want to let Christian do something but sort of thought he had to.
Like…he wasn't really happy about what he was
going to say. But he said it, anyway. "Nobody
would be able to take you. We'd be a family, me,
you, your mom. It's the perfect answer."

Christian thought about it. Having her living
here wouldn't be that bad. She was a good cook,
and…he'd kind of liked it when she hugged him.
And the way she listened to him.

The gross part was that she and Uncle Nolan
would share a bedroom. Christian did *not* want
to think about what they'd be doing in there.

Uncle Nolan wasn't doing this because he was
gooey over Dana. He'd said he would fight dirty
to keep Christian with him, and marrying her
was how he would do it.

Guiltily, he asked, "What if you start wishing you *weren't* married to her?"

"Not happening." Uncle Nolan seemed confident. It was like after the car accident, when
Christian was so scared and Uncle Nolan walked
in and said, "You'll live with me from now on."
Nobody would dare argue with him.

"You haven't asked her, have you?"

"No." He smiled a little. "You have to court

a woman. Right now she'd think you were the only reason I was asking."

"And she might say no."

"Right." Uncle Nolan pushed away from the counter. "Since we don't want that, you need to get lost again Friday night."

"I'll call Jason right now."

Laughing, Uncle Nolan handed over his phone. "Somehow, I thought you'd be on board."

DANA HAD GONE all out, cooking a pot roast in her Crock-Pot, using tiny new potatoes bought at a fruit stand and baking biscuits from scratch. A cherry pie, made from local cherries, cooled on the counter. Focusing on the menu had held her nervousness at bay.

Mostly at bay, she conceded, a little rueful as she listened for Nolan. Now that the biscuits were in the oven, she couldn't seem to tear her eyes from the clock.

At 6:29 p.m. she heard a car stop outside. At 6:30 p.m. on the dot, the doorbell rang.

If you chicken out, it's just dinner, she told herself.

When she opened the door for him, the first thing she noticed was his damp hair. Second was the freshly shaved jaw. *For me.* The butterflies in her stomach swirled into panicked flight, not calmed by her extreme awareness of him. She should have said something, stepped back so he could enter, but instead she looked at him: the pale lines beside his blue eyes that crinkled with a smile or against the sun, thick, dark lashes, an old scar at the angle of his chin, the bulky muscles of his shoulders and the strength of his neck.

He looked at her, too, his eyes darkening and a muscle jumping on his jaw. But when she gulped and said, "I'm sorry, I'm keeping you standing on the doorstep," he only smiled and walked in.

"Smells good," he said easily. Before she could retreat, he dipped his head and kissed her lightly, his hands running up and down her arms.

Dana fled for the kitchen. Under his amused gaze as she fussed over getting the meal on the table, she rhapsodized about the fruit market she'd discovered and how much produce was grown locally.

"There's a reason the Willamette Valley seemed like the promised land to so many settlers," he commented, obviously willing to cooperate.

"We're not in the Willamette Valley, are we?" As if she cared.

"Let me take that." He removed the heavy Crock-Pot from her hands and set it in the middle of the table. "No, our climate is a little more arid, but we're close enough. Some of that produce isn't grown right here. We're best known for our orchards."

At the sight of the biscuits, hot from the oven, he made a pleased sound. Dana realized the effort she'd put into this meal hadn't been only to distract herself; she was ridiculously happy to see him dish up and start eating. She'd loved feeding Craig when they were first married, but cooking just for herself was nothing but a chore.

Nolan ate voraciously, no surprise given that he'd admitted to not having lunch. He had been shorthanded, with his afternoon part-timer calling in sick.

"She was probably late writing a paper due tomorrow," he said with a tolerant shrug. "It happens. I use a lot of college kids, but they're generally reliable."

Although they hadn't yet run together, he knew she tried to get out at least three times a week and suggested some trails she might not have discovered. "Evenings or weekends, I often use the high school track. Nobody minds. I avoid pounding the pavement. My knees took enough wear and tear humping heavy packs in mountainous country."

"I've read that soldiers these days carry something like a hundred pounds in gear." She couldn't imagine.

"More like a hundred and thirty, forty pounds," he said, sounding unconcerned, "between the body armor, gear, weapons, pack." He buttered another biscuit. "I'm a big guy. It was easier on me. If we were trying to move fast, I'd add extra to help out a smaller guy."

Why did she suspect he had *always* loaded himself down to help his teammates? A man who'd let his career go in a heartbeat because the boy he believed to be his nephew needed him, Nolan Gregor was a born protector. She could so easily see him throwing himself over a grenade to save others. She shivered, knowing he'd be willing to die for other people, grateful that his intense, protective drive had instead led him to take early retirement.

Guessing he would rather she not verbalize any of that, she limited herself to "You weren't kidding about that wear and tear on your knees, were you?"

"Backs go, too."

"Do you miss it?"

He'd speared a potato with his fork but didn't lift it to his mouth. "Sometimes," he said after a minute. "Mostly the other guys. I don't have friends here of the same caliber."

"Have you stayed in touch?" she asked softly.

He took the bite, maybe to give himself a moment. "Sure." Pause. "It's tough when I hear about the casualties. There's some guilt." Those big shoulders moved, not so much in a shrug as in discomfiture.

"If you'd been there, you might have died instead. Or too." Her throat felt tight.

His eyes held hers. "Could be I'd have saved someone else. Kept us from making a mistake." His mouth quirked. "You don't have to tell me how arrogant that sounds."

Smile trembling, she shook her head. "Confident."

He laughed. "Is there a difference?"

"Don't you think so?"

She watched him mull that over. "Of course there is," he said finally. "Every service has leaders who think they know it all. Foul-ups are always someone else's fault. Men die, the colonel gets promoted to general." His anger was quiet but unmistakable.

"You must have known some cocky young guys, too."

"That's swagger, not confidence. If they survive a first mission or two, they get over it."

"Were you ever…?"

"Cocky?" At close quarters, his grin was devastating. "Now, come on. You know me. What do you think?"

His sense of humor was contagious, and she said, "Of course you were."

"And I'm one of the survivors."

Dana wanted to know more. His wartime experiences were a big part of what made him the man he was. But she knew if she asked, he'd respond with more of the usual funny tales. The gut-wrenching stuff, the loss of friends, the experience of killing, he would choose to tell her someday or he wouldn't.

And that presupposed this relationship endured, became something intimate enough for him to want to open himself to her. And even then she knew there was a lot he would never talk about.

"Another helping?" She nudged the handle of the ladle toward him. "If you don't put some more away, I'll be eating it for days."

"You know—" he rubbed his belly "—I think I may be at capacity. Guess I should have brought Christian after all."

"Oh, sure," she said with mock seriousness. "He wouldn't have left me any leftovers."

"Kid can eat," Nolan agreed. His voice changed, deepened. "Can't say I wish he was here, though."

"No," Dana whispered. She cleared her throat. "No."

"Dana—"

Nervous, she interrupted. "I have cherry pie for dessert. And ice cream if you want it." Oh, heavens—she sounded like an upbeat waitress confiding the day's specials.

Creases formed between Nolan's dark eyebrows. "Can we wait for a bit?"

"Of course." She jumped to her feet. "Coffee?"

"Thanks." He sounded inexplicably gentle. "Let me help you clear the table."

They worked together as the coffee brewed.

Before she'd snapped the top on the plastic container of leftover pot roast and potatoes, Nolan was already scrubbing the Crock-Pot.

"You're a guest," she protested. "You already have to do this at home—"

He smiled. "Nope. That's what a kid is for."

"Nolan."

He laughed at her chiding tone. "I cook, he cleans. He cooks, I clean. I never get any argument."

"Really?" Hearing her own amazement, Dana laughed, too. "My brother and I squabbled until he went to college about who had what chores. We still do it a little bit when we're both home."

A shadow passed over his face. "Marlee and I did some of that. Except…"

"You were always protective of her."

"Spoiled her, is what you mean." He avoided her scrutiny by concentrating on rinsing the ceramic Crock-Pot lining. "You'd be right."

Dana wanted to convince him that he had no reason to feel guilty about his sister, but this wasn't the right time for that, either—and she wasn't the right person.

Instead, in unspoken reassurance, she touched his forearm, bared by a rolled-up shirtsleeve, and looked around. "Done! And so is the coffee."

They took their cups into the living room. He sat at one end of the sofa and patted the middle cushion next to him. With only the tiniest hesitation, she sat beside him and set her coffee cup on the table. Nolan tugged her toward him. Dana relaxed, his arm secure around her, her face tucked in the crook of his neck.

"You smell good," she murmured.

Amusement rumbled in his chest. "You wouldn't have thought so if I'd come straight here from work."

She lifted her head to see his face. "Why not?"

"Worked my ass off today." He kissed the tip of her nose, then let his lips travel to the ridge of her brows, her temple, her cheek and jaw. Her eyes drifted closed as she just *felt*. This wasn't the kind of kiss that should have aroused her, but it did.

"Dana." His voice came out rough, his breath a sigh against her ear.

"Mmm?"

"Were you planning to ask me to stay tonight?"

She quit breathing. The moment of truth. *It's too soon*, she wanted to cry, but was it really? All of those lunches, dinners over the past month, the small touches during the weekend days she spent at Wind & Waves. The way his gaze always found her, lingered. In the midst of all her confusion, she couldn't doubt that he wanted her. His focus was so intense, even when he was talking to someone else, she knew he was always conscious of where she was, what she was doing.

In the end, it was no decision at all. "I was," she admitted.

His gaze traveled her face, much as his lips had. "And yet you look terrified."

She smiled weakly and laid a hand on his hard cheek. "It's been a long time. I'm entitled to some nerves."

"Tell me you've had someone."

She shook her head.

His hand on her upper arm flexed even as his eyes closed. "Damn it, Dana."

She swallowed. "I know this is probably a little off-putting…"

His eyes opened, the flare in the blue depths hot enough to singe her skin. "No. Nothing about you is off-putting. I need to get a grip. That's all."

She slid her hand to his neck, kneading the taut muscles. "I was married. I had a kid." This was important to say. He already saw her as wounded, she knew. Enough was enough. "I'm not made of porcelain."

Suddenly a wicked smile appeared. "Okay." He gripped her waist and lifted her onto his lap, swinging her around so that she straddled him. Her squeak of surprise never had a chance to rise from her throat. He kissed her with new tenderness, playing with her mouth, letting her play with his. She explored, slipping her fingers into the ruffled silk of his hair, touching that small scar, testing the powerful muscles that ran from his neck to his shoulders.

Her skin felt tight, her blood thick. He kissed her until she couldn't have said where they were. When he pulled back to breathe, eyes blazing, she began to undo the buttons on his shirt. However clumsy her fingers, he only watched. When she finally parted his shirt and laid her hands on that broad, muscular chest, his eyes closed again, this time in what looked like pleasure. She swept her hands in circles, found his nipples, curled her fingers in his chest hair. She lingered on his scars but chose not to ask about them.

"You're beautiful," she whispered.

Nolan laughed huskily. "Not sure that's the right word. Now, for *you*—" he yanked her knit shirt over her head "—it works." The next second, he cupped her breasts in those huge hands, rubbing gently. Dana felt herself undulating at the pleasure.

He made a guttural sound, found her bra's hooks and tossed it away. And then he arched her back over his arm and closed his mouth over her right breast, sucking in a rhythm that had her hips rocking.

Dark blood slashed his cheeks when he looked up. "Bedroom."

It wasn't a question. He rose, lifting her effortlessly. Dana grabbed on around his neck and tightened her thighs about his hips, moaning as his every stride rubbed her against his erection. She was so ready by the time he stopped next to her bed. When he lowered her to her feet, she reached for the snap on his jeans as he did the same on hers.

They became tangled, laughed, but somehow the rest of their clothes were gone. Nolan yanked aside her covers and laid her back across the bed. Then he did nothing but look at her, his eyes almost black.

And…he *was* beautiful. Maybe that wasn't the right word for a man, but she was overwhelmed by so much muscle. Craig had been long and lean, not powerful. Not compelling by his very presence.

Nolan broke, a raw sound escaping his throat as he came down on top of her. Even then, he held his weight on his elbows, protecting her.

His mouth descended on hers with a ferocity she answered. The pleasure of feeling his rougher skin against hers made her moan and arch upward to feel *more*. Becoming frantic, she wrapped a leg around his muscular thigh and struggled until the tip of his penis pressed her opening. And then she pushed up—

But he broke away. "Condom."

She whimpered. He was right, but… "Hurry."

He found the packet he must have brought, tore it open and covered himself in a matter of seconds. But he came down beside her, seemingly determined to torture her. He went for her breasts again while his fingers stroked between her thighs, circling, pressing, tangling in her curls. She fought for control. "Please. I want—"

And finally, *finally*, there he was, pushing inside her, filling her, until he was buried to the hilt. Hanging over her, his lungs pumping, he went still. "Yes?"

Her "Yes" came out strangled.

He began to move, slow, deep, then faster and harder, while she clutched him and strained to match his rhythm. Her whole body tightened in agonizing bliss…until he thrust even deeper, and she shattered. He followed, his body bucking, his teeth showing, his blue eyes never leaving hers.

And, of course, instead of slumping down on top of her, he rolled to rest his weight on his shoulder. But he took her with him, holding her close.

And she was suddenly afraid she was about to cry.

CHAPTER FOURTEEN

PACING HIS LIVING ROOM, Nolan still couldn't believe Dana had broken down the way she had after they made love. Three days later, he remained shaken, thinking about it. She insisted it was just another kind of release, and he believed her, but...her tears had unnerved him.

Mopping her face, she'd finally told him in a soggy voice, "I just never thought I'd be so happy again."

"You put your life on hold."

She'd tried to smile and failed. "I guess I did."

Alone and brooding, he made another circle of the room, stopping to look out the front window. Dana would come in when she dropped Christian off from her first swim lesson, wouldn't she?

One of the things that kept Nolan tense was wondering what Christian would do if somebody he knew saw her with him. Whether Christian knew it or not, he was well on the road to accepting Dana. As far as Nolan knew, however, he hadn't told even Jason about the shock of that blood test. Did he think he'd never have to?

Irritated with himself, Nolan settled on the couch with his laptop. He hadn't even asked to go with them; this was something for the two of them. Stewing wasn't getting him anywhere. He should at least try to be productive.

Checking out new products was a never-ending task. Most of his rental customers at Wind & Waves were at an intermediate level, but on the retail side, people didn't tend to spend the bucks to outfit themselves entirely unless they were dedicated to the sport. If he let his product lines get stale, he'd lose the really serious windsurfers, the ones who competed, who were out on the river in the dead of winter. So he browsed suppliers' websites, following rumors of a new, higher-strength thermoplastic that intrigued him.

At the sound of a car in the driveway, he held his breath. A minute later, Dana and Christian came in the front door. She'd dried her hair, which lay loose and shiny. Christian's hair still dripped onto his shirt.

"How'd it go?" Nolan asked, as casually as if he hadn't spent the evening as antsy as a man whose wife was in labor.

Dana made an awful face.

Christian rolled his eyes. "I think she lied about those lessons."

"I did too finish the intermediate class!"

"Finished," Christian scoffed. "But did you *pass*?"

"Of course I did!"

Christian's mouth opened but before he could continue the childish exchange, Nolan laughed. "Enough already. How many years ago was it that you took that class?"

"Uh…" Her eyes shied from his. "I might have been twelve or thirteen."

"Christian's age."

Her son gaped.

"Something like that."

"And how much swimming have you done since?"

"I've splashed in a lake or river a few times."

He shook his head. "So, you've forgotten how to swim."

After a sulky moment, she collapsed onto an easy chair. "I guess so. Or maybe it was the near drowning. Tonight I was about as relaxed as a board."

"Windsurfing boards have some flex."

Christian howled with laughter. Dana narrowed her eyes at both of them.

"There must be something that scares *you*."

"I told you I don't love heights," Nolan reminded her.

"While mentioning that you jumped out of airplanes, anyway. That's so helpful."

Christian came to the rescue. "Even if she was scared, she did okay."

She sighed. "He means I dog-paddled from one side of the pool to the other."

"Next time, you won't be so nervous."

Even Nolan blinked at the encouragement, coming from this kid he thought he knew.

"Did Jason call?" Christian asked, reverting to form.

"Yes, I told him you'd call him back."

"Where's the phone—" He spotted it on the side table, grabbed it and thundered upstairs.

Dana laughed. "Thank you for the lesson. Good night."

Nolan saw her wistful expression as she looked after Christian.

"This all feel unreal?"

Turning her gaze to him, she didn't even try to hide her vulnerability. "He teased me. He touched me, without being asked."

She sounded awed, but he read something else.

"But?"

"I need to get past thinking about how much I lost. Feeling angry because I should have watched every swim lesson *he* took, cuddled him, trimmed his hair, helped him sound out words. What I had tonight is a gift…"

"C'mere." Nolan set the laptop onto the coffee table and held out an arm.

She all but flung herself across the room, diving into his embrace.

Rubbing his cheek against her head, he said, "You have every right to feel all those things. You did lose. Why *wouldn't* you be angry?"

"Because anger might keep me from feeling the joy I should in what I do have." A voice shouldn't be able to sound bruised, but hers did.

"Weren't you joyful this evening?" he asked quietly.

A little silence. She twisted to stare at him. "So much I felt like I'd been pumped full of helium. I was sure I *couldn't* sink to the bottom of the pool."

Nolan smiled and tucked her back in. "How could you help it?"

Neither said anything for a long time.

"You shouldn't understand," she said at last.

He'd thought about this. "I've had to face the possibility that I'll lose him."

"Oh." Dana pressed her lips to his chest. "That makes sense."

He laughed. She punched him lightly.

"Focus on the years ahead," he said. "You can help him when he's struggling with a class, live with the angst of his first romance, be in the bleachers for his first basketball game."

"Can I?" Voice suddenly brittle, she straightened, withdrawing from the circle of his arms. Her smile was sad enough to jab a painful spike into his chest. Not hard to guess what she was thinking. The rebuff of her tentative appearance at the open house would continue to haunt all of them.

"Things are changing," he said as gently as he could.

She nodded and rose to her feet. "Time for me to get home."

"Dana, I haven't heard him talk the way he did tonight in a long time. You should be flattered."

She hid deeper emotions and did smile. "After he told me I lied about ever having taken a swim lesson?"

"Yeah, but he also said you did okay. High praise."

"Yes." She shivered. "That's quite a scar."

"It is. He's lucky no tendons or ligaments were severed. Fortunately, it was more of a glancing blow without a lot of heft behind it, since Jason is as scrawny as Christian is. Still, there was so damn much blood…"

She didn't press for details, seeming to understand how painful the memory was. Instead of commenting, she glanced toward the stairs. "Will you tell him I said goodbye?"

"Sure." He pushed himself to his feet and walked with her to the door. "Was Christian helpful at all?"

"He was actually really patient." She stopped

on the porch and turned back to him. "He kind of surprised me. I thought he'd be embarrassed to be seen hanging out with someone my age, but he didn't seem to mind." She frowned. "Although mostly the people there were adults swimming laps, or mothers and fathers with little kids." The frown melted into an impish smile. "When I got out of the pool, one man checked me out. He'd be dead if Christian had laser vision."

"When I admitted we were seeing each other, I told him you're a beautiful woman. All he could think to say was, 'But she's my mother!'"

Dana giggled.

Satisfied that she remembered good things were happening, Nolan tipped her chin up. "Let's shock the kid if he comes downstairs."

The way she lifted her face to his, with no hesitation, letting him see her trust, provided more satisfaction.

He kept the kisses playful—but still went to bed frustrated as hell.

Unless they started having quickies during the lunch hour, he would be spending a lot of time frustrated in the foreseeable future.

CHRISTIAN AT HER SIDE, Dana searched the crowd at the arrivals gate. No baggage had yet appeared on the airport carousel, so it was reasonable that her parents hadn't made it here yet.

She hadn't told her parents Christian had agreed to come with her. He had either volunteered or been pressured by Nolan. Nolan just smiled when she asked. And Christian... Well, if he hadn't wanted to come, she would have expected him to be sulky. Instead, she would swear that beneath the facade of indifference, curiosity and even excitement brewed.

Dana had been spending more and more time with him and Nolan. When she suggested her parents schedule their visit for the week after school let out in late June, even Christian agreed.

So here they were. And her parents *had* to be somewhere in the airport, too, since her mother had texted as soon as they landed.

"Dana?"

She whirled at the sound of her father's voice and threw herself into his arms. "Dad!" Her mother was next, but she remembered Christian and pulled back.

Her father was smiling at his grandson, but a tear tracked down his cheek. "You don't know what this means," he said in a choked voice.

Christian ducked his head, then peeked at his grandmother, who was crying openly.

"He looks so much like Peter did at that age." Her father swallowed.

"Like you, too, Dad," Dana said. Christian had become so much his own person to her she was shocked to see how much he did take after her father.

"I think I have to hug you," her mother told the currently shy boy, just before enveloping him in her arms. Thank goodness she had the sense to release him quickly, too.

Dana struggled for her own composure. "Mom and Dad, meet Christian. Christian, your grand-parents. Shari and John Hayes."

Her mother shot her a quick look, probably because *Christian* had come out so readily, instead of *Gabriel*. *My Gabriel*, she thought, but without as much sadness as she'd expected.

At the introduction, his "Um" went deep, the "hi" a few octaves higher. As always, he turned red at the loss of control.

Her father cleared his throat. "It's a pleasure, son."

The carousel jerked to life, providing a welcome distraction. Once her dad grabbed their baggage, Christian took the handle of one of the suitcases and willingly slung the strap of a laptop case over one shoulder. Dana's father was too macho to let her take anything, leaving the two women with only their purses. When Dana teased her dad, he just laughed.

Christian's shyness didn't last as long as she expected. By the time she drove past the Welcome to Lookout sign, he was talking with her dad about climbing Mount Hood, which on this sunny day dominated the skyline. High and sharp, it was still snow covered.

"Uncle Nolan said he might take me this summer," Christian said. "He wants Dana to come, too. Maybe we can do it while you're here."

"I'd love to make the climb," her dad admitted, "but it might be too late to arrange."

"Count me out," her mother said promptly.

Christian argued. Peter and Dana had often climbed with their father, but her mom had always balked.

"Maybe Jason could come," Dana suggested without thinking.

Christian's expression lit...then dimmed.

After parking in Nolan's driveway, she took a moment to press a hand to her breastbone to ease the deep ache before releasing her seat belt. No one else noticed, not even Christian—she hoped.

For all the ground they'd gained, he wasn't ready to claim her as his mother.

NOLAN EMERGED TO greet Dana's parents, liking them on sight. Since he'd seen plenty of pictures of them, it shouldn't have been such a blow to see how much Christian looked like this man.

He concentrated instead on picking out which pieces Dana had taken from her parents. The shape of her face and her eyes were from her mother, height and smile and coloring from her father. Athleticism, too, he had gathered. Shari Hayes had stayed slim and active but spent her time in the garden. She'd apparently never been an athlete like her husband and both children.

He felt new pangs when he saw the wonder on their faces when their gazes rested on Christian.

Christian raised the idea of climbing Mount Hood. Dana's father thought they could extend their stay, if that would make it possible.

Nolan's first instinct was to suggest they aim for next summer, but Christian's eagerness got to him. It would be a great experience, he had to admit. Three generations…and him.

"I'll see what I can do," he finally agreed.

"Will we need to hire a guide?" John Hayes asked. "If so, I'm happy to kick in—"

"No, I've made the climb half a dozen times." He frowned. "I'm probably the only one who is already outfitted."

"I am," Dana said. "I brought everything but crampons and rope. I thought I might want to ski or climb."

"I can have my son collect my gear and ship it overnight," John said. "Cheaper than renting. It occurs to me some of Peter's winter clothes might fit Christian and save you buying when he's still growing. I'll ask him."

After putting in a pizza order—the Gregor family go-to—they made plans for her parents to visit Wind & Waves the next day. Dana had yet to see either Christian or Nolan windsurf, so they agreed to go out, while her father thought he'd rent a kayak.

"Why don't you come with me?" he asked her, looking surprised at her grimace.

"I don't actually swim very well," she admitted. Nolan was impressed when Christian didn't hoot at the understatement. "Even with a vest... I don't think so."

Good decision, he thought, without saying it out loud.

Of course, there were exclamations from her parents, who apparently hadn't noticed her evading all sizable bodies of water.

The evening proved surprisingly pleasant, given the undercurrents. Dana's parents didn't show any wariness with him. When Christian was out of earshot, they all talked briefly about what measures Craig Stewart might take. Shari's rage at the man who'd abandoned her daughter was more overt, but Nolan saw a cold light in John's eyes, one he fully understood.

He also saw that this family touched easily and often. They tried to restrain themselves where Christian was concerned, but it took an effort. His grandfather wanted to throw an arm over his shoulders, his grandmother wanted to ruffle his hair and even kiss his cheek. Nolan appreciated their self-restraint.

The climb would erase some of those boundaries. If he could make a success of the expedition, it might cement his place as part of this family, too.

That slotted into his plan just fine.

TWO DAYS LATER, Jason's father took four boys, including Christian, to Sky High Sports, an indoor trampoline park in Portland. Since Dana had to work, her parents decided to drive along the Columbia Gorge.

Nolan met her at the park near her agency for lunch. They nabbed the picnic table farthest from the playground. He tugged her onto the bench beside him.

"Thank God we're alone," he exclaimed.

She laughed. "My parents just got here."

They had insisted on taking a room at the Lookout Inn, although she'd intended to go ahead and buy another bed, since she'd presumably need a guest room in the future.

"This will give us some independence and you some space," her mother had declared. "We'll do some fun things while you're working. I might even make your father take me out for a romantic dinner one night."

When she told Nolan that, he nuzzled her neck. "Tell me when. We'll have a romantic dinner at home."

"With Christian?"

"It's never hard to convince him he wants to spend the night with a friend."

It sounded good to her. Making love with Nolan was addictive. Seeing him so often and not being able to do more than steal a goodnight kiss was hard. If her parents really extended their stay, it could be a long two weeks.

Prying the lid off his container of chili, he said, "I have to ask."

She looked at him curiously. "Ask what?"

Nolan met her eyes. "Have you told your parents about us?"

"I… Yes." Last night, but she didn't want to tell him that she hadn't sooner. She hadn't even chosen the time. When she walked them to their room at the inn, her mother had speared her with an all-too-familiar look and asked bluntly.

"What did you say?" he asked.

"I said we're dating."

"Dating?"

She narrowed her eyes at him. "What was I supposed to tell them? That we're having steamy sex whenever we can get away from my son?"

He reached for her hand and laced her fingers with his. Voice deep, he said, "You could say that we're in a relationship."

Dana found herself searching his face for something she hardly understood. "Is that what this is?" she whispered.

"A serious relationship."

It scared her how serious her feelings were. Sometimes she thought she'd already toppled in love with this man. Other times she worried that he was the first attractive man she'd met after the ice broke—after she found her son. The idea of them as a family was undeniably seductive. And, yes, that worried her, too, because it wasn't reason enough to become involved with someone.

"I think they'll come to their own conclusions," she said, avoiding a real answer.

He watched her for a minute, almost somber, then nodded.

They'd started to eat when he said, "Your parents don't know how much you kept hurting, do they?"

Unnerved by his discernment, she said, "No."

"How did you fool them?"

"I…didn't go home as often. When I did see them or one of us called, I talked about friends, things I was doing, how proud I was to have lost weight."

"Even though losing weight was never a goal."

"I look so different. I let them believe I was trying to take better care of myself. And I was, in a way. I made myself eat. And running was my only effective stress reducer."

Nolan took her hand, the tenderness in his

eyes almost her undoing. "Did you have anyone you could really talk to?"

She made herself look away. "I didn't want anyone. I had to be strong."

He squeezed her hand but didn't say anything. When she looked back at him, it was to see new creases on his forehead. They ate in silence for a few minutes, Dana wishing she knew what he was thinking.

"I'm prone to letting things fester," he said suddenly.

They had that in common. "Marlee?"

"Yeah."

She waited.

"The happier I am, the guiltier I feel."

A gigantic knot formed in her chest. "Is that because it's me you're happy with?"

He kept frowning toward the playground. "Partly. I can't deny it. But also…the better I get to know you, the angrier I am at her. At what she did to you. Sometimes I think about what I'd say to her." He made a raw sound. "But then I remind myself how unproductive that would have been. All she'd have done was take off. I used to worry about her when she was gone. Think about what could happen to her. Now? I don't know if I could bring myself to care."

"Don't say that," she begged, although…who was she to talk, carrying as much hate as she did for a mentally ill woman who had killed herself rather than face what she'd done?

She had never seen Nolan's eyes so bleak. "It's the truth."

"If she hadn't died…everything would be different." Despite the warmth of the day, Dana felt cold. "How could we have any kind of relationship? Or…or cooperate the way we have?"

He released her hand, turned to straddle the bench and leaned toward her, touching his forehead to hers. "We'd have gotten here, anyway. You're…something new in my life. I took a hit the minute I saw you."

"You mean that?" she whispered.

"I do." He kissed her gently. "If Marlee was still alive, Christian would have had more of a dilemma."

"He would have had to reject me," she realized. "He couldn't have let himself hurt her that much."

Nolan straightened, that bleak honesty still apparent. "For his sake, I'm glad she's dead."

"Which makes you feel even guiltier."

He nodded. "I'm a mess."

"Maybe this—" she waved her hand between them "—us, isn't such a good idea."

"You're wrong." His voice was low and passionate. "It's the best idea I've ever had."

"Really?" How pathetic she sounded.

"Really." This kiss escalated until she forgot they were in public, until she gripped his shoulder with one hand while the other dug into his muscular thigh. She whimpered when he ripped his mouth from hers. "Don't have second thoughts," he said raggedly. "Promise?"

Somehow, Dana nodded. She fought to hold back tears, her body ached for him, and her heart seemed to have doubled in size, a painful sensation. She felt too much, all at once. Was it ever like this, with Craig? She couldn't remember. His betrayal wiped out everything that came before. "No second thoughts," she managed to say.

He just held her until the need for tears had passed.

"WHAT ARE YOU DOING?"

Startled by Dana's voice, Nolan looked up. "I thought you were helping Christian with his social studies paper."

She had stopped just inside the living room. "We talked it out. I think I helped him develop his idea." Laughter lit her face. "He would have loved it if I'd agree to sit next to him supplying the words, too, but I declined."

Nolan smiled, even though he didn't much feel like it. On the surface, the evening had been good. Dana and her parents had come to dinner. John and Shari had left half an hour ago, while Dana stayed at Christian's request. Figuring they would be at it a lot longer, Nolan had decided to sort some more of his own parents' stuff, a task he'd put off too long. It had been easy to do until he'd learned Christian wasn't a Gregor. Now he wanted to bring his parents back, say, *What were you thinking?* Going through their papers was the closest he could come.

This evening, he'd been hit by guilt and even a little anger, something that hadn't happened in a while. There he and Christian were, happy and surrounded by Christian's real family. Marlee had lost so much. Telling himself she deserved to lose Christian hadn't soothed his dark mood.

"Is something wrong?" Dana asked quietly.

"No. Just—" What? How could he say, *Christian never responded to Marlee the way he does to you*? Even putting it into words would be tantamount to admitting he was bothered to see the growing closeness between her and Christian. And how irrational was it that he also *wanted* to see that growing closeness?

She took a step back. "I should head home."

"No." He started to stand, papers slipping from his lap. Dropping back down, he said, "Please. Come talk to me."

She hesitated before taking the cushion at the far end of the couch. "What is all that?"

"Mom and Dad's stuff. Right after they died,

I didn't have time to go through anything non-essential. I paid bills. I dumped everything else into rubber tubs and carried them to the attic."

Dana stared at him for a moment, then turned her head to look around as if she had never seen the living room—this house—before. Her voice sounded odd when she said, "This is your family home."

He leaned back, not liking her expression. "It is. It wouldn't have made much sense to sell the house and buy another one."

"No." She gave her head a small shake. "It just never crossed my mind…"

"Why does it bother you that this was my childhood home?"

"I don't know." She couldn't quite hide that she was troubled, though she sat with her back straight and her hands folded on her lap, as if a serene pose would fool him. But then she said, "I suppose… I don't love the idea that this house was your sister's, too. That everything I touch, she touched. That when you and Christian watch me cooking in your kitchen, you both must see her there, too. And your mother."

"That's the beauty of a family homestead." He shrugged. "Which is overstating reality here, since my parents didn't buy the place until Mom was pregnant with Marlee and they needed a bigger house for two kids."

"This is a little more complicated than the turnover of generations," Dana snapped. He hadn't heard that sharpness from her in a long time.

"It is," Nolan admitted. "I assumed you knew. And I admit it didn't occur to me that you'd have a problem with it."

"I shouldn't." Tension shaped every line of her body.

He didn't know how to handle this, especially after the stress he'd felt tonight, a kind of double exposure. Marlee cleaning the kitchen with Christian. Marlee sitting at that same table with him. Dana there instead, doing everything better than his sister had.

What came out surprised him. "I don't love sleeping in my parents' bedroom. When I came home for good, I got rid of their mattress, even though it was in decent shape. Even so…" He frowned at the fireplace, where his mother had always displayed framed family photos.

"Didn't you have your own bedroom?"

"Huh?" He focused on Dana. "Oh. No, it became Christian's. I didn't mind. When I was home on leave, I slept here." He patted the sofa. "It pulls out."

"If the house is three-bedroom, you could have—"

He started shaking his head even before she finished. "No. Marlee's room is…"

"Marlee's room."

Was that sympathy he saw on her face? "I guess so."

"Have you even cleared it out?"

He frowned. "Some. I had to step carefully getting rid of her things."

Dana nodded, expression now unreadable. "What's this you're looking through now?"

She didn't want to talk about Marlee. That made two of them.

"Miscellaneous. Which is why it went into the attic. I always knew Mom kept everything. Never occurred to me I'd be the one having to go through it all."

"Are those love letters?"

He glanced down to see the bundle of envelopes tied with ribbon. "Don't know." He picked it up. "No, Mom and her sister exchanged letters for as long as I could remember. Aunt Patricia died—" he had to think "—six or seven years ago? Something like that. She'd held on to at least some of Mom's letters, no surprise because Mom kept Aunt Patricia's, too. See what I mean? Never threw anything away."

Dana laughed. "So these are your aunt's—"

"Nope. They're probably in here, too, but Patricia had a daughter. She sent these back to Mom." He looked ruefully into the overflowing tub. Maybe *he* could use the same pretext to ship some of this crap to other people. Who would undoubtedly be as thrilled as he was.

"Then you have cousins?" Dana sounded surprised.

"Nobody on Dad's side. Two first cousins on Mom's, Patricia's kids. I guess I met them once or twice when I was a kid. Haven't seen either since. Patricia didn't fly. My parents weren't big on travel, either." He looked down at the letters. "I suppose I'll keep these in case Christian..." He didn't finish. *In case Christian wants to hear his grandmother's voice again.* Not his grandmother.

On a surge of anger, he shook off the voice. His parents *were* Christian's grandparents in every way that mattered. He wouldn't let Dana or her ex-husband take that away from his family.

Whatever his expression showed, Dana's became wary. She rose to her feet. "Maybe you should skim those. Could be your mom and her sister did nothing but complain about their husbands. Or they talked about the weather and prices at the grocery store, and why keep that?"

This time, she did leave. He walked her out, kissed her until his confusion was vanquished and watched as her Subaru disappeared into the night, wishing she'd gone up to bed to wait for him instead.

Then, pausing only to see how Christian was

coming on the great social studies paper, Nolan returned to the living room and tonight's quota of the detritus of his parents' lives.

Dana was right; to be thorough, he shouldn't keep stuff he hadn't at least glanced at. He gathered several other bundles of letters his mother had written Aunt Patricia, discovering they were in the order they had been sent. Nolan flipped through until he found a postmark date six weeks or so before Marlee brought home "her" baby boy.

He untied the ribbon, carefully removed the handwritten pages from the envelope and started reading.

CHAPTER FIFTEEN

TWO HOURS LATER, Nolan wished he'd never begun. Mom *knew*, was all he could think. Sick to his stomach, he shook his head. No, it was more accurate to say his mother had *guessed* that baby Christian was not her daughter's.

He rested his head back on the sofa, closed his eyes and brooded.

His mother had probably told his dad what she was thinking. He couldn't imagine she wouldn't have.

Her handwriting had become shaky.

I see nothing of Marlee in this baby, Patty. Nothing from our family. I know that's not evidence. He could take after his father. But that combined with the lack of bond between them convinces me that they're strangers to each other. I can't believe I just wrote that. It frightens me to death. But what can I do but talk to Marlee?

Why hadn't she contacted authorities? A muffled sound escaped him. If she'd ever had the baby's blood tested, she would have known. Why hadn't she? *Why?*

"Marlee won't talk about Christian's father at all," she wrote a few weeks later.

> She sounds traumatized, as if having a baby was more than she could handle emotionally. She had a housemate, another woman who had a baby of her own. Marlee confesses to having let her do more for Christian than she should have. She told me she was scared. If all of this is true, I don't understand why she didn't come home sooner. This was the longest she's ever stayed away. She's always run home when she knew she was in real trouble. So why not this time?

Nolan ground his teeth. *Gee, Mom, did it ever occur to you she had to find a baby the right age and gender to* steal?

In the end, his credulous, too-loving mother had decided her doubts were silly. The way Christian was shooting up in height reminded her so much of Nolan at that age. He was going to be just as good at sports as Nolan, too! And look how Marlee loved her little boy, Mom marveled. Why, once she was back on her medication, she was a wonderful mother!

If she had listened to her instincts, she could have saved Dana years of suffering.

Then his parents wouldn't have had Christian to love and protect.

And, no, he couldn't flip that on end, not now that he'd gotten to know Dana's parents. Christian would have had loving grandparents either way. He'd have had Dana instead of a crazy mother.

I wouldn't have had Christian.

He'd wouldn't have moved into this house, bought Wind & Waves. He would likely be—where?—Afghanistan? Somalia? Some war-torn part of the world. Saving the world, was how he'd always thought of it. Windsurfing would still be a very occasional hobby taken up in his teenage years and now indulged during brief leaves.

His next thought felt like a bullet to the chest. *I'd never have met Dana.*

With a heavy sigh, Nolan opened his eyes and stretched to relieve taut muscles.

There was no going back. Would he ever tell Dana about what he'd read? How could she not be furious? Hate his parents as well as Marlee? He didn't like knowing how self-centered he was to wonder whether the new knowledge would damage his relationship with her.

And Christian. Damn. Was this anything he needed to know?

Tempted though he was to shred this whole pile of letters, he didn't like dishonesty. He'd have to tell Dana. Christian...probably not. Or, at least, not until he was a whole lot more secure in his identity.

Strangely, while reading those letters had disturbed him, he also felt some of his guilt lifting from his shoulders. Maybe, he thought with grim humor, because he'd been able to dump it on his parents.

Except he knew better. It was more as if he could see that Marlee's last weeks had been only one knot on a long rope studded with knots. Maybe an inevitable one. He wasn't sure he'd had any real choice over how he handled her. He couldn't in good conscience have let the issue of Christian's real identity slide.

After a minute, Nolan tied the ribbons around the two bundles of letters he'd read and dropped them back in the tub. Then he put the lid on it. It could go to the back of the attic.

DANA'S MUSCLES BURNED as she planted the ice ax and kicked her foot into a step already formed by other climbers in the steep, snow-covered chute that was aptly called the Pearly Gates. They weren't alone on the mountain, even though they'd deliberately chosen a Thursday after the Fourth of July weekend. A group from a climbing school was ascending right behind them. Fortunately, she was too tired to look over her shoulder; think how embarrassing it would be to discover they'd been seething with impatience for hours.

She'd turned off her headlamp a little while ago. The sky was a pearlescent pink that shimmered off the ice formations. A burst of light had just appeared above the rocky wall. Sunrise.

Climbing through the night had been a strange experience, narrowing her world to the circle of light cast by her headlamp and to grunts and occasional voices coming from ahead of her on the rope.

Because of Christian, they had carried tents and sleeping bags and camped out partway, just above the Palmer Snowfield. Though he had been insulted that Nolan thought he wouldn't be as strong as the adults, he was not only young, he wasn't a runner. Now, praying the summit really was at the top of this chute, Dana was grateful they hadn't tried to make the ascent in one go.

"Everyone okay?" Nolan called back, as he did regularly.

Dana found enough voice to say, "Yep."

"Yeah!" Christian yelled.

Her father, just ahead of her on the rope,

laughed. He was in his late fifties, and *he* didn't sound tired, she thought, disgruntled.

Climbing in the dark was safest, with the snow firm beneath an icy crust instead of treacherously soft. Nolan had dragged them out of their tents at one thirty in the morning, insisted they have a bite to eat and a hot drink, and had them gear up. They had strapped on crampons and roped up for the first time, too. Dana had just enough experience herself to see how careful Nolan was being for Christian's sake.

And for mine. He paused frequently to look back. At rest stops, he'd spent time at her side, his voice low and…intimate as he urged her to snack.

The long, dark hours during the climb had been conducive to thinking. When Nolan first told her that his mother had suspected Marlee's baby had been stolen, Dana had been so angry she'd had to hide her shaking hands so he wouldn't know. But he'd also told her the rest of what his mother had written, and understanding and acceptance had gradually taken away the anger. Dana had barely become acquainted with Christian, and yet she knew what Nolan's mother had felt for her daughter.

She wouldn't want to believe Christian had done something terrible any more than Marlee's mother had. She'd do the same, latching on to any tiny reason to be able to dismiss those suspicions.

Lifting her gaze now, she discovered Nolan had disappeared from sight. Then Christian did, too, and an instant later she heard him whoop. Her dad laughed again, said, "We made it," and, reinvigorated, Dana stamped her way up the last bit to emerge on the snowy approach to the top.

A minute later, they were there, standing at the edge of the summit ridge.

And…oh, my.

Dana trailed the others, her head swiveling as she took in the extraordinary view, made sublime by the soft, glowing colors of sunrise. No wonder they'd timed their ascent to be here now. No wonder.

"Awesome!" Christian yelled.

"Highest point in Oregon," Nolan said. "One of the best views of Mount Jefferson, too."

Another volcano, it rose sharp pointed and snow clad to the south.

They plopped down on the snow to rest, Nolan nagging them all to snack on the trail mix and candy bars they'd brought and handing around a bottle of water. He pointed at Mount Adams to the north, close but situated in Washington State. Saint Helens was less visible, but she stared in fascination, anyway.

"Could we go up there someday?" she asked. "Have you been, Christian?"

"Uh-uh. That'd be cool."

"I haven't been in years, but I hear the devastation is still apparent," Nolan said. "We'll plan on it."

After making them apply sunscreen and put on wraparound sunglasses to protect their eyes from the glare of the sun off the glacier, he finally got them moving again to begin the long descent. He was hustling them, she knew, because he wanted to get below the Bergschrund, a huge crevasse, before the warmth of the day made the passage more dangerous.

Dana had forgotten that going down was even harder on the thigh muscles than climbing up, but the exhilaration of success carried them, and at least now they could see where they were going and pause to study the crystalline beauty of huge ice formations and the oddly flat, distant world at the foot of the mountain.

The sight of the crevasse, with its mysterious depths, chilled her. She wanted to grab Christian when he inched forward for a better view, but then Nolan laid a calm hand on his shoulder, and a minute later they left it behind.

The sun rose, the glorious early morning color vanishing into a day warm enough for them to peel off layers of clothing. Dana itched—literally—to remove her helmet, but even the traverses across steep snowfields could be dangerous. One misstep and she'd plummet. If she couldn't stop herself quickly by digging her ax and toes into the snow, she could potentially pull her father off his feet, too, and then Christian. Could Nolan hold them all?

Probably, she thought, wrinkling her nose, but she didn't want to find out.

On rest stops, he not only pushed food and water at them but made them all slap on copious quantities of sunscreen.

The descent from where they'd camped was an anticlimax. Snow became skimpy. The lift towers for the ski area, off to one side, were an odd punctuation in an otherwise primitive landscape.

Even Christian groaned when they reached Nolan's big SUV. Dana sagged against the fender, resting on her pack. Laughing, Nolan unlocked the doors, heaved his own pack—by far the heaviest, of course—into the back and took Dana's from her next.

"Fun?"

She grinned at him. "It was amazing. But you know what?" She waited for his raised eyebrows. "Once is enough."

Smiling, he touched a finger to her cheek. "I think you got too much sun."

"You're sort of burnished, too." Oh, she wanted to lay a hand against his face, feel his stubble, but she was very aware of Christian and her father watching. She looked at her son, who couldn't seem to stop grinning. He'd already taken off his helmet.

With stiff fingers, Dana did the same.

"Hot bath, here I come," she announced.

"Hot *tub*, here I come." Her dad gave her a quirky grin. "Why do you think we're staying at the inn?" With a chuckle, he easily dodged the elbow she aimed at his midsection.

Tiredness caught up with them during the drive. Dana was glad not to be behind the wheel. She kept nodding off.

Nolan left her father at the inn first, then drove to her house. She looked in the backseat to see that Christian was sound asleep, cheek flattened on the window. He didn't stir even when Nolan collected her pack from the rear and slammed the hatch door.

Of course he insisted on carrying it in for her, keeping only the helmet and mountain locator unit, both rented. He set the pack down inside and pulled her close. Dana leaned gratefully, loving his strength, longing for him to stay.

"I wish you were coming home with us," he grumbled, echoing her fantasy, but then kissed her gently and gave her a small push. "Bath and nap."

She smiled at him. "You, too."

Nolan started to leave but swung back. This kiss was rougher, fueled by what felt like frustration. It didn't last long enough for her to respond.

"Thank you," she said this time, knowing he'd understand. She'd always have this—an unforgettable twenty-four hours spent with her father, her son...and the man she was very much afraid she loved.

He nodded, said, "You're welcome," and left her swaying with exhaustion in the middle of her living room.

"LIGHTS OUT," JASON'S mom called.

"Mo-om," he protested. "It's not *that* late."

She knocked lightly before opening the door and poking her head in. "It's midnight. I don't care if you talk quietly, but *I* have to work to-morrow. So sleep tight." She flipped the switch, plunging the two boys into darkness.

Jason's mother was a Realtor, which meant she worked on weekends, when other people had time off to look at houses. Jason's parents were both cool. Even his little sister wasn't that bad. Christian used to be jealous of Jason's family, but he didn't have to be after Uncle Nolan came home for good.

When he was staying overnight, Christian always slept in a sleeping bag on a thick pad on the floor next to Jason's twin bed. He lay there now, looking up at the ceiling. He knew everybody was probably getting tired of him talking about the climb two days before, but he couldn't help himself.

"Mount Hood was amazing. Now I really want to be a mountain climber. My gra—" He gulped to a stop. "I might get to go to Colorado next summer and climb in the Rockies."

He heard Jason roll over to peer down at him. "Who do you know in Colorado?"

"It's…" Suddenly he hated lying, but he did it, anyway. "Someone Uncle Nolan knows."

"Like from the army?"

"I guess." He hurried on. "Although climbing there is different."

"Because the mountains aren't volcanoes."

"I don't know if they have glaciers. You should have seen the ice formations!" Guilt seized him. "I bet Uncle Nolan would take us both up next summer."

Jason was quiet for a minute. "I wish I could have gone with you."

"He said…" Christian had to swallow. "You know. That he didn't want too many inexperienced climbers, and there were these other people."

His mother and his grandfather, who'd both done lots of climbing. Christian had been the only one who *didn't* know what he was doing. The whole way, he'd been roped between Grandpa Hayes and Uncle Nolan, because they were the two strongest climbers.

This time, the silence went on so long, Christian wondered if Jason had gone to sleep. Except he knew he hadn't.

They were best friends. *I should have told him*, he thought glumly. If he had, Jason could have gone, too. Only now it was too late, which made it even harder to say, *See, it was my mom and my grandad who went with us, only it's not the mom who died. This one is my* real *mom.*

Christian had kept secrets before. Nobody had known how often he stayed alone because his mother flipped out and took off. Or that she did drugs and probably slept behind Dumpsters in alleys when she was gone. Or even that she wouldn't say *anything* about who his dad was. When he was younger, he'd made stuff up about this father who'd died, so he couldn't be part of Christian's life. All his friends and teachers knew was that his mother was weird.

Telling this secret would mean admitting she was so crazy she'd stolen him from his real parents. But that wasn't why shame crawled inside him. The bad thing was he was going to *have* to tell everyone. Dana lived right here, and she was over at his house all the time. She'd want to come when stuff was going on at school next year.

As bad as telling Jason the truth would have been when Christian first found out, it was going to be worse now. If it had been the other

way around…would *he* understand why Jason
had lied to him for so long?

Christian curled on his side because his stomach hurt. "Jason?" he whispered, in case his
friend was asleep.

"Yeah?"

"There's something I should have told you.
I guess I thought it would all go away." Which
was the truth. He'd thought *she* would go away.
Except now…he didn't want her to.

He took a deep breath and started. "You remember how much I bled, that time we were
fooling around with the ax?"

SATURDAY, LUNCHTIME ARRIVED and Christian had
yet to show up at Wind & Waves. Nolan decided
that as soon as his current customer quit dithering over sails, he'd call Jason's house to track
the kid down. Damn it, he knew rule number
one: keep Nolan updated.

On this, the Hayeses' last day in Lookout, John
had taken a kayak onto the river again, while
Dana had joined her mother. Nolan watched from
the window as they departed together in Dana's
Subaru.

Her parents were nice people. He thought the
visit had gone well, overall. Christian had behaved decently, spending a fair amount of time
with his grandparents, who'd been willing to
take him on some outings to the North Clack-

amas Aquatic Park, which had waterslides, a wave pool and a rock-climbing wall, and to a pirate-themed mini-golf course, where apparently Grandpa had beaten the pants off Christian *and* Grandma. He'd even called them *Grandpa* and *Grandma*—when he had yet to say *Mom* to Dana.

And Nolan could hardly wait for these people to go away.

As he rang up the purchase at long last, the bell attached to the door tinkled.

"Uncle Nolan?"

"Here," he called.

Looking sheepish, Christian appeared between aisles carrying a small white bag. He stepped aside for the customer to pass, then said, "Jason's dad stopped and bought us burgers and fries. He bought you some, too."

Realizing he was starved, Nolan signaled to Sara that he was taking a break. Despite the gray, misty day, he carried his lunch outside. Christian trailed him and sat down, too.

"Is Grandpa back yet?"

"No. He seems to know what he's doing, so I'm not worried about him."

Squirming just a little, the boy nodded.

"I was starting to worry about you," Nolan added.

"I'm sorry. We were having fun, and…" Christian gave up, his sidelong glance nervous.

"You thank Jason's dad?"

He nodded.

Nolan unwrapped the cheeseburger and took a big bite. Damn, that tasted good.

"I told Jason."

Nolan heard, but it took him a couple seconds to process. Swallowing, he stared at Christian. "About Dana?" And there was an oversimplification of a vastly complex subject, he thought.

Christian nodded.

"What did he say?"

"He was kind of blown away."

"Weren't we all," Nolan said drily.

Christian fidgeted some more. "I guess now I have to tell my other friends. And then *everyone* will know."

"I'll go to the school before your first day to make them aware of what's going on. For Dana's sake." When Christian didn't respond, Nolan asked gently, "Why now?"

Misery filled Christian's brown eyes. "I had to do it *some*time. And…I felt bad 'cause Jason could have gone with us up Mount Hood if I had told him sooner."

Guilt over deceiving his friend but not hurting Dana's feelings?

But Christian continued, "And…you know. I want her to be able to come to my birthday party. And school stuff."

Her. He still couldn't say it. Given his own

tangle of feelings for Marlee, Nolan understood why.

"You decided when that birthday party will be?" he asked quietly.

"If I'm going to tell everyone—" Christian gave an awkward shrug "—I guess it should be my real birthday."

Nolan smiled at him. "I'm proud of you."

Color flooded Christian's cheeks, and he suddenly jumped to his feet. "There's Grandpa! I think. Has anyone else rented a kayak today?"

"One couple, who took a double."

"That must be him." Christian loped toward the beach, leaving Nolan to gobble his lunch before the next emotional hit.

DANA'S MOTHER PLOPPED onto the king-size bed in the hotel room, bunched some pillows behind her and stretched out her legs. "Sit. Get comfy. I don't know when your father will get back from paddling his way to the Pacific Ocean."

Dana laughed. "I hope he doesn't get quite that ambitious."

Humor sparkled in Shari's eyes. "Oh, well. His absence gives us time to talk."

"About subjects Dad told you to leave alone?" Dana guessed.

No guilt crossed her mother's face. "Did we *ever* tell your father everything we talked about?"

Well, no. And there was a time Dana had

been grateful to share secrets with her mother. Today she felt more than a little wary. Her parents were leaving in the morning. Lunch today with just Mom had been fun. She'd believed herself safe from exactly the talk Mom clearly had in mind.

Resigned, Dana dropped her purse on the small round table by the window and chose one of the chairs, in case she needed a quick getaway. "What?"

"I'm your mother."

Uh-oh. "I know you're my mother." Dana rolled her eyes, feeling very teenage. "There's something you want to say."

Instead of amusement, she saw worry.

"I suppose," her mother said slowly, "I'm wondering about Nolan. Your relationship with him."

Dana went very still. Neither of her parents had ever questioned her about Craig. They'd welcomed him with warmth and had been thrilled when he asked her to marry him. "You don't like him."

"How could we not?" Shari said. "He's been nothing but kind. For Christian, he's everything a father should be."

Dana waited.

"It's just…hasn't this happened awfully fast?"

"I met him four months ago. I moved to Lookout over two months ago. It's not like we've announced an engagement." Initially stung, she felt her temper mounting. "We're…interested. Seeing each other separate from the time I spend with Christian. Is there an appropriate timetable I somehow missed hearing about?"

"I didn't mean that as criticism."

"Sure you did."

"I suppose your father was right and I should have kept my mouth shut," her mother murmured. "It's just…"

If it had been anyone else, Dana would have walked out. Even stormed out. "You think I've grabbed on to him because he's convenient."

Her mother blinked. "Well, no. It's *his* motivation that concerns me. You're Gabriel's biological mother. There's no question you'd win in a custody battle."

"So he's decided the best way of ensuring he doesn't lose Christian is to put on a convincing show of being madly in love with me," she said slowly.

"I love you. I don't want you hurt. Just…hold on to enough skepticism to be sure, that's all. Is that so unreasonable for me to ask?"

Her skin felt tight. Dana stood. "I take it you don't believe there's any other reason he'd want me. And, yes, I know I'm too thin and sad too often and…and damaged. Thank you for the reminder."

Looking horrified, her mother pushed herself up. "You know that's not what I meant!"

"Do I?"

"Aren't I entitled to worry about you?"

Then where were you the past eleven years? But that wouldn't be a fair question. *She* had opened the distance, not her parents.

Dana summoned her dignity. "What you don't understand is that he carries a lot of pain inside, too. We…match. And that's all I have to say."

Ignoring her mother's pleas, she picked up her purse and left. Outside, she saw her father, wet and sunburned, crossing the parking lot. Instead of going to him, she slipped behind an SUV until she was sure he'd made it to the lobby before hurrying to her car.

During the drive home, she didn't let herself think.

Not until she was safe in her sanctuary did she allow the hurt to swell or acknowledge the sharp claws of doubt.

CHAPTER SIXTEEN

THEY ALL WENT out to dinner that night. Iron-
ically, her parents chose the same restaurant
where Nolan and Christian had taken Dana her
first night in Lookout and insisted on picking
up the tab despite Nolan's good-natured protest.

"You've done plenty to make this a memora-
ble visit," Dad said. "This is a modest thanks."

Given their early morning flight, the good-
byes were said in the parking lot outside the
restaurant. Nolan politely shook hands before
stepping away. Dana had the fleeting thought
that he looked very alone as he waited for her
and Christian. As, of course, he was. He had
no one but Christian...and Christian had a big
new family.

Her father threw an arm around her son and
murmured something in his ear that had him ducking his head but smiling. Her mother squeezed
Dana hard.

"I hope you know I said what I did because
I love you."

Vision blurring, Dana nodded. "I love you, too, Mom."

As they drove away, Christian tipped his head. "Are you *crying*?"

She sniffed. "Yes."

"How come? I mean, you didn't live with them, anyway."

No—or see them that often. "They're farther away now," she tried to explain. "I think—" *I'm feeling again, after eleven years of numbness laid atop pain.* Not something she wanted to say. "It'll probably be Christmas before I see them again. That's a long time."

Nolan placed a hand on her back that warmed her through her thin cotton cardigan and camisole.

Christian got quiet, which she appreciated.

Before starting the engine, Nolan asked if she'd like to come home with them, but Dana shook her head. "I need to take a long, hot bubble bath and weep a little." And try to get over being mad at her mother. "Thank God tomorrow is Sunday and I can sleep in," she said with a sigh.

By Monday she'd be feeling a little ashamed because she was glad her parents were gone. The visit had been wonderful except for the new tension between her and her mother, but it had also been exhausting. And it had taken her away from Nolan.

Dana was annoyed to have let her mother's suggestion throw her into turmoil. She *knew* how much Nolan wanted her, and he expressed his gentle awareness and concern for her so often, with touches and words.

Somehow, though, she hadn't quite succeeded in prying the sharp hook of doubt from her heart. *Time*, she told herself. Trust would build. Nolan was too honorable a man to create a huge lie to secure what he wanted.

As she was getting out in front of her house, Christian blurted from the backseat, "You can come to dinner tomorrow night, can't you? She can, right, Uncle Nolan?"

"She can," he said, amusement rich in his voice. "Whether she *will*…"

It was just the note she'd needed. Laughing, she said, "I can *and* will. Thank you. Shall I bring anything?"

"Nah, I think it's time to let Christian impress you with his culinary skill."

"Tacos," her son said. "My tacos are really good."

"One of my favorite foods." Which was true. "Good night."

The SUV stayed put at the curb until she unlocked her door, flipped on the light just inside and turned back to wave.

Of course, the minute she was alone, she wished she weren't.

"YOU WERE RIGHT," Dana said, smiling at her son across the dinner table. "Your tacos were wonderful."

Grinning, his cowlick sticking up at the crown of his head, he looked young, a boy instead of a near teenager, Nolan thought, with some regret.

"I guess I should learn to cook something else now, huh?"

She laughed. "That's a plan. By the time you're living on your own, you'll want to have a good, solid repertoire of at least seven meals. Repeating in the same week? Not so good."

"I'll eat out."

"I'd like to think," Nolan interjected, "that you'll be eating dorm food for a few years."

"I bet it's gross."

Only half listening, Nolan returned to a worry that stuck like a burr. Late in her parents' visit, something had changed between Dana and her mother. He'd asked, and she had refused to talk about it, which made him think the quarrel had been about him.

And, damn, that made him feel edgy.

The climb had been good; he hadn't gotten any odd vibes from Dana's father. Up to and including goodbye hugs, her mother was all sweetness and light with him, but he didn't trust it, or her.

He reminded himself of how much Dana had hidden from her parents over the years. They couldn't be that close. How much would she let her mother's opinion influence her?

He was being paranoid, Nolan decided. She wasn't behaving any differently toward him than she had before her parents' visit. Dana gave every appearance of being relaxed and happy. She and Christian were having a good time, that was all. She *should* be concentrating on him. That was what this was all about. Nolan and Dana would have time for each other later.

Yeah, when? his cranky side demanded. He hadn't made love to her for a seemingly endless two weeks. Her parents never did have that romantic dinner out. Instead, Dana and often Christian had spent damn near every evening with them, often without Nolan.

The Hayeses were gone. Things would get back to normal.

"I want to do something different for my birthday party this year," Christian said out of the blue. "I wish we could go climbing."

Nolan shook his head. "I can't accept liability for other people's kids, not to do something like that. We could go to someplace with an indoor rock-climbing wall, but we'd need to get signed permission from all the parents." He hesitated. "Are you sure your friends would all enjoy that, anyway? It's not for everyone."

Christian screwed up his face. "Ryan would

probably hate it. And maybe Eric. He's kind of clumsy."

"What about a hike?"

"I want to do something *cool*!" In an instant, he was sullen, more teenager than little boy. "Different from everyone else."

"What have your friends done for their birthdays lately?" Dana asked.

"Oh, sometimes, you know, just an arcade and cake. Jason wants to go back to the water-slides. He's really into that. Dieter's birthday was in February. His dad got four tickets to see the Trail Blazers play."

Dana's brow wrinkled. "Is that basketball?"

"Uh-huh. And once Kieran's dad took a bunch of us to see the Winterhawks. That's ice hockey."

"So...no summer professional sports around here."

He shook his head. "Except minor-league baseball, and I don't care about baseball."

Well, crap. Christian wanted this birthday to be a big deal, maybe because of the reveal of his new identity, maybe just because it was his twelfth. Heck, the increasingly volatile hormones could be blamed for just about everything.

"It's a long drive, but what if you went to the ocean?" Dana suggested. "Flew kites, I don't know." Her voice had petered out at Christian's obvious lack of enthusiasm.

She'd given Nolan an idea, though. "You know, I'm getting a load of sand delivered."

The sand on his "beach" was largely washed away over the winter. Having a private beach helped sell his business, so he renewed the sand regularly. It was worth every penny.

"Yeah?" Christian said.

"I could change the delivery date." Or have another load dumped. "What if you had a sand-sculpture-building party? Not little-kid sand-castles but big, awesome creations. You could divide into teams."

Christian's eyes widened. "Remember the picture of the dragon?"

"I do. And the charioteer with two horses."

"Yeah! You can make a car or a...a..."

"Octopus!" Dana exclaimed. "Or even a cas-tle. I saw a picture of one with an open arch. I don't know how they do that."

"I don't, either," Nolan said, deciding it was time to scale back the grandiose dreams. "I imagine some of those take days and skill we don't have, but I'll bet you and your friends could come up with some good ideas that *are* doable."

"But...what if it rains?"

Nolan grinned. "Then we go out for pizza, I'll hand out tokens for the games, and we'll come back to the house or to Wind & Waves for cake."

"July is mostly good weather," Christian said thoughtfully.

Dana's breath caught. "July?" she echoed.

"Oh. Yeah. Um…" Cheeks pink, he did some squirming. "Since that's really my birthday."

Her eyes held desperate hope. "But…then everyone…"

Christian swallowed. "I told Jason. And I'm going to tell my other friends. About…you know. You."

"Really?"

Seeing tears welling in her eyes, Nolan hastily grabbed a clean napkin and handed it to her. "Really," Nolan said, smiling at her. "We'll let the school know. Mom."

Her mouth formed an O. Then she buried her face in the napkin and cried. Christian stared helplessly at her. Nolan pushed back his chair, circled the table and sat next to her so he could pull her forward to lean against his chest.

"I'm sorry," she mumbled. "I'm just…happy!"

Christian looked askance. "That's *happy*?"

Nolan found himself chuckling as he stroked her hair. "Yep. Live and learn, kid."

"But only a *girl* would do that. And I don't like girls."

And suddenly Dana was laughing, too. Feeling his wet shoulder, the vibration of her laughter, the smooth silk of her hair against his cheek, Nolan smiled.

"It won't be long until you do." Somehow, he came to be looking at Dana instead of Christian when he finished. "Trust me."

Her puffy eyes holding his, Dana offered him a shaky smile. Her lips formed near-silent words that were only for him. "I do."

All Nolan's anxieties fled.

DANA FELT LIGHT as air when she went home that evening. Her mother's worries had been a kind of infection, leaving her feeling as if she had the flu, complete with aches and tiredness. Tonight, looking into Nolan's eyes, she had let it all go.

Giddiness filled her.

Mom. Christian had told his best friend about her. He intended to tell all of his other friends in time to celebrate his birthday on July 17, which wasn't very far away.

She loved the sandcastle idea. It felt…magical. The way she felt. This was the first birthday she'd celebrate with him. She wanted it to make up for all the ones she'd missed.

At the sound of muffled ringing, she hurried to the kitchen to dig her phone out of her purse. Nolan.

"Hi," she said.

"Hey. Ah, Christian just got an invite to a sleepover tomorrow night. This one from Ryan."

"The clumsy friend?"

"No, that's Eric. Ryan is scrawny and into computers. He's played soccer, I think, but I suspect his father encouraged that."

"The classic geek."

Nolan laughed. "Yep. Fortunately, Christian has some geek in him, too. I'd like to see him reading more, but he's buried in his laptop half the time."

She opened her mouth to ask if Christian had been begging for a phone to extend his digital reach...but realized she didn't care. Not right this minute. What Nolan had really called to tell her was that *they* could have a sleepover tomorrow night, too. They'd both have to get up early for work the next day, but so what?

"Would you like to come to dinner?"

"I would love to come to dinner." He hesitated. "I don't want you feeling obligated, but I like the days you're around at work, too."

He was talking about Saturday, even though she'd be around all day Sunday for the birthday party. "Free," she teased.

"That doesn't hurt," he agreed, a smile in his voice. But the smile was gone when he said, "I just like knowing I can turn around and there you'll be. I'll see you cocking your head as you puzzle over all the jargon some young hotshot is throwing at you and the smile that brings him to his knees the same way it does me. Or your back as you walk away. Your amazing legs and the sway of your hips and the way you carry yourself, with such pride."

She clutched the phone, a tightness growing in her chest. Nobody had ever said anything like this to her.

"I love the sight of you soaked to your knees and sandy, feeling good because you just pulled off something else you've never done before." His voice dropped another octave. "Then there are the times I turn to find you looking at me. My head empties of whatever I was thinking. There's just you."

When he fell silent, Dana whispered, "You've made me cry again." She blinked hard.

"And I'm not there to put my arms around you."

"Tomorrow." She took a deep breath. "*And* Saturday. Because...I like spending the day with you, too, even if we hardly have a chance to talk."

"Good." He made a ragged sound—a cleared throat? "I don't plan to do a lot of talking tomorrow night."

Pleasure squeezed deep in her abdomen, had her toes curling. "Sleep tight," she said, sultry in a way she didn't recognize.

"Fat chance," he said hoarsely. "Good night, Dana."

He was gone. She stood in the middle of her kitchen, aching for him.

He couldn't have said all that if he didn't mean it. Not Nolan. She'd been right to let go of the suspicion her mother had roused.

And she needed to get to bed, considering how little sleep she was likely to have tomorrow night.

THURSDAY EVENING, CHRISTIAN appeared in the living room without the usual preamble of feet stomping on the stairs. Instead of sitting down, he hovered in the doorway. "That was my father. On the phone."

Nolan nodded. He'd recognized the caller's voice. Resented having to hear it. For all the neutrality he struggled to present to Christian, Nolan had developed a deep antipathy for the man who intended to take his place.

His attitude wasn't helped by the fact that Craig Stewart hardly acknowledged his existence. From the beginning, Dana had understood she needed to build a relationship with him, not only with her son. She had talked to him. Listened to him. Craig didn't so much as say, *Hi, Nolan. Gabriel available?* No, it was always a crisp *May I speak to Gabriel?* His tone suggested irritation that he had to go through an intermediary. Nolan was surprised he hadn't bought an expensive smartphone for Christian and shipped it to him.

Nolan set aside his laptop. "He have anything special to say?"

"I told him about my birthday party." Christian looked unhappy. "He wants to come."

Oh, hell. If anything would spoil the day more than a cloudburst, that would be it.

"What did you say?"

"I didn't know what to say!" Christian cried. "I just…" His voice dropped to a mumble. "I don't know what I said."

Uh-oh. "We'd better warn Dana."

"He sounded kind of mad." Christian hunched his shoulders. "I called her…you know. *Mom.*"

Yes! Now if Christian would only call her that to her face.

Nolan dragged his mind back to the man he considered enemy number one. "He didn't like that?"

"He got really icy and said he'd talk to her."

Nolan clasped his hands behind his head when what he really wanted to do was lunge for his phone. He nodded at it. "Why don't you give her a quick warning call?"

Christian's eyes went to the phone, but he kept hovering where he was. "Do you think I should?"

Nolan raised an eyebrow.

The kid dragged himself over. Instead of

taking the phone to make his call privately, he plunked down at the other end of the sofa and dialed.

Nolan maintained the pretense of relaxation.

After a minute, Christian set down the phone. "It's busy. I'll bet it's him."

Nolan bet it was him, too. The SOB who had gotten over the loss of his son in no time at all and ditched his wife because she wasn't willing to move as fast. And, sure, that might not be entirely fair; Craig hadn't carried the baby for nine months, and he hadn't stayed home days with him. Or, Nolan suspected, gotten up nights with his son. He had to get his rest, after all, because his work was so important. Had he so much as changed a diaper?

Nolan was a little ashamed to admit he hoped not. He resolved to ask Dana.

"She can handle him," Nolan said. "Don't worry about it."

The brown eyes beseeched him. "What if he wrecks my birthday?"

"How can he?" Nolan said simply. Sure as shooting, the jackass would bring the perfect birthday gift: a smartphone. "Him being there will be more uncomfortable for Dana than it will be for you." He smiled. "You'll be too busy building…?"

"A dinosaur," Christian said with a burst of enthusiasm. "I was thinking, like, a stegosaurus's back, only I have to figure out how to do the triangles that stick up."

"You might find some how-to advice online," Nolan suggested. "You probably should look and share what you learn with all your friends." Who had all thought the idea of building sand sculptures was awesome.

Christian bounced to his feet. "I'll do that right now." Halfway out of the room, he turned back. "I told you Dana is going to bake the cake, right?"

Nolan smiled. "You did."

"I bet she makes a great one!"

This time, those oversize feet thundered on the stairs.

DANA STEWED FOR half an hour before she let herself call Nolan.

"Hey," he said. "Did your jerk of an ex reach you?"

"You knew?"

"Christian tried to call to warn you. Apparently Craig got to you first."

Sitting in her big upholstered chair, she drew her knees up. Because it was comfortable, she told herself, not because she needed comfort.

"Did he tell Christian he's coming out here?"

"For his birthday."

"Craig is furious because I hadn't let him know that Christian—excuse me, *Gabriel*—

has decided to admit I'm really his mother. It didn't help that Christian told him about my parents' visit." She sighed. "I can't really blame him about that. They shouldn't have had the chance to see him before Craig did. He's Christian's father."

How strange that it seemed wrong, even offensive, to call her son by his birth name. *And I swore I'd never think of him by the name* she *gave him.*

But *she* was Nolan's sister. A deeply troubled human being. Christian had loved her. When forced to see the truth, she'd killed herself.

Dana almost felt…pity for Marlee Gregor. Not that she'd ever admit as much to Craig.

And Christian… Well, that was who her son was now.

"It was inevitable he'd show up," Nolan said, sounding wonderfully unperturbed. "Do you suppose he'll announce he's filing for custody right when we're lighting the candles?"

Almost able to see it, she hugged her knees. "It's dumb that I've let him become some kind of bogeyman. I loved him. I married him." Her voice softened. "He loved Gabriel, too."

His silence made her think about what she'd just said. Did he not like her saying she'd loved Craig?

"You're never dumb. I don't want to hear you saying that," Nolan said sternly.

It was her turn to gather her thoughts. "He could take Christian away from both of us."

"How can he, if we stand together?" Nolan said, his voice so tender she closed her eyes and imagined it was a touch, warming her skin, giving her courage. "You're his mother. I'm the only father he's ever known. And no judge would disregard what a boy Christian's age wants."

"No. Of course not. I may be wrong about what Craig intends, anyway. No matter what, he should get to know his son."

"I agree. Which is why I grit my teeth and hand the phone to Christian every time the guy calls."

She was able to laugh, stepping back from the cold anger in every word Craig had spoken. Saying good-night, Dana felt amazement at how much had changed since the first time she came to Lookout and met hostility from both Nolan and Christian. Now Nolan spoke as if standing together was a given. And Christian had told his friends about her. He *wanted* her around. He hadn't called her *Mom* yet, but he would. He would.

In a way, she'd be glad to get this first meeting with Craig over with.

CHAPTER SEVENTEEN

DANA PATTED WET sand into place. She was having a blast, and to heck with Craig. If he wanted to sulk, let him.

Somewhere along the way, the sand sculpting had been opened to parents, too. Some had joined in, while others formed an enthusiastic audience. If she turned her head ever so slightly, she'd be able to see Craig, standing at a distance from anyone else. Apparently crawling around in the sand was too undignified for him. The impression he gave was one of impatience. With a hint of sadness, she remembered a trip to Galveston Island in Texas, when the two of them, young and in love, had built a sandcastle. They'd stayed, hand in hand, to watch the tide turn and the castle wash away until only smooth sand remained.

He'd been so patient with her late in the pregnancy, when her feet and ankles swelled and she needed help getting up. And in the months after they brought Gabriel home, too. Craig had called at least once a day to be sure they were all right, brought takeout dinners a couple of evenings a week. He would sit for hours with Gabe asleep against his shoulder, his expression tender.

The man he'd been would have joined the dad team, which seemed to be trying to build a giant football helmet. Or he'd be going from group to group, like Nolan was, urging sunscreen on the boys, encouraging and helping and laughing.

Maybe the fault was hers, because she hadn't suggested Nolan give Craig a role today. It hadn't occurred to her yesterday evening during that first tense encounter.

Craig hadn't liked her being there. She couldn't tell him Christian had begged her to stay. It had been odd seeing him after so long, still handsome, still lean and athletic. Her first thought had been a startled *He has Christian's eyes*. Which she knew, of course; the first time she saw Christian, she'd thought he had Craig's eyes. Now... this man was a stranger. It didn't feel as if it had been him she'd kissed, made love with, laughed and quarreled with.

If he had shown any hint of regret when he looked at her, she might have felt old guilt, for shutting him out in the depths of her grief. But all she saw was a cool assessment, followed by faint irritation.

Even the parents of Christian's friends all

knew now that she was his mother and that his father would be here for his birthday party. The ones who were watching instead of playing in the sand were probably sneaking peeks at him. Maybe self-consciousness was what gave him that aloof, snobby air.

Nolan crouched beside her and held out the tube of sunscreen. "You're turning pink," he said, sounding amused.

Dana sank back to her haunches, wiped her sandy hand on her shorts and accepted a white glob from him. As she started spreading it, he offered some to the three other women working on the octopus that reached one long, tentacled arm toward the water. All three accepted.

Then he dabbed some onto the tips of her ears. "Having fun?" he asked in a low voice.

"Yes." She glanced toward the stegosaurus. "Is Christian, do you think?"

Nolan nodded. "This was a hit. You notice how many people have walked over from the inn to watch? Not to mention every customer at the store. Pictures are probably all over the internet already."

"Too bad we have such a killjoy here," she muttered.

Nolan followed her gaze. "He's an idiot. If he'd joined in, he would have scored points with

Christian." He shrugged. "Do you suppose he's as much fun at his daughters' birthday parties?"

She laughed at his careless dismissal of her ex-husband. "Maybe *their* parties are appropriately dignified."

He pushed his sunglasses up so she could see his eyes. "You mean their mom isn't crawling around in the sand, ass waggling, getting sunburned and, hey, having fun?"

She narrowed her eyes. "Waggling my ass?"

His wicked grin sparked a whole lot of *in*appropriate ideas in her. The soft rumble of his voice in her ear didn't help. "It may be just me noticing."

She gave her hips a tiny wriggle, just to be mean. "What a shame the house will be filled with preteen boys tonight. How many is it? Ten?"

Nolan groaned. "You sure you don't want to spend the night?"

"Not a chance. A, I wasn't invited, and B, it's a manly job. I'd kill the atmosphere."

Ryan's mother nudged her shoulder. Laughing, she said, "Quit flirting. You're the mastermind. We need you."

"Right. Moms rock."

"Moms rock!" the other three chanted.

The nearest boys jeered as, laughing, Nolan beat a retreat.

Forty-five minutes later, all four women fell back when the piercing whistle blew.

"Time!" Nolan called. When everyone quit sculpting, he said, "This wasn't a competition, so we should admire everyone else's work." He held up a phone. "I've taken pictures and will email them to everyone." He half turned toward the other parents. "Anyone else who gets a good one, please do the same."

"I think I've been turned on the spit a few too many times," Dana said, feeling heat in her face.

"Me, too." Jason's mother, Ellen, touched her nose gingerly. "I swear I added suntan lotion every half an hour. How can I be burned?"

"I'm not," Tomás Acero's mother said smugly. "That's what you get for being so pasty."

Dana stuck out her tongue and giggled when she saw Ellen doing the same.

Above her, her son exclaimed, "Yours is awesome! Uncle Nolan, did you see Mom's octopus?"

"Hey!" Juanita Acero complained. "There were four of us."

Dana grinned at her. "But I'm the mastermind, remember?"

Laughing, Sylvia flicked sand at her. Dana bent sideways to avoid it.

And then she heard it again. *Did you see Mom's octopus?*

Mom's.

Me. He called me Mom *in front of everyone.*
And she absolutely could not cry here and now.

NOLAN WATCHED DANA absorb the casual way
Christian called her *Mom*. She met his eyes,
stunned pleasure on her face.

And then she had the sense to scramble to
her feet and say, "I want to see yours," instead
of making a big production out of the moment.

He took a look around, too, although he'd
been able to watch all the sand creations from
the get-go.

Christian's stegosaurus had been a more ambitious project than the octopus, and the boys
had accomplished miracles. The one actual cas-
tle was impressive, as was a sports car. And the
football helmet—well, at least it had a recogniz-
able Seahawks emblem on the side.

The nonparticipant parents now wandered,
too, as did some of the inn guests and other
strangers. There were catcalls, laughter. And
satisfaction.

Finally, Nolan whistled again and said, "Let's
go back to the house for pizza and cake. Any
of you parents who want to join us, feel free."

He heard Christian saying, "At least there's
no tide to wash these away," and hoped no older
teens would feel compelled to destroy their creations. It wouldn't shock him—but this was pri-

vate property, the beach protected from sight by the building that housed Wind & Waves.

What would be, would be.

He saw Christian hesitating, obviously wondering what he should say to his father, and made a point of walking over to Craig Stewart. "You're welcome to ride along with us. I can run you back later."

The man nodded stiffly. "Thanks, but I think I'll drive myself."

"I'd suggest Christian ride with you, but the rental company might not appreciate all the sand." The kid was coated in it.

Craig glanced at his son, his eyebrows rising above dark glasses a lot pricier than Nolan's. "You have a point."

O-kay. Nolan took that as permission to sling an arm around the birthday boy's shoulders and steer him toward his old Suburban while Craig set off on the path that led to the inn parking lot.

"I think this was a winner," he murmured, and had the gift of a dazzling grin in return.

"Yeah!"

Parents usually ditched their kids at these affairs, but at least half decided to come along. All eight adults who'd indulged in building a sand-something stayed. Most were sunburned, while the boys, who spent more time outside, looked okay. Only Ryan, the nonathlete of the bunch, was a dangerously bright pink despite Nolan's best efforts.

Jason's dad had volunteered to pick up the pizza. Nolan called and doubled the order. The boys who spent the night would want more later. Everyone stuffed their faces, sang a loud and unharmonious Happy Birthday, and scarfed down cake and ice cream, too.

Some of the parents left before the present-opening began. Nolan was very aware that Craig was standing right beside Dana. So close his shoulder must have been brushing hers. Nolan wouldn't have admitted to anyone that he was annoyed. Did the guy plan to cut her from the herd so he could talk to her? Or did he envision the two of them sharing this touching moment?

Ashamed, Nolan had to admit he could understand that. They *should* be able to share an experience neither had likely believed would really happen.

Christian started ripping, the other boys huddled around, riveted. The scene didn't look so different from elementary school and even preschool birthday parties.

No surprise, a lot of video games and a couple of movies, but a few of the presents were more creative. Ryan gave him what appeared to be wood pieces packed in a square but was apparently a puzzle that turned into a robot. The crowd clearly approved of a fiber-optic lamp and a universal charging station.

Christian had saved gifts from family for last. Dana had bought him a pair of top-quality binoculars, something he'd wanted so he could better watch performances out on the river. He let out a whoop that warmed Nolan's heart. He seemed happy with the new sail Nolan gave him, also on his wish list. And finally...yep, there it was. A smartphone from Dad.

As excitement broke out, Dana's rueful gaze met Nolan's. A couple of the boys already had their own phones, but it was clear all of them wanted one. Christian hadn't even reacted to the tag: To Gabriel, from Dad.

Craig smirked. Or that was the way Nolan chose to categorize his satisfied smile.

The remaining few parents mock-grumbled on their way out the door.

"More ammunition for Jason," Ben said with a sigh.

Nolan clapped him on the back. "Not my fault."

Dana wished him a pleasant evening with a smirk of her own and fled. Unfortunately, her ex-husband walked her out. Though it took some determination, Nolan didn't let himself dwell. Instead, he closed the front door and went back to the boys.

THE PHONE SHOULD have been the best present ever, but after seeing the look on his father's face, Christian had kind of shivered, too. Dad just wanted to be able to get to him without having to ask permission from Uncle Nolan. He'd been smug because his present was the best, too, which Christian resented.

He didn't think he liked his father.

Instead of hanging out with friends or helping Uncle Nolan at Wind & Waves, he had to spend the next day with his father. *Just* his father, which freaked him out. Why couldn't Mom come along? Or…well, he could see that Dad didn't like Uncle Nolan and even sort of understood why. But Mom and he used to be married!

The good part was, his father rented a catamaran, so he and Christian went out on the river. Uncle Nolan didn't want to take his money, but Christian's father insisted.

"The day's on me." He locked stares with Uncle Nolan, who finally nodded.

Christian liked sailing, but his father wanted to do the important stuff, like he didn't think a kid would know how.

"I keep my sailboat at a marina on Nantucket," he said casually. "It's a thirty-foot Catalina, meant for day sails." He glanced around the Hobie. "A little fancier than this. We'll go out in it when you're with me. I'm thinking a couple weeks on Nantucket Island in August. What d'you say?"

"I don't know." But he did. He didn't want to go, even though the sailing part might be fun.

"Well, I plan to talk to Mr. Gregor and your mother this evening. It's time we quit playing games."

His father did know what he was doing on a sailboat, that was obvious. Otherwise, he tried to get Christian to talk about himself, and when he wouldn't, *he* talked. He did something important with money that Christian didn't really get, but it sounded like he was rich. He promised to show Christian pictures of his house— "We have your bedroom all set up"—and his wife and daughters.

"Angela and Elizabeth go to a private school. I can't imagine what kind of education you've been getting in a small town like this." He kind of sneered when he said that.

He did have season tickets for both the New England Patriots *and* the Boston Bruins, the ice-hockey team. He claimed to have a private box at Gillette Stadium, where the Patriots played. Christian could hardly imagine what that would be like.

His dad didn't like basketball or baseball but went to those games sometimes to "network." Whatever that meant.

Christian was glad when they got back to Wind & Waves, furled the sail and helped pull the Hobie out of the water. When they went back up to the store, Uncle Nolan looked them over and asked if they'd had a good time.

He shrugged.

"Excellent!" his father said, slapping him on the back. "I told him about the Catalina I have at our place on Nantucket and what good times we'll have sailing it."

"Glad you have some experience," Uncle Nolan said. "The Columbia has some wicked winds and currents."

"Nothing like the nor'easters we have in New England." He glanced at Christian. "Grab your duffel. We can clean up at the inn and have an early dinner."

Christian nodded and went to the break room. Behind him, he heard the two men talking quietly, although he caught only a few words. *Seven o'clock* and *attorney*. Fear cramped in his chest. He knew who'd said *attorney*.

His father was leaving tomorrow. He'd made it sound like a big deal because he'd taken the two extra days off to make a long weekend. "Can't do more than that," he'd said, so all Christian had to do was get through dinner. Uncle Nolan said if he and Mom stood together, Christian would be able to stay in Lookout.

And he knew they would. So he didn't have anything to worry about.

He took a deep breath and came back out. "I'm ready," he told his dad.

"Do you hear me?" Nolan said, looking hard at Christian.

"I have to stay in my bedroom, until you call me down to say goodbye to him," Christian recited obediently, although his expression was anything but. "It's not fair!" he burst out. "You're talking about *my* life. Why can't I be there?"

Nolan had never been so tempted to say, *Because I said so.* He hoped those words never crossed his lips.

"I understand how you feel," he said instead, still making sure his tone had no give. "But we may say things we don't want you to hear."

"What things?" Christian asked, still sulky.

"Legal threats. This is not the kind of discussion any parent wants to have in front of their kid. Whether you like it or not, we three adults have to work something out. You've had your say. I'm guessing even your father knows you want to stay here. Now the three of us have to come to an understanding, or we'll end up in court, where a judge can make decisions none of us like."

The doorbell rang. Nolan raised his eyebrows. With a sound that might have been a sob, Christian whirled and thundered up the stairs. His bedroom door closed with a loud bang and Nolan winced.

It was Dana who'd arrived, but Craig Stewart's rental car was turning into the dirt-and-gravel driveway, so they waited for him on the porch.

"Did he and Christian have a good day?" she asked, watching her ex-husband park.

"They got through it," Nolan said tersely. "The idea of going sailing was a good one, except I think it was intended to one-up me. He made sure Christian knew he has a fancier boat, docked at his place on Nantucket."

"Even a shack there must cost a fortune!"

"When they got back from dinner, Christian looked pretty closed up—" He nodded at the man striding up onto the porch. "Craig. Come on in."

He brought coffee for all of them, and they sat in a semicircle in the living room, he and Dana at each end of the sofa, Craig in an easy chair facing them. The guy wore chinos, a polo shirt and dock shoes, no socks. The watch looked like it would simultaneously tell the time everywhere from London to Abu Dhabi or Pretoria as well as to the depths of the ocean.

"I hope you had a good day with Christian," Dana said, breaking the ice.

Those eyebrows rose smoothly. "I might have if he knew how to talk."

She smiled. "He did a lot of mumbling and shrugging with me at first. Once he gets to know you, he can talk your ear off."

His cool gaze met hers. "But that won't happen long-distance, will it?"

Nolan held his silence, letting her handle this for now.

"Craig, with us divorced, the best you could hope for is visitation, anyway."

He leaned forward. "Are you so sure the courts wouldn't award me custody? I can afford good private schools, he'd have a stepmother and he'd live with his sisters."

"Why waste time negotiating when you can threaten?" Nolan observed.

Craig cast him a hostile look. "I don't even know why you're here. You have no legal standing."

"Haven't you heard that possession is nine-tenths of the law?"

The guy snorted. "If you're not going to take this seriously—"

"Oh, I take it very seriously." Nolan let him hear the army ranger. "Christian is, for all practical purposes, my son." He held up a hand to silence the jackass. "He's happy and established here. He grew up in this house." Not entirely true, but close enough. "He loves me. If a judge were to ask where he wanted to live— and with a kid Christian's age, that question *will* be asked—he'd say here. That carries a lot of weight."

Craig shifted his attention to Dana. "You caved?

You're the woman who swore you'd never give up! You would bring your son home or die trying. And now you're fine with tiptoeing around the edges of his life?"

Nolan's temper simmered at the attack, but Dana only shook her head.

"What I'm *fine* with is giving Christian time to get to know me. To accept that I'm really his mother, that I love him. I'm *fine* with respecting his wishes. No matter what we wish, he's not that baby anymore."

He grunted.

Dana said, "If you go on this way, you'll alienate him. Is that what you want? He's too old for you to mold, Craig. He's a strong individual already. That doesn't mean it's too late for you to become his father if you bring him slowly into your life and quit threatening his sense of security. I want a son who will someday choose to bring his wife and children home to me at Christmas. That wouldn't happen if he was forced to live with me."

"But this way, he'll never live with you, will he?"

Nolan saw her tiny flinch but the guy hadn't damaged her poise.

"I've been spending a lot of time with him." She smiled. "He's giving me swim lessons, Craig. You wouldn't believe how sweet he is. I help him and Nolan one day a week at Wind & Waves. I was involved in planning his birthday party. He talks to me." Her voice broke at the end. "I can't have back everything I lost. But I found him! He calls me *Mom* now." She lifted her chin. "If you try to take him from me, I'll fight you tooth and nail."

Nolan had seen shifting expressions on the guy's face that suggested she was getting through to him. Now Craig said urgently, "We could share custody."

Nolan tensed until he saw Dana shaking her head.

"Christian doesn't remember being taken, but the trauma has to be there somewhere in his psyche. He does remember not being able to depend on his mentally ill 'mother.' With Nolan overseas, Christian lived much of the time with his grandparents. Do you know what it must have done to him when they were killed and Marlee was badly injured? Nolan gave up his career for Christian's sake. Because of Nolan, Christian finally had stability…until that blood test, when he found out he isn't who he thought he was. I think one more move would break him."

Lines on Craig Stewart's face deepened, making him seem more human. As if he might have it in him to be likable. After a minute, he rubbed the back of his neck and sighed. "I get your point. But he's our son, Dana! To find him and have to leave him where he is..." He shook his head.

Figuring his moment had come, Nolan reached across the cushion separating him from Dana and took her hand. "You need to know that I'm hoping the three of us will be a family." He ignored her startled look. "That one of these days soon, Dana will be living here, too. If you don't fight us, I guarantee we won't stop you from seeing Christian. I think once he knows you're not trying to yank him away, he'll want to get to know you." Time to lay out a lure. "He said you'd talked about a couple-week vacation later this summer, him joining your family."

Craig didn't move for a suspenseful minute.

Nolan looked at Dana again. "Is what he says right?"

Her fingers tightened on his. "Yes," she said steadily.

"This isn't some ploy to get rid of me?"

Her breath took a funny hitch, but she didn't display any doubt. "Of course not."

Craig swore, but not as if he meant it. "All right. I'll let it lie for now. Let's talk visitation."

They negotiated. Nolan couldn't help thinking that, whatever the result, Christian had reason to resent what they were doing here. This *was* his life laid on the table like so many poker chips, and he wasn't allowed any say over what pile each chip went in. But Nolan also didn't see any realistic way they could allow him that say, not now. As he got older, he could negotiate with his father. All of them would have to figure out how to work around summer jobs, girlfriends, sports. For now… Craig was his father, and Christian should find out what kind of man he was.

"You let us know what two weeks work for you in August. He doesn't have any other set plans."

"I'll pay for his ticket if he flies out for Thanksgiving."

"If we can have Christmas."

Spring break. Next summer. Phone calls. They laid it all out, terms in a business contract. The experience was unpleasant…but Nolan consoled himself they were doing the best they could, for all of their sakes.

DANA MAINTAINED HER COMPOSURE, even walking Craig to the door, Nolan being tactful enough to stay behind in the living room.

"If you want to say goodbye to Christian…" she thought to say.

Craig shook his head. He opened the door but turned back to her. "You really love this guy?"

She tried to smile. "Yes."

"Okay." He smiled, but crookedly. "Despite everything, it's been good to see you. I hope

this works out, for your sake." He nodded toward the living room.

"I'm trying to have faith," she told him.

"You always were able to have more than I
could."

His quiet admission rattled her. "I know I was
so obsessed—"

"Don't even say it." His voice was choked.
"Let the past go, Dana." He bent quickly, kissed
her cheek and said, "I'm sure we'll be seeing
each other." Then he walked quickly out to his
car without looking back.

She closed the door, such a tangle inside she
didn't know what she felt. Happy—of course
she was. But so much else, too. And...she desperately needed to be alone for a minute.

As she hurried toward the downstairs bathroom, Nolan rose from his seat on the sofa.
"Dana?"

She flapped her hand toward the bathroom,
hoping he'd assume her desperation had a different cause.

The moment she locked herself in, she closed
the toilet seat and lid—men!—and sank down
on it, curling forward and burying her face in
her hands.

Christian is safe. Nothing could be more
important.

Nolan— No, she wasn't ready to think about
what he'd said yet.

Craig had revealed himself to be the decent, even kind man she remembered after all. The grief in his eyes as they said goodbye… Why it hurt, Dana didn't know. His frustration with her, impatience that became irritation, those memories had lingered until they overpowered everything that had come before. It was bittersweet to be able to acknowledge that they had failed each other, and they both knew it. *I can let it go.*

She drew a breath that filled her chest and was able to straighten, letting her hands fall to her lap.

Nolan. *I'm hoping the three of us will be a family.*

Had he really meant it? He'd implied as much, talking about a serious relationship, but she hadn't quite let herself believe in it. She trusted him, but…she hadn't dared in so long to be happy that she was having trouble reaching for it now.

She kept breathing until all the emotions untangled themselves and left… She wasn't sure. Peace, maybe.

Had Nolan told Christian yet? Dana popped to her feet, suddenly eager.

She'd just let herself out of the bathroom when she heard Christian say, "I can stay here with you? Really?"

Nolan's deeper voice. "Really."

The earsplitting yell made her smile.

"*Yes!* Yes, yes, yes!"

Nolan laughed. "Glad to know you're happy."

"It was because of Dana, wasn't it?"

"It was."

Christian's back was to her as she entered the living room. "You did it," he exulted. "You said you'd get her on our side. You swore you'd fight as dirty as you had to, and you did."

She felt as if she'd walked into her baby's bedroom to find him gone all over again. There was that out-of-body moment. *It can't be.* Frozen in place, she couldn't decide if her heart was still beating. If she *wanted* it to beat.

Nolan was grinning. And Christian…

Dana. He'd said *Dana*, not *Mom*.

Oh, dear God. She took a step backward, and Nolan saw her.

Shock transformed his face. "Dana!"

She shook her head and backed up. Christian swung around, too, but she didn't let herself see his expression. Instead, she turned and ran.

Kitchen. Purse. Front door. Nolan was there to block her, but when she struck at him, he lifted his hands and backed away.

Somehow, she made it into her car, got the key in the ignition and drove.

CHAPTER EIGHTEEN

"BUT I DIDN'T MEAN—" Christian stared after his mother in horror.

"You did." Hearing his harshness, Nolan closed his eyes. What was he saying? *He* was to blame, not this boy. *He* had let Christian think—

Don't lie to yourself. The strategy had been his. It had never been only that; he'd wanted Dana from the first day, when she walked into his business. He liked her. He had truly believed they could be happy together. Now, gripped by panic, he knew he loved her. Had for a long time. His pursuit of her hadn't been about Christian in weeks, if not months.

If ever.

He wasn't a hearts-and-flowers guy. He'd never been in love. He was comfortable thinking in terms of strategy, practicality. He'd told himself they fit, that the three of them as a family solved problems for them all.

He was a fool.

"Uncle Nolan?" his nephew whispered.

"Give me a minute," he said, his voice like gravel.

"She thinks everything was a lie."

No shit.

"I'll call her," Nolan said. "Tell her—" His throat spasmed closed. Exactly what was he going to tell her?

"I'm scared."

Nolan let himself look at a boy who was learning a hard lesson. "Yeah," he said roughly. "Me, too."

He found his phone and sank down on the sofa, gripping it tight as he rehearsed openings. *You misunderstood.* Like she'd buy that. *What you heard was a joke.* Uh-huh. *I'm sorry?* He was.

Finally, he made the call. Of course she didn't answer. He was very conscious of Christian standing stricken in the middle of the living room. This was one of those moments when he looked painfully young. Skinny and awkward.

Beep. "Dana, I think you misunderstood what you heard. I did tell Christian I'd fight dirty back at the beginning, when I didn't know you and all I was thinking about was protecting him." He took a breath. "You have to know we're long past that. That what Christian and I both feel for you has nothing to do with being sure we'd win when we took on your ex-husband. Please." He bent forward to hide his face, pinching the bridge of his nose between forefinger and thumb. "I need to talk to you, Dana," he finished raggedly. "Please give me a chance." *Beep.*

"What if she goes back to Colorado?"

"She'll listen." Nolan tried again. "She loves you."

"You mean she used to." Christian ran for his bedroom.

Nolan jerked when the door slammed. He didn't have it in him to offer any more consolation. What could be more useless, when he couldn't convince himself there was hope?

He sat for a long time, asking himself all the same questions Christian probably was. What if she never wanted to see them again? She could be packing right now, with the intention of leaving Oregon first thing in the morning. The people at Helping Hand would be disappointed to lose her, disappointed in her, but that wouldn't prevent her getting a job in Colorado, where she had connections.

On a flash of agony, he wondered whether she'd gone to the inn instead of home. She could have knocked on Craig's door and said, *I've changed my mind. Let's file for custody.* Or even said, *He hurt me.* Nolan had seen the way the guy looked at Dana today. There'd been bittersweet knowledge in Craig's eyes; he knew what he had thrown away. Would they— No!

Damn it, no. Even if Stewart would cheat on his wife, Dana wasn't that kind of woman.

She could call in the morning to formally request visitation, preferably in a way that kept her from coming face-to-face with Nolan. Or *she* could file for custody, while graciously allowing him an occasional weekend. Right now, if she asked for custody, he thought Christian felt guilty enough to pack and move into her small home without argument.

She might feel she'd been better off with dreams of finding her son than with the reality of a boy who'd participated in a plot to use her to get what he wanted.

Nolan shot to his feet. At the foot of the stairs, he stopped only long enough to call, "I'm going to Dana's."

When he reached her house, he found it dark. He jogged up to her porch to ring the bell, wait, ring it again, then pound on the door.

"Dana! Let me in."

Not a whisper of sound came from inside. But he knew—she was in there, all right, huddled on her sofa or in bed, covering her ears. Crying. Or, worse, too shattered for tears.

His chest heaving, he flattened his hands on her door and rested his forehead against it. He wasn't sure he could make himself go home. He couldn't imagine sleeping. But…she wasn't

going to relent right now. He couldn't stand on
her porch all night.

And Christian would need him.

Feeling old and very tired, Nolan turned away
and started down the steps.

A SMALL VOICE inside insisted that Nolan and
Christian couldn't have faked everything. No
boy was that good an actor. And Dana had a
hard time believing Nolan could have made love
to her with such urgency, such tenderness, such
need, if he didn't care about her at all.

But she wasn't ready to listen to that voice.

After making it home, she hadn't so much
as brushed her teeth. She'd stripped to her underwear, crawled into bed and pulled the covers over her head. Curling into a ball, she felt
childish, but there was no one to see her.

When her phone buzzed, she guessed who the
caller was. When the doorbell rang, she pulled
the pillow over her head, too, and kept it there
until Nolan gave up and went away.

Sometime during the night, she uncurled and
lay stiff, staring at the ceiling as she moved
past thinking she never wanted to see either of
them again.

Given Christian's age, connecting with him
had been too easy. She had moved to Lookout
only—she had to count—ten weeks ago? Or was
it eleven? He'd hurt her feelings a few times,

but really he had come around with astonishing speed. She should have been suspicious.

And why hadn't she questioned Nolan's motivations? Initially hostile, he had done a one-eighty and become her new best friend. Supportive when it came to Christian, eager to spend time with her, happy to include her in their lives. She had deluded herself to think he appreciated her willingness to meet him halfway. It stung—no, worse—when she forced herself to meet head-on her credulity in believing that he'd be attracted to *her*, out of all the women in the world. Really? Was she that dumb?

Apparently, the answer was yes.

She never did sleep. Dana dragged herself to the bathroom the next morning, cringed at the sight of the zombie she saw in the mirror and stepped into a hot shower. After dressing, she drank a cup of coffee and nibbled a piece of toast.

At work, she managed to laugh when everyone exclaimed that she had to be coming down with something. "Insomnia," she explained, "but if I'd taken the day off and napped, I'd have ended up really turned around. This way, I'm guaranteed to sleep like a log tonight."

They bought it, thank heavens. Grateful she had no classes to teach, she spent the morning meeting with a few clients and sharing ideas with Meghan about how to help an unwed pregnant teenager.

Noon arrived. She hadn't brought a lunch. She wasn't hungry but was contemplating getting something small when someone knocked lightly before pushing the door open.

Nolan's shoulders almost brushed each side of the doorframe, blocking any view behind him. Dana stiffened. It was a moment before she could force herself to look at his face. When she did, she suffered a shock. Every line had deepened. His eyes seemed to have sunk farther back into their sockets. He hadn't slept any better than she had.

She would not soften. "Afraid the master plan is endangered?"

"Did you listen to my message? Or Christian's?"

"No."

He lifted a bag. "I brought lunch. Will you talk to me?"

Dana closed her eyes, shaken by that low, deep voice, imbued with so much she didn't want to hear. With her feeling so vulnerable, this was the worst possible time for him to show up. Someone had driven a spike through her temple this morning. The ibuprofen she carried in her purse hadn't touched the agony. All it had done was make her queasy. How could she deal with Nolan when she felt like this?

But I'll have to eventually. Why not get it over with?

"All right." She grabbed her sunglasses but left her purse locked in her drawer and allowed him to usher her out. They walked in silence the two blocks to the small park. She didn't let herself look at the cheerful young mothers or the giggly kids running from merry-go-round to slide to swings.

Nolan set the sack on the picnic table. He handed her a bottle of water, followed by a cup of what she prayed *wasn't* chili. She couldn't even pretend to eat that. A paper sleeve held a scone. Lemon, her favorite.

Dana pried the top off, relieved to see soup. It looked like lentil, which ought to be safe enough.

"Christian cried after you left," he said abruptly.

She lifted her head. "You expect me to believe that?"

"It's the truth. He thinks this is his fault."

"When really it's yours. No boy his age could come up with a scheme so nasty. Either that, or you embroidered it substantially after the two of you dreamed it up." Lashing out felt unexpectedly satisfying. "I'd like to think he didn't suggest you—" she stopped herself from saying something really crude "—have sex with me."

"You have to know us making love had nothing to do with Christian."

"Do I?" Suddenly afraid she was going to throw up, she sipped her water and concentrated on taking slow, deep breaths.

"There are some things you can't fake."

"I wouldn't know."

Nolan bent his head. He swallowed, scrubbed a hand over his face and looked at her again, his eyes holding devastation.

"I've told you a lot about myself," he said slowly. "I think I said once that I'm happiest when I have a mission."

Oh, God. Why hadn't she taken that as a warning?

"When you first called, defeating you and Christian's father became my mission. I did tell him then that I'd do whatever I had to."

"Fight dirty."

He inclined his head, his eyes not leaving hers. "I knew almost immediately that I couldn't do that. You'd suffered too much already, and yet you carried yourself with such dignity. I could see you had somehow held on to hope for all those years. There was no way I could hurt you."

Her laugh ached. "And yet."

He reached across the table as if he couldn't help himself, then slowly withdrew his hand when she pulled hers away.

"I think...the need to fulfill the mission kept humming in the background, even when

I thought I'd discarded it. Christian knew I wanted us to be a family, but I never came out and told him, 'I'm not saying that because it gives us the most certainty of staying together.'"

"You wanted us to be a family," Dana echoed. "What a perfect way to say it was *all* about Christian."

He nodded. He held her gaze, his eyes burning. "You're right. I kept thinking of our relationship that way, even though—"

Please don't let him say it, she begged. Not now. Believing him right now wasn't remotely possible.

"I fell in love with you a long time ago."

She put the lid back on the soup, then set it in the sack and the scone on top. Then she swung her leg over the bench and stood, grabbing the sack. "Thank you for the lunch. You may tell Christian he's free to call me or…stop by to see me." She nodded and walked away.

Nolan didn't come after her.

WITH THE SUN setting so late now, Uncle Nolan let Christian ride his bike to friends' houses in the evening as long as he'd be home before dark.

After leaving his bike on Mom's lawn, he sat down on the porch steps to wait for her to come home. Uncle Nolan said she hadn't even listened to the messages they'd each left. Christian's stomach felt as if he'd swallowed a bunch of river water. Didn't she want to hear what he had to say?

He'd been there for only, like, fifteen minutes when her red Subaru appeared. He thought she'd seen him, because it hesitated partway down the block. What if she didn't want to talk to him and just kept driving? But she parked in the driveway and sat for a minute without moving. Eventually, she pushed the door open, got out and walked across the lawn toward him.

"Christian."

He rose to his feet, feeling shaky. "I came to say I'm sorry."

She didn't say anything immediately. Finally, she nodded. "I think you need to be honest with me."

"I will be."

She passed him, going up the steps. He hovered as she unlocked the door. Would she close it in his face? But she said, "Come on in," and he hurried after her.

"Let me take off my heels." She dropped her purse on this little side table and went down the hall to her bedroom.

Christian shifted his weight from foot to foot and began thinking she was taking an awful long time. When she reappeared, she'd changed from her work clothes to jeans and a sweatshirt. She barely looked at him, but he followed her to the kitchen.

"You're…" He hesitated.

His stomach clenched at her blank stare. He swallowed to keep down this acid taste.

"You're kind of scaring me," he blurted.

As if she hadn't heard him, she said, "There are cookies in the jar and soda and milk in the fridge."

For once, he poured himself a glass of milk, thinking it might settle his stomach, and one for her, too. He put a few cookies on a plate and carried that to the table, too, even if he was the opposite of hungry.

His mom seemed surprised to see the milk appear in front of her, but she did take a sip, then a longer swallow. When she put the glass down, she focused on him for the first time.

"Christian, from what I heard, it's pretty clear you still wish I wasn't in your life."

"No! That's not true."

Her smile looked sad. "I won't promise to go away no matter what you say. You are my son, whether you like it or not."

"That's not—"

She talked right over him. "Would you be happiest if I went back to Colorado and you just came for a short visit once or twice a year? Or if I stay in town and we do things together sometimes and maybe you occasionally spend the night?"

He struggled not to cry. "No! I want…I want

everything like it was. With you and me and Uncle Nolan. I thought—" he gulped "—you might marry him."

"As part of the plan?"

"No!" He'd said that a bunch of times, but she hadn't listened. "It wasn't like that. He kept saying if all of us stood together, my dad wouldn't be able to take me away from you and Uncle Nolan. But…Uncle Nolan, he wouldn't lie, like you're thinking he did," Christian continued desperately. "He looks at you all gooey. My friends pretend to gag. But I like it, even though I don't tell them that."

"So exactly how did your uncle 'play dirty'?"

"I…don't think he did. I don't even know why I said that!"

"Did he send you here to talk to me?" Her voice was hard. "Be honest, Christian."

"He doesn't even know I'm here." He held his breath, waiting to see if she believed him.

She looked at him for a long time, not even blinking. And then she closed her eyes and sighed. She seemed to sag, her head bending forward like it was too heavy for her to hold up.

"He looks like he did after my mom…" He gulped. "You know, his sister killed herself. Like the most terrible thing in the world happened. He thinks this is his fault, too, and it's not! It's mine. I said something stupid, and now you don't trust us." He grabbed the hem of his

T-shirt and used it to wipe his eyes, hoping she was still looking down and didn't see. But when he lifted his head, he saw that she had, too. Her face was twisted with some emotion, but he couldn't tell what it was.

"Why don't you have some cookies? They're good."

"I don't— My stomach feels all—"

"Mine, too." Her smile was sort of crooked. "I'll think about what you said, okay?"

"I like it when you come to Wind & Waves and have dinner with us and…" He couldn't say the rest. That he wanted a mom who talked to his teachers and watched his games. Stuff his other mom—Marlee—had never done.

Her eyes were wet, too. She used the back of her hand instead of her shirt to catch tears. "Okay, Christian. Please don't look so worried. I've loved you since the day you were born. There isn't anything you could do to make me quit loving you."

"Even if, I don't know, I killed somebody or started taking drugs or…?" He ran out of ideas.

Suddenly she was smiling as if she meant it. "Even if. I might be mad at you, but that's different."

His nose was running now. He lifted his hem again but then caught her eye. "Um, I guess I should…"

She actually laughed. "Paper towels are on the counter."

He jumped up and grabbed one, blowing his nose. He was crying like a baby, but he didn't care. He felt great! He hadn't ruined everything after all.

After he threw the wadded paper towel in the trash, he said, "I could make tacos tomorrow night again. If...if you'd come to dinner."

Mom looked startled, and then her eyes went unfocused for a weird minute. Finally, she blinked and he knew she was seeing him again. "Thank you for the invitation, Christian. I think...I'd like that. If your uncle doesn't mind." Momentarily, she sounded stern. "If he does, you need to let me know. I'd rather have honesty than any more pretense."

"We weren't ever pretending."

She nodded slightly, not as if she totally believed him, but as if she needed to think about it, the way she'd said.

He never did eat any cookies, and as he rode his bike home, he suddenly realized he was starved.

DANA WAS COMING to dinner.

Too jumpy to sit down, Nolan prowled the living room, with an occasional detour to the kitchen to check on Christian's preparations.

She was coming to dinner. He couldn't wrap

his mind around the idea. What did it *mean*? Had she forgiven him? And Christian? Or did she just want a civil setting for a painful conversation?

She'd been so sure he was lying to her, but she had agreed to have dinner here, anyway. Nolan shook his head in bewilderment.

This time when he passed the front window, he saw headlights. A car turning into the driveway. It had to be her.

"Dana's here!" he called.

Christian replied; Nolan didn't take in what he said. He moved away from the window so she wouldn't think he was pathetic.

The doorbell sent a jolt through him. When he let her in, she smiled at him, a little cautiously, but any kind of smile surprised him.

"Dana."

"I brought dessert." She thrust a dish at him. "Blackberry cobbler."

His stomach growled, probably because he hadn't eaten much in two days. Dana laughed and went with him to the kitchen.

Christian turned from the stove. He'd already grated the cheese and it looked like he'd just dumped the chicken strips into hot oil. They exchanged shy greetings that still left Nolan without a clue.

"Would you like some wine, or…?" he asked.

"Not right now, thank you."

"Shall we go sit down in the living room?"

Her fingers curled tight, then straightened. So she *was* nervous. "Thank you."

They were all being polite, when she'd spent enough time here it felt as if she belonged.

She surprised him again by sitting at what he'd come to think of as "her" end of the sofa instead of choosing a chair well distant from him. Tucking one foot under her, she faced him at the other end. The middle cushion felt as wide as the Columbia River.

"I have something to say."

God. Here it came. "All right," he said warily.

"I need to apologize for overreacting." Dana shook her head when he opened his mouth. "I didn't like what I heard, or the expressions on your faces. You were celebrating because you'd put something over on Craig."

She was right. That was how juvenile they'd been. Christian had an excuse; Nolan didn't.

"Christian...upset me," she continued, her gaze unwavering. "It meant a lot that he'd started to call me *Mom*. Hearing him revert to *Dana* the minute he got what he wanted..." She gave her head a little shake. "But I was hurt most of all by the idea that you'd befriended me from the beginning to get me on your side. Even worse was thinking you'd set out to use my attraction to you to cement my support."

"I didn't." He couldn't let her keep thinking—

"Yesterday I asked Christian to be completely

honest with me. I'm asking the same of you. I can handle the truth. Later—" she gave an awkward shrug "—it would be much worse."

That she even felt she had to ask was killing him. Voice raw, he said, "Dana, what I told you yesterday was true. Every word. I swear."

Her eyes searched his in a way that left him feeling emotionally naked.

"Hey. Dinner's ready," Christian announced from the archway.

Nolan jerked. Dana's pupils shrank, then dilated. The timing couldn't be worse. But he stood and said, "Smells good."

Dana forced a smile and rose, too.

Dinner took an eternity. Nolan made himself eat even though his stomach kept spasming. Christian was proud of his cooking and excited that Dana had agreed to come. She smiled and chatted with Christian, at least pretending interest in what Jason or Ryan or Dieter said and which of his new video games had been awesome.

When they had all finished, Christian said eagerly, "We have ice cream to put on top of the cobbler, right, Uncle Nolan?"

He smiled. "We do, but can we wait for a bit? I'm pretty full."

Christian opened his mouth to complain, met Nolan's eyes and said, "Sure. Dieter said to call. So…" He eased out of the kitchen and then thumped his way upstairs, displaying unexpected understanding.

Nolan looked at the dirty dishes on the table and saw that Dana was doing the same. Then she giggled. "I think I've volunteered for KP a few too many times."

Nolan laughed, too. "You're not cleaning the kitchen tonight. Let me get the coffee started."

She did clear the table while he poured coffee and got out creamer. They both sat down again and looked at each other, neither reaching for their cups.

"Sunday," she whispered, "was worse than when I realized Craig was seeing another woman. Worse than when he told me he wanted a divorce." Her fingers twisted together. The pain in her eyes gutted Nolan. "When I thought it was all a lie... The way you touched me and looked at me and—"

He shoved back his chair and circled the table, pulling her to her feet. He wanted to haul her into his arms and never let her go, but he had to make her believe him first. "These two days, knowing what you thought—" he swallowed with difficulty "—that you might never forgive me... These were the worst days of my life."

It was the truth. He'd been an idiot not to have recognized what he felt until he'd screwed up and lost her. He had no defense.

"Please," he managed, hearing how broken his voice was. "I love you, Dana."

Again she looked deep. When she let out a cry and threw her arms around his neck, it felt as if his heart had just burst open. Messy, painful, exhilarating.

She pressed her lips to his. There was no finesse. Their teeth clanked together; he tasted blood from her lip or his, he didn't know. Finally, finally, he got it right, deepening the kiss, gripping her butt to lift her, exultation more powerful than any physical hunger.

They spun in a circle, kissing until they had to come up for air, then diving back in again. "I need you," he managed to say at one point. And she whispered the words he craved.

"I love you."

They thumped into a wall. He wanted to tear off her jeans, unfasten his and bury himself inside her. It still wasn't all physical. What he felt was more primitive than that. His hips rocked and she moaned.

Thud, thud, thud.

A part of his brain knew what that sound meant. The rest of him didn't care. He somehow squeezed a hand between them to cup her breast.

"Love you," he said gutturally.

"Can we have cobbler now?"

The cheerful voice calling down the stairs

had the effect of a cattle prod. Nolan groaned, tore his mouth from Dana's and whispered, "Can we ditch him?"

"He'll be in the kitchen any second."

Nolan said something obscene, but he also retreated a few inches, not letting go of her.

"Oh, there you are." This time the voice came from right behind him. "Are you *kissing*?"

Nolan started to laugh.

"What's funny about that?" Christian asked indignantly.

Nolan couldn't quit laughing.

Dana punched him. "We were kissing."

"Oh. You mean you're not mad anymore?"

She succumbed, too. Hooting and giggling, they clung to each other like a couple of drunks staggering out of a tavern.

"I guess I should go away, huh?"

At the tentative, possibly offended question, Nolan shook his head and turned. "Hey. Come here."

Christian took a slow step, then another. Nolan held out an arm and pulled this boy he loved so much into an embrace shared by all three of them. "We don't want you to go away," he said, his voice low and rough. "Even if privacy can be hard to come by for parents."

"Parents?" Christian's head came up, his hope as naked and vulnerable as anything Nolan had ever seen in Dana's eyes. "You mean…?"

"I do mean." He hadn't asked, but all he had to do was look at her to know what her answer would be. "Cobbler sounds good to me," he heard himself say, ushering Dana back to the table.

Once they'd eaten... Christian was a big boy. He'd be okay home alone for a couple of hours.

* * * * *

LARGER-PRINT BOOKS!

◆HARLEQUIN *Presents®*

GET 2 FREE LARGER-PRINT NOVELS PLUS 2 FREE GIFTS!

PASSION GUARANTEED SEDUCTION

REQUEST YOUR FREE BOOKS!
2 FREE WHOLESOME ROMANCE NOVELS IN LARGER PRINT
PLUS 2 FREE MYSTERY GIFTS

☀☀☀☀☀☀☀☀☀☀☀☀☀☀☀☀☀☀☀☀☀☀

HEARTWARMING™

❋❋❋❋❋❋❋❋❋❋❋❋❋❋❋❋❋❋❋❋❋❋

Wholesome, tender romances

YES! Please send me 2 FREE Harlequin® Heartwarming Larger-Print novels and my 2 FREE mystery gifts (gifts worth about $10). After receiving them, if I don't wish to receive any more books, I can return the shipping statement marked "cancel." If I don't cancel, I will receive 4 brand-new larger-print novels every month and be billed just $5.24 per book in the U.S. or $5.99 per book in Canada. That's a savings of at least 19% off the cover price. It's quite a bargain! Shipping and handling is just 50¢ per book in the U.S. and 75¢ per book in Canada.* I understand that accepting the 2 free books and gifts places me under no obligation to buy anything. I can always return a shipment and cancel at any time. Even if I never buy another book, the two free books and gifts are mine to keep forever.

161/361 IDN GHX2

Name _____ (PLEASE PRINT) _____

Address _____ Apt. # _____

City _____ State/Prov. _____ Zip/Postal Code _____

Signature (if under 18, a parent or guardian must sign) _____

Mail to the **Reader Service:**
IN U.S.A.: P.O. Box 1867, Buffalo, NY 14240-1867
IN CANADA: P.O. Box 609, Fort Erie, Ontario L2A 5X3

* Terms and prices subject to change without notice. Prices do not include applicable taxes. Sales tax applicable in N.Y. Canadian residents will be charged applicable taxes. Offer not valid in Quebec. This offer is limited to one order per household. Not valid for current subscribers to Harlequin Heartwarming larger-print books. All orders subject to credit approval. Credit or debit balances in a customer's account(s) may be offset by any other outstanding balance owed by or to the customer. Please allow 4 to 6 weeks for delivery. Offer available while quantities last.

Your Privacy—The Reader Service is committed to protecting your privacy. Our Privacy Policy is available online at www.ReaderService.com or upon request from the Reader Service.

We make a portion of our mailing list available to reputable third parties that offer products we believe may interest you. If you prefer that we not exchange your name with third parties, or if you wish to clarify or modify your communication preferences, please visit us at www.ReaderService.com/consumerschoice or write to us at Reader Service Preference Service, P.O. Box 9062, Buffalo, NY 14240-9062. Include your complete name and address.